The Unlikely Spy

A Gareth and Gwen Medieval Mystery

THE UNLIKEY SPY

by

SARAH WOODBURY

The Unlikely Spy
Copyright © 2014 by Sarah Woodbury

This is a work of fiction.

www.sarahwoodbury.com

Cover image by Christine DeMaio-Rice at Flip City Books
http://flipcitybooks.com

To Dan

My partner in crime for more than thirty years

Pronouncing Welsh Names and Places

Aberystwyth –Ah-bare-IHST-with (the 'th' is soft as in 'forth')

Bwlch y Ddeufaen – Boolch ah THEY-vine (the 'th' is hard as in 'they'; the 'ch' as in in the Scottish 'loch')

Cadfael – CAD-vile

Cadwallon – Cad-WASH-lon

Caernarfon – ('ae' makes a long i sound like in 'kite') Kire-NAR-von

Dafydd – DAH-vith (the 'th' is hard as in 'they')

Dolgellau – Doll-GESH-lay

Deheubarth – deh-HAY-barth

Dolwyddelan – dole-with-EH-lan (the 'th' is hard as in 'they')

Gruffydd – GRIFF-ith (the 'th' is hard as in 'they')

Gwalchmai – GWALCH-my ('ai' makes a long i sound like in 'kite; the 'ch' like in the Scottish 'loch')

Gwenllian – Gwen-SHLEE-an

Gwladys – Goo-LAD-iss

Gwynedd – GWIN-eth (the 'th' is hard as in 'the')

Hywel – H'wel

Ieuan – ieu sounds like the cheer, 'yay' so, YAY-an

Llanbadarn Fawr – shlan-BAH-darn vowr

Llywelyn – shlew-ELL-in

Maentwrog – Mighn-TOO-rog

Meilyr – MY-lir

Owain – OH-wine

Rhuddlan – RITH-lan (the 'th' is hard as in 'the')

Rhun – Rin

Rhys – Reese

Sion – Shawn (Sean)

Tudur – TIH-deer

Usk – Isk

Cast of Characters

From Gwynedd
Owain Gwynedd – King of Gwynedd (North Wales)
Rhun – Prince of Gwynedd (illegitimate)
Hywel – Prince of Gwynedd (illegitimate) and Lord of Ceredigion
Cadwaladr – Owain's younger brother, former Lord of Ceredigion
Gwen – spy for Hywel, Gareth's wife
Gareth – Gwen's husband, Captain of Hywel's guard
Mari – Gwen's friend, Hywel's wife
Evan – Gareth's friend
Gruffydd – Rhun's captain
Goch – A soldier
Rhodri – A soldier
Meilyr – Gwen's father
Gwalchmai – Gwen's brother
Rhys – Prior of St. Kentigern's monastery, St Asaph

Tangwen – Gwen and Gareth's daughter
Gruffydd – Hywel and Mari's son
Elspeth – Tangwen's nanny
Bronwen – Gruffydd's nanny

From Ceredigion
Cadell – King of Deheubarth
Angharad – Cadell's niece
Pedr – Prior of St. Padarn's monastery
Iolo – a cloth merchant
Madlen – Iolo's niece
Sion – gatekeeper at St. Padarn's
Morgan – Hywel's steward
Pawl – tavern keeper

1

Late August 1146

Gwen

Gwen peered into the courtyard of the monastery before venturing across the hot cobbles into the mid-afternoon sun, which shone out of a rare deep blue sky. Heat radiated off the stones, and Gwen moved towards the garden, seeking the breeze coming off the brook. She'd swept up her brown hair into a chignon, but sweat clung to the tendrils at the back of her neck.

The guesthouse lay to one side of the large square, which was fronted on the road by a gatehouse and a long stone wall. The monks' quarters, church, and college of priests were opposite, as far from the guesthouse as possible while still remaining in the same compound. Given her hour-long struggle to get her daughter to go to sleep, Gwen had to admit the genius of that decision.

In point of fact, that distance was not because the monks feared to hear a crying child but was left over from when Norman monks, who viewed women and children with a certain degree of hostility, had occupied the monastery. Now that Hywel ruled Ceredigion, the monastery had been restored to the native Welsh Church. Still, the presence of young women and children in the guest quarters made some of the older monks uncomfortable, and Gwen had been trying as best she could to keep Tangwen quiet and out of the way. She'd failed utterly at both today.

For the moment, however, Tangwen was asleep, and Gwen's fourteen-year-old maid, extravagantly named Elspeth, remained with her. Gwen hoped her daughter would sleep for at least two hours. To say Tangwen was overtired after all the activity of the last few days was an understatement.

Unfortunately for the monks' peace of mind, Gwen's adorable baby girl was the least of the monks' problems this week. Travelers filled the guesthouse, with more coming every hour. At Prince Hywel's request, the abbot had agreed to suffer through the presence of whatever women came to stay with them, regardless of their seductive beauty.

And it wasn't just the guest quarters at the monastery that were filling up. Aberystwyth castle, the villages of Aberystwyth and Llanbadarn Fawr, and the entire surrounding area were full to bursting with travelers who had arrived at Prince Hywel's invitation. He'd put out a call to every corner of Wales for bards to travel to Ceredigion for a music festival with him as the host. Even King Owain—along with Gwen's father, Meilyr, and brother, Gwalchmai—were journeying from Aber for the celebration.

Gwen (and Prince Hywel too) had hoped they would have arrived already, since the festival had opened that morning. Given the distances involved and the number of people traveling, however, it was hard to judge how long any journey would take. Regardless of when they arrived, they would stay for a week afterwards, which was some consolation. Gwen had missed her father and brother in the two months she'd lived in Ceredigion.

As Gwen stood in the shadows of the guesthouse, a party of riders entered through the monastery gate and halted on the cobbles. Gwen stood on tiptoe to look past them, hoping Gareth might be among the stragglers. He wasn't, and Gwen sighed in disappointment. Then a frazzled stable boy ran to hold the bridle of the lead horse, and the hosteler, a fat, balding monk in charge of the wellbeing of guests, waddled out of the chapter house to greet them.

Although Gareth had not come, Gwen smiled when she recognized Prior Rhys riding in at the tail end of the group. His soldierly bearing was unmistakable even underneath his bulky monk's robe. He wasn't in Aberystwyth for the festival but had come because his abbot had sent him to St. Padarn's to consult with the members of the college of priests on a spiritual matter. Gwen hadn't seen him since the evening meal the night before, and at the sight of him, she lifted her hand and finally stepped into the hot sun so she could greet him.

But instead of allowing her to come to him, Prior Rhys dismounted and ran to her, hitching up his robe to reveal the breeches and boots he wore underneath. Just looking at the weight of his clothing made Gwen feel hotter. In addition, his behavior was unusual enough to turn her expression from a smile of greeting to a frown of concern.

"Where might I find your husband?" Rhys said when he reached her. He was of the same generation as Gwen's father, but unlike Meilyr, Rhys's age was revealed not in a burgeoning paunch but in the lines on his face, evidence of many years spent outdoors in the wind and sun. At the moment, his bushy eyebrows had drawn together, making the lines on his forehead more pronounced than ever.

"He was at the castle last I heard." Gwen sidled back to the guesthouse wall so she could stand in the shade. She also wanted to put a few more feet between Rhys and the new arrivals, who were shooting curious glances at the prior. She didn't want him to be the subject of anyone's entertainment, and, had they known him at all, they would have realized that something was very much wrong for him to behave with anything less than absolute dignity.

"I already checked. Both he and the prince were absent. I had hoped to find them here."

Gwen shook her head. "I haven't seen Gareth since this morning. What's wrong?"

"Do you have someone to keep an eye on Tangwen?" Rhys said.

"Elspeth is sitting with—"

"Good. You must come with me." Rhys took Gwen's elbow and urged her across the cobbles to his horse without waiting for her to finish her sentence. He paid no attention at all to the guests, who were now openly staring as they passed. Hoisting himself into his saddle, he held out his elbow for Gwen so she could mount behind him.

She didn't question him, merely took his proffered arm.

The hosteler, however, gazed up at both of them, open-mouthed. "Whatever is the matter? Where are you taking Lady Gwen? What should I tell the abbot?"

Rhys made an exasperated sound at the back of his throat. Glancing at the guests, none of whom were making any pretense of minding any doings but his, he leaned down to speak to the hosteler, lowering his voice so nobody else could hear. "The body of a man has been found in the millpond."

"He's dead?"

Generally 'body' implied 'dead', and Rhys didn't deign to answer in words but simply nodded.

The hosteler stepped back, shocked and sputtering. "But—but—"

"Just tell him," Prior Rhys said.

Then, as Gwen clutched Rhys around the waist, the prior turned the horse toward the exit. Once underneath the gatehouse, however, Gwen said, "May I please have a moment?"

Rhys stopped to allow Gwen to lean down to the gatekeeper, who had come out of his small room next to the gate in response to all the commotion. He was an aged man with white hair and hunched shoulders. "Sion, would you tell my husband or Prince Hywel if he arrives that I have left with Prior Rhys on an urgent matter?"

"Where am I to say you've gone?" Sion said.

Gwen glanced at Rhys, who spoke for her. "The millpond."
The millpond had been carved out of the north bank of the Rheidol
River, southeast of the monastery. Everyone in the region brought
their grain there to grind, though it was most often used by the
castle and the monastery, since they had the most land planted in
grain.

"Of course, Prior Rhys," Sion said. Gwen didn't know that
the gatekeeper could actually see the prior at that distance, but
Rhys had a distinctive gravelly voice that Sion would have
recognized. "Go with God's blessing."

"Thank you," Rhys said and then continued under his
breath as he spurred his horse out onto the road, "We're going to
need it."

Once on the road, he skirted another group of travelers,
some walking, one driving a cart, and two on horseback. This party
was bypassing the monastery in favor of continuing south to the
castle and the festival grounds.

Instead of following them, at the crossroads Gwen and
Prior Rhys headed east towards the mountains. A half-mile farther
on, they turned into a clearing in front of the mill, a stone building
built on the edge of its pond. Several empty carts were parked by
the entrance, and the giant water wheel spun as the water flowed
past. A small group of people had gathered near the edge of the
millpond.

At Rhys's and Gwen's appearance, the man in the center,
who'd been crouching low over something on the ground, looked
over his shoulder. It was Prince Rhun, Hywel's brother and the

eldest prince of Gwynedd. His bright blond hair was lit by the afternoon sunlight that filtered through the green leaves overhanging the pond. Even with a dead body at his feet, Rhun's blue eyes remained bright. Gwen had seen this prince somber, but not often. Prince Rhun had been in Aberystwyth longer than Gwen, escaping (he said) his stepmother's matchmaking.

Prince Rhun had confessed to Gwen upon her arrival that circumstances had reached such a dire point in Gwynedd that his father had decided to become involved. He'd warned Rhun before he left that if he didn't find a wife for himself by the Christmas feast, King Owain was going to allow Cristina to choose one for him.

Recognizing Gwen, Rhun stood. "Thank the Lord the prior found you."

Two monks, instantly recognizable in their undyed cloaks, and two men, wearing the breeches and sweat-stained shirts of laborers, surrounded the body. The monks had kilted their robes and were soaked to the waist, implying that they'd waded in to retrieve it. Although some monasteries employed day laborers or lay brothers—peasant members of the order who were restricted to agricultural work—this monastery required everyone to work and made no distinctions among types of labor.

Rhys and Gwen dismounted, and Gwen studied the dead man from a few feet away before approaching Prince Rhun and the others. The body lay in the dirt and grass beside the pond out of which it had been dragged, far enough away from the water that it didn't lap at its feet. At other murder scenes, how and when the body was moved could make a difference between solving a murder and allowing the murderer to walk free. Today it didn't, since this wasn't the spot where he'd died. Nobody had yet said the word *murder,* but Prior Rhys had to suspect that the man's death wasn't an accident, or else he wouldn't have come to fetch her.

Gwen hadn't been involved in an unexplained death since before Tangwen's birth. Men had died in Gwynedd since then, but none mysteriously as far as she knew. And she would have known: while Prince Hywel was absent and living in Ceredigion, she'd served as a liaison between Hywel's spies and King Owain. Gareth had sworn more than once that he would protect her from these investigations. But since he wasn't here, Gwen was fully capable of stepping into his place, even if she couldn't be pleased that a dead man had been found in the millpond.

"What happened?" she said.

One of the men, larger than most, with thick muscled arms characteristic of heavy labor, scoffed. "He drowned."

Prince Rhun pinned the man with a gaze that would have shot right through him had it been an arrow. "Start at the beginning. Tell Lady Gwen what you know."

Gwen wasn't surprised at the man's dismissal of her question. Until they learned more of her, most men treated her that way. Rhun, however, was a prince, and the man's face flushed red to be chastised by him. He didn't defend himself but merely ducked his head in apology. "Yes, my lord."

"What is your name?" Gwen said.

"My name is Bran. I work the mill," the man said. "I'm the journeyman, though I know more about milling than the miller." He made a motion as if to spit on the ground but stopped himself at the last moment.

"So you've been here all day?" Gwen said.

"Since early morning," Bran said. "I had a short break at noon, but I've been grinding since just after dawn."

"That means you've been inside all day?" Gwen said.

Bran nodded. "It is necessary to pay attention all the time in case something goes wrong. I didn't notice anything amiss out here until young Teilo came running in to tell me about a body in the water. I don't know how long it'd been there. I didn't notice anything this morning or after my noon meal, but I didn't look hard either."

"Thank you." Gwen looked at Teilo, the other laborer not dressed as a monk. His brown hair was cropped close to his head, and like everyone else, sweat beaded in his hairline. He wore a filthy shirt that might have once been the color of cream, brown breeches cut off at the knees, and bare feet. In regards to the heat, he had to be the most comfortable of all of them. "What did you see?"

Teilo looked as if answering the question physically hurt his throat, but he cleared it and said in a low whisper, "I was coming by like I always do—"

"From where?" Prior Rhys said.

Teilo swallowed, and his eye skated from Gwen to Prior Rhys and back again. As with Prince Rhun, Prior Rhys's authority was unmistakable. "From swimming in the river with my friends. We've all worked in the fields since dawn." He said these last words somewhat defensively.

Gwen didn't care if he was avoiding work and didn't blame him for wanting to cool off in the river. "On our way here we passed a water hole full of caterwauling local boys. You'd been among them?"

Teilo nodded.

"My boys would have loved it." Gwen gave a rueful smile at the thought. Gareth had formally adopted their two wayward charges, Llelo and Dai, who were fifteen and twelve. The adoption meant they were now sons of a knight and no longer destined to be herders like their grandfather or a trader like their father. Consequently, their training to be soldiers had begun.

Since neither Gareth nor Gwen had kin of their own to provide guidance for the boys, Prince Hywel had arranged for them to fall under the care of Cynan, his twenty-three-year-old half-brother. Cynan had been fostered by King Owain's sister, who was married to the King of Powys. Recently, King Owain had made Cynan custodian of Denbigh Castle, north of Rhuddlan. From there, he and his two younger brothers, Cadell and Madoc, protected eastern Gwynedd for their father. Dai and Llelo had been welcomed into the garrison, and Gareth was confident they would learn to be knights there.

It had been two months since she'd seen them, and Gwen missed her sons. She planned to visit Denbigh upon her return to Gwynedd in the autumn.

She motioned with her hand to encourage Teilo to continue his story. "You were walking by and ...?"

"And I saw him, bobbing about in the reeds," Teilo said.

"Face down or face up?" Gwen said.

Teilo's face went blank for a moment, but then he said, "Face down."

She needed to ask these kinds of questions, even if they appalled the men, so she tried to ignore their shock. She looked at the two monks. "You two retrieved him?"

They nodded.

"Can you show me exactly where he was floating?" she said.

Prince Rhun answered for them. "He was under the trees, over there in an eddy."

One of the monks then pointed east, to the opposite side of the pond from the mill. The Rheidol River flowed from east to west, emptying ultimately into the sea. Upstream, a portion of the river had been diverted into a man-dug channel to form a pond here, in order to provide a steady supply of water to the water wheel that ran the mill.

Gwen turned back to Prior Rhys. "While I examine the body, would you mind following the others around the edge of the pond to see if you can discover the place where the dead man went in? It would be good to know the exact spot." Gwen remembered from an earlier investigation how uncomfortable the prior had been to witness her examination of a corpse. She would avoid discomfiting him this time if she could.

A smile hovered around Prior Rhys's lips—perhaps in acknowledgement of what she was trying to spare him—but he nodded and gestured to the two monks that they should lead the way. The journeyman begged off, saying he had to get back inside the mill. Gwen watched him go, telling herself not to distrust the man just because he was resentful of his position.

Teilo went with the monks, but before Prior Rhys himself moved away, Gwen caught the edge of his sleeve. "I don't want to tell you what you already know, but Gareth would want me to say this: try to make sure they don't trample whatever evidence has been left."

A smile twitched at the corner of Rhys's mouth.

"Sorry." Gwen looked down, chastising herself for even mentioning it. Prior Rhys had been a soldier and spy before she'd been born. She had no business telling him what to do.

"I value your counsel, Gwen," he said. "I will do my best."

"Thank you."

Prior Rhys turned away to follow the other men around the millpond, and Gwen eyed Prince Rhun, who was hovering over her. "Are you ready for this?"

"I've seen dead bodies before, Gwen." He looked at her carefully. "You must know that I have killed men."

"Yes, but—" Gwen broke off as she thought of how best to say what she meant. Rhun had killed men in war. Gareth had too, of course. But murdering a man—and the sight of a murdered man—was different in both thought and deed, and a man who could kill another man in the heat of battle might find himself squeamish at the sight of the same man dead beside a millpond on an August afternoon. "I know you've seen murdered men before, but it's a beautiful day and maybe you have other tasks that need your attention."

"One—" Prince Rhun held up his right forefinger, "I'm not leaving you alone here with a dead body and men you don't know, and two—" up went the second finger, "I'm interested. I have witnessed the beginning of investigations before—Newcastle comes to mind—but I had other duties there that prevented me from seeing the whole of it."

"Well—" Gwen took in a breath and let it out, accepting that Rhun meant to stay and deciding not to worry about it, "—if you mean it, we might as well get started."

"What do we do first?" Prince Rhun said.

"Well, first of all, we should acknowledge that this man didn't drown.

.

2

Gwen

"He wasn't murdered for his money either," Gwen said, though it was too soon to declare the *why* of his death, which had to come after the *way* of it.

"What? How do you know any of that?" Rhun looked from the body to Gwen and back again.

"My lord, look at the whole of him. He wears a threadbare coat, his soles are thin, despite the three boot makers who have taken stalls at the fair, and his purse is flat and still tied to his belt." Gwen crouched beside the body and carefully removed the purse in order to peer inside it. It contained nothing much: a bit of string, a few small coins, and a fire starter. Nothing to kill a man over, nor anything to indicate the man's identity. Rather than encumber herself with it, she tied the purse loosely back onto his belt.

"If I take a step back, I can see what you mean about his wealth," Rhun said, "especially about the purse. But why do you say he didn't drown? How can you tell that just by looking at him?"

"A drowned man would have spent days in the pond, much of it on the bottom. This man hasn't done that." Gwen gestured up and down the length of the body. "If he'd spent any time in contact with rocks or debris, his nose, forehead, and chin, along with his knees and the back of the hands, would show evidence of it."

"So you're saying the man was dead before he went into the water?" The prince was looking at her intently.

"Dead men float; drowned men sink," Gwen said. "A drowning man dies because he pulls water into his lungs—he breaths it in—and once he dies from it, the weight of the water inside him causes his body to sink. He ends up on the bottom of whatever body of water he fell into. It is only after some days have passed that fumes inside the body cause it to bloat, and float, and eventually rise to the surface again. It's like blowing up a pig's bladder into a ball for children to play with."

Gwen glanced up at Prince Rhun, whose mouth had formed an 'oh', though no sound came out. She plowed on. "In this instance, this man's body is stiff with rigor, which happens within half a day of death. That's not enough time for any real decay or bloating to occur. As you said, he died *before* he went into the pond."

Rhun finally managed to speak, and when he did, his voice was normal in tone. "I'm guessing the murderer didn't know this, or he might have found a different means of disposing of the body."

"I would say you're right," Gwen said.

Rhun's brow furrowed. "What if he'd died naturally and just happened to fall into the water on his own?"

"You mean, perhaps his heart failed or illness overtook him as he was standing on the edge of the water?" Gwen said.

Rhun's lip curled. "When you say it that way, it sounds foolish. Nobody dies that quickly."

Gwen put out a hand to the prince, not quite touching his arm. Rhun thought she was mocking him, but she hadn't meant to. "As I said, the issue is whether he was breathing when he went into the millpond. If he was still alive, even if he was dying, his lungs would have taken in water. He would have sunk to the bottom, and after a few days there, he would not look like this man does."

"He would look much worse. I can see that." Rhun nodded. "Can you tell how long ago he died?"

"He is very stiff." She gently lifted one of the man's arms, though it didn't want to move.

"I would have thought soaking in the water would prevent him from stiffening up," Rhun said, and then made an appeasing gesture of his own. "And don't look at me the way you did before."

"How did I look at you before?"

"Pityingly," Rhun said. "I'm asking questions because I want to know what you know."

Gwen looked down at her hands, taking a moment to compose herself. Then she raised her head. "I apologize, my lord. I didn't mean to offend you. And I certainly don't pity you. Sometimes I get so wrapped up in what I'm seeing that I don't think about what I'm saying. Truthfully, it is helpful to me for you to ask these questions because it clarifies what's in my own mind."

Rhun gave a small smile, looking pleased, and Gwen was hugely relieved to see that she hadn't offended him, or at least he wasn't offended any longer.

She went back to the body. "I would guess that he died in the early hours of the morning, roughly half a day ago. Rigor will vary depending on the temperature of the water. Right now, the water here is about as warm as it ever gets, but it still isn't warmer than the air."

Rhun leaned out and put a hand into the pond. Shaking the excess water off his fingers, he wiped them on his breeches. "The river flows down from the mountains. Even with this heat, the millpond carries a chill."

"He probably would have decomposed faster had he not been thrown in." Then Gwen beckoned to the prince, since he looked as if he was about to move away, thinking they were done. "There's more, my lord."

"More?"

Gwen held back a smile, knowing he wasn't going to like what she was about to do—and opened the man's eyelids with her forefinger and thumb. The revulsion on Rhun's face was almost comical, and he made an involuntary motion with his hand, as if to suggest that she shouldn't have touched the dead man's face.

Gwen ignored his reaction. "You can tell a great deal about how a man died from the condition of the eyes."

Rhun swallowed down whatever protest he'd been about to make and joined her, kneeling in the dirt beside the body. Beads of sweat dampened the hair at his temples, but another quick glance at him told Gwen that he'd been telling the truth earlier: he was hot, as they all were, but he wasn't squeamish.

"When a man drowns, tiny red or brownish spots form in the eyes. Gareth thinks the change has something to do with what happens when a person is deprived of breath. He's seen it also in the eyes of men who've been strangled. Regardless, this man doesn't have those spots."

Rhun gazed intently into the dead man's face. The prince didn't seem to have anything to say, so Gwen continued, "Did the monks close his eyes?"

"They did. His eyes were open when he came out of the water. How did you know?"

"When eyes dry out, a splotchy brown line forms in the whites," Gwen said. "I'm not seeing that here. Nor have his eyes turned opaque. I'm guessing that this man died somewhere very close by and was put in the water immediately after."

As Gwen let go of the dead man's eyelids, Rhun reached out a hand and widened them again. His revulsion seemed to have left him.

"But even without all that, I know the man didn't die from drowning." Intentionally keeping her face expressionless so Rhun couldn't see the triumph in her face at her discovery, Gwen gingerly poked her finger through a slit in the man's shirt, right under his left breast. "He was stabbed in the chest."

Rhun bent forward, lifting the shirt to show the wound beneath. "You're right." Then he frowned. "Why is there so little blood on his clothing? The front of his shirt is stained with mud and blood, but not nearly as much as I might have expected from a stab wound."

"That is very observant of you, my lord," Gwen said, "and I can explain that too."

"I can't wait to hear it."

Gwen just managed not to smirk at his sarcasm. "You must have noticed that when you stab a man, if you keep the blade in his body, blood doesn't really flow from the wound until you remove it. The sword—or the arrow—acts as a plug."

"I have seen that," Rhun said. "I may not know much about murder, but I've seen death in battle. Usually men don't die quickly, especially from such a small stab wound. And yet, this man barely bled at all."

"You're right," Gwen said, "but if the murderer waited until the man was dead to remove the blade, the blood would hardly have flowed from the wound. The instant the heart stops, the body stops bleeding. And if he fell on his back, and the murderer let the body set for a moment, the blood would have pooled away from the wound. Then he could have put him into the pond face first. The blood near the wound would have done little more than seep out the gash, and the water would have washed most of that away."

Gwen was glad to see that Rhun was looking at her with an expression that was closer to awe than horror. "You're amazing, Gwen."

She tsked through her teeth. "Gareth would have realized he hadn't drowned within moments of looking at him too. The blade was thin and narrow, but you can't hide a death wound like thi—" She broke off with a gasp she couldn't suppress as she bent to study the wound more closely. It very much resembled one she'd seen before—on the road to Dolwyddelan, three years ago almost to the day.

"What is it, Gwen? What's wrong?" Rhun was looking at her with concern.

She shook herself. "Nothing, my lord. It's nothing."

"It isn't nothing. You practically jumped out of your skin," Rhun said.

Gwen suppressed the impatient growl that rose to the back of her throat. Rhun might not have much experience observing the details of murdered men, but he had always been good at reading people. Gwen traced the line of the wound, her finger a hair's-breadth above it because in this instance she didn't want to touch the skin if she could help it. "Do you see the way the wound is ragged here? The blade had a notch in it."

Rhun leaned closer to look, putting his nose six inches from the man's chest. "I see what you mean, though if you hadn't shown me, I wouldn't have noticed." He paused. "Murder, like you said."

"This is definitely murder." Gwen sat back on her heels. Hywel wasn't going to be happy to learn that someone had been murdered on the eve of his festival, unless he himself had done it. Her heart sped up a little to think about it. *Please God, let it not have been him.*

Rhun rose to his feet, and she looked up at him. "My lord, we need to keep this quiet if we can—for as long as we can."

Rhun looked down at her. "The man is dead. How do we keep that quiet?"

"I didn't mean his death," Gwen said. "I meant that it was murder. Everyone will believe that he drowned, and for now, it might be better if the murderer didn't know that we know that he didn't."

Rhun laughed under his breath. Gwen didn't know what he was laughing at, so she hurried to explain. "Prince Hywel taught me to give out as little information as possible. If someone knows more about the death than he should, he might be the murderer."

"If the murderer is here for the festival, he might have hoped to have been long gone before the body surfaced." Rhun said.

Gwen chewed on her lower lip, thinking that the prince was looking a little too fascinatedly at the body. Simply because they'd often been called to investigate it, Hywel, Gwen, and Gareth had learned the ins and outs of murder, but there had been something wholesome about Rhun's unfamiliarity with it. Gwen was starting to regret besmirching Rhun's innocence with her long lecture about the differences between a drowned man and a murdered one. And if Prince Hywel had anything to do with the murder, it would be best if she could find a way to keep his brother far, far away from it.

For now, that wasn't going to be possible, especially since Prior Rhys appeared at the edge of the trees a moment later and waved at them.

"Let's get one of the monks back here to guard the body," Prince Rhun said. "It looks like the prior has something to tell us."

3

Rhun

Although Rhun had participated in several of these investigations at which Hywel excelled, he'd never been one to trek around in the mud looking for clues to the killer. As he and Gwen headed around the edge of the pond, following Prior Rhys, Rhun truly appreciated for the first time the necessity for speed, discretion, and the careful placement of feet.

The undergrowth around the pond was thick and prolific, with vegetation everywhere he looked. This week of heat had been preceded by a month of rain, and the woodlands were a long way from drying out. As Rhun stumped through the ferns and bushes on a well-worn path, Rhun found himself admiring Prior Rhys's skill in preventing Teilo and the monks from trampling whatever evidence might have been left behind. At the same time, he knew exactly what the prior had done to achieve it: he had a way of looking at a man that sent shivers down his spine. And if Rhun, a prince of Gwynedd, felt that way, one would be hard pressed to find an illiterate peasant who could withstand it for more than a few heartbeats.

"What have you discovered?" Gwen said when Prior Rhys stopped in a small open space near the water's edge. She, apparently, remained unintimidated.

Prior Rhys indicated the ground in front of him, giving no indication he objected to Gwen's straightforward demand. "Some blood and scuffed earth."

"What do they tell you?" Gwen said. "It's pretty clear from the body that the man was stabbed."

If Rhun hadn't known it before, he was learning it now: when Gwen focused, very little could deter her from her chosen path. Some might claim that doggedness was a man's trait, but Rhun knew quite a few women with that characteristic, some of whom had far less tact than Gwen. Rhun's stepmother, Cristina, came instantly to mind, and half-shuddering, Rhun pushed away her image.

Hywel had teased Rhun only this morning about his quest for a wife, wondering how he was going to find one stuck away in the backwater that was Aberystwyth. What Hywel didn't yet know—and Rhun wasn't going to tell him until things had progressed much farther than they so far had—was that he was well on his way to finding his own wife.

Rhun had been spending the summer supporting his brother's rule of Ceredigion, and in so doing, Rhun had traveled multiple times at Hywel's behest to visit Dinefwr Castle, the seat of King Cadell of Deheubarth. Relations had been more cordial than Rhun (or Hywel) might have expected, considering that Hywel was ruling Ceredigion, which Cadell considered part of Deheubarth and rightfully under his jurisdiction.

While Rhun had been overtly supporting Hywel's agenda, he had also been pursuing his own. Cadell had a niece, Angharad, who had caught Rhun's eye. When Cadell had agreed to attend Hywel's festival, the king had also promised that Angharad would accompany him to Aberystwyth.

But even if Gwen had known about Angharad, Rhun's romantic prospects were the last thing that she was concerned about right now. Rhun, however, hoped that this murder would be cleared up quickly, before Angharad arrived. He didn't want anything to distract him from her, even as—almost against his wishes—he could feel a growing sense of obligation to discover who had murdered this poor, unnamed peasant.

Prior Rhys seemed to be feeling it too. He bared his teeth in a silent grimace as he looked through the overhanging branches, thick with leaves this time of year, to the millpond. "Stabbed is it? What do you say to the idea that the dead man and his killer conversed in this small space?" He made a sweeping motion with his arm to indicate the area under the trees a dozen feet from the edge of the pond. "They argued, one man stabbed the other, he fell, and then the murderer dragged the body into the pond, hoping to wash away the evidence."

"I can see it," Prince Rhun said. "He hoped the body would sink as drowned bodies are supposed to."

Prior Rhys raised his eyebrows.

"Thus Gwen explained to me just now," Rhun added. "The killer would have wanted to put time and space between him and the body immediately. Hiding the evidence was one way to do that. He should have buried it instead."

"It takes time and effort to dig a grave deep enough to bury a man, time the murderer may not have had," Prior Rhys said. "Not to mention a shovel."

"It would have been difficult to keep quiet about it this close to the road and the monastery too," Prince Rhun agreed. "The millpond must have seemed like an easy solution."

"Prior." Teilo was back, ducking his head in obeisance. "We haven't found anything else."

Prior Rhys nodded. "Thank you for your efforts." He dismissed the monk to help his brother monk guard the body. Then he sent Teilo off too, with a warning not to gossip about what he'd seen. Given Teilo's bright eyes, Rhun suspected the warning fell on deaf ears. It was a good thing Teilo hadn't witnessed Gwen's examination of the body because the story he would tell would be that the man had drowned, just as they wanted.

Prior Rhys looked at Gwen. "If the murderer left the area, we may never catch him."

"We can't think that way," Gwen said. "Hywel always tells me to pull on any thread that's offered and unravel it to see where it leads. If the murderer has left Aberystwyth, we will know soon enough."

Prince Rhun's brows came together. "That would make the murderer a newcomer to the area—"

"Since the alarm hasn't been raised about the dead man's absence, he appears to be a stranger too," Prior Rhys said. "Plenty of strangers here for the festival."

"Yes," Prince Rhun said, "but if the murderer is one of the visitors to the festival he won't have left yet. Gwen told me that if our dead man had drowned, he would have stayed under the water for days, giving the murderer enough time to see the festival through and depart before the body was found."

"How do we know the stab wound was what killed him? Not all such wounds are fatal." The prior had turned to face Rhun, and it was with a small degree of surprise that Rhun realized the prior was taking him seriously. Rhun had always felt that Rhys considered him something of a spoiled princeling, dismissing him in favor of Hywel, who was more clever and less open than Rhun.

It had never bothered Rhun that the prior had assessed him thus and found him wanting—or at least it hadn't bothered him very much. Rhun knew that his father looked upon him with favor. He was the *etifedd*, the first born son and heir to the throne. It was his birthright to be favored. Rhun could give way in favor of his younger brother once in his life.

Still, in his own mind, Rhun had never meant to play the princeling or take for granted what God had given him, which was why he was pleased to see Prior Rhys speaking to him man-to-man. Rhun didn't like having his qualities questioned, especially by someone whom he himself admired.

"Gwen says the man was dead before he went into the water," Rhun said.

Rhys made a *huh* sound at the back of his throat. "Regardless, there doesn't appear to be much blood."

"If he died quickly, there wouldn't have been," Rhun said.

"Why is that?" Prior Rhys said.

"Because corpses don't bleed."

Prior Rhys's eyes actually twinkled. "You learn quickly."

"Gwen is a good teacher."

Ignoring their exchange entirely, Gwen had been standing with one arm around her waist and the fingers of the other hand to her lips, studying the crushed vegetation. Then she bent into a walking crouch and began moving around the small space, her hands on her knees and her eyes on the ground. "Gareth tells me that if you really want to kill a man without leaving a trace, you slice him between the bones at the back of his neck." She rubbed at the back of her own neck to show the two men where she meant. "He will immediately drop to the ground, and his death will be nearly instantaneous. There will be very little blood to scrub away, and you'd hardly have touched the body."

Prior Rhys moved out of Gwen's way, looking upon her with amusement. Rhun didn't know whether to be horrified or impressed anew that she knew so much about effective methods of killing men. He was glad, regardless, that she was with them today. Though he'd sent Prior Rhys to find Gareth, Gwen was proving to be more than adequate to the task before her.

Thinking to help, Rhun bent to observe the soil and dead leaves that had been scraped in a path from the base of a tree to the pond. The marks ended at the water's edge. He frowned. "Is the level of the pond higher than it was last night or earlier today?"

Gwen remained bent over, but she turned her head to see where Rhun was gesturing to the plants growing beneath the level of the water—plants that wouldn't normally have grown under water at all.

"The water clearly ebbs and flows," Prior Rhys said, understanding Rhun's point immediately. "Would the murderer have known that and could he have used it to his advantage?"

"You have good eyes, my lord," Gwen said.

"Perhaps I should ask the mill master," Prince Rhun said. "It should be he who controls the level of the water coming from the river through the sluice gates."

Gwen straightened. "That's a good idea."

Rhun didn't feel like Gwen was mocking him, though he could tell that his assumption of responsibility amused her. He hadn't been able to hide how surprised—even shocked—he'd been at her knowledge of death, and how little about it he knew himself, despite his experience with war. He'd been beside her for all of an hour and already he knew more about murder than he'd learned in the dozen battles he'd led and from the men he'd killed.

He was ashamed to realize it.

Whether a man died in battle or of old age, Rhun had viewed death as a definitive process. But he'd been wrong about that. Death in battle might be violent, but death by murder was an evil thing, with darkness at its center.

"Please come find us when you've spoken with him. Prior Rhys and I will continue to search." Gwen glanced at the prior, who nodded. "Even if the others found nothing of interest, it might be worthwhile to look again. We can't pass up the chance that the murderer left a token of himself here. A cloth caught on a branch or a footprint could help us discover who he is."

"You're assuming the murderer is a man." Rhun was turning away as he spoke, but he caught Gwen's *whuf* of surprised laughter. Smiling, Rhun continued through the trees back towards where the dead man lay.

Gwen called after him. "I was assuming, my lord. We would do well to remember not to!"

Still laughing to himself, Rhun waved a hand above his head in acknowledgement of her comment but didn't turn around. This murder had well and truly caught his attention. He wanted to help with the work. And truthfully, the miller might respond to his authority better than to Gwen's. Gwen was the wife of a knight, but Rhun had met the miller in his ramblings around Aberystwyth over the last few months, and the man had an attitude that was common to many middle-aged men: he'd reached a point in his life where he was sure of the world and his place in it. A young woman investigating a murder might very well rub him the wrong way like a cat stroked tail to head.

The miller hadn't been present at the discovery of the body, making it unlikely that Rhun would find him in the mill itself. But as Rhun came out of the trees near the clearing, a few yards from where the monks still guarded the dead man, the miller drove a one-horse cart into the clearing and halted. Spying the monks, he leaped from the cart and loped towards the water's edge.

Then he caught sight Rhun and pulled up, blanching. "My lord! I heard there's been some trouble." He looked from Rhun to the monks and back again.

"You could say that," Rhun said.

To Rhun's mind, the miller was currently at the top of his (admittedly short) list of suspects. The miller knew his pond well. He could have killed the man and raised the level of the water in the pond in hopes of hiding evidence of where the body had gone in. Prior Rhys had so quickly discovered the exact spot where the man had died, despite the water level, because Gwen had been on hand with a working knowledge of what was to be done. If Prior Rhys hadn't hastened to bring her to the scene and prevented the monks from carting the body back to the monastery right away, much of the evidence that could ultimately point to a killer could have been lost.

In addition, if Rhun himself hadn't known that a dead body thrown into the water wouldn't sink to the bottom, it was easy to believe the miller wouldn't have known it either.

The miller had moved a few more paces towards the monks, his eyes on the body on the ground. "Is that—?" He couldn't take his eyes off it. He put a cloth to his mouth, and his throat contracted.

"A dead man, yes," Rhun said. "Would you be so kind as to look into his face and tell me if you recognize him?"

"Of course, of course." The miller mopped his sweating brow.

Rhun might have read guilt in the action, but it was a hot afternoon. He should delay any conclusion until he learned more. One of the monks had laid a handkerchief across the dead man's face, and now he removed it.

"Do you know him?" Rhun said.

The miller bent over the body for a moment and then straightened, clear relief sweeping across his face. "No, my lord. No, I don't."

"Are you sure?" Rhun said.

"I'm sure. I was afraid for a moment—" He stopped.

Rhun pounced on the man's hesitation. "What were you afraid of? If you know anything about his death, I need to know it right now."

"I know nothing." The miller shook his head vehemently back and forth. "I was going to say that I've been waiting for my apprentice to return from his aunt's house in Borth." He gestured helplessly to the body. "Even were I unsure of this man's features, this body isn't missing a hand."

"Excuse me?" Rhun said. "Your apprentice is missing a hand?"

The miller waved a hand dismissively. "He's a good worker nonetheless."

Rhun was sure that Gareth or Gwen would have done a better job at hiding their surprise, but he took a breath and soldiered on nonetheless. "Did you have some particular reason to think this was your apprentice?"

"Not-not really. I expected him back from Borth this morning, but he hasn't come. When I learned a body had been found, I feared the worst. But this isn't he." The miller clasped his hands in front of him to stop himself from wringing them.

The miller was genuinely concerned, and Rhun felt his sympathies rising, despite the fact that the miller's information was turning out not to be worth very much. The miller put the cloth back to his mouth. He had turned a distinctive shade of green.

Rhun pointed to the water's edge a few feet away. "If you are going to be sick, please move away."

The miller swallowed hard and lifted his eyes towards the sky. "I am well enough."

"What can you tell me about the millpond?" Rhun said.

"What do you need to know about it, my lord?"

"Is the water level higher today than yesterday?"

"Ach, yes." The miller flapped his cloth. "I always raise it when I have a large amount of grain to grind. And with the orders from both the monastery and the castle that came in two days ago because of the festival, I knew I'd be grinding day and night throughout the week."

"How quickly does the water level rise once you increase the width of the sluice gate?"

"It takes some hours," the miller said. "It's a constant battle to get it right, and don't get me started on what it's like in the spring during the floods."

"I'm sure it isn't easy," Rhun said appeasingly. "Does anyone guard the mill at night?"

"My apprentice sleeps in the loft," the miller said.

"The one who went to Borth?"

"The same," the miller said.

Rhun just managed to refrain from rolling his eyes. "So you're telling me that nobody was sleeping in the mill last night."

"No, my lord. Nobody."

"Where were you just now?"

"I had business in the village. My journeyman is more than capable of running the mill in my absence."

Rhun was convinced that the miller's business had included more than one tankard of mead, but he didn't mention it. He wanted to keep the miller cooperative, not confront him with shirking his duties. Rhun glanced at the body, thinking of what question to ask next. So far the miller had explained about the water level in the millpond, which Hywel probably already knew but had been able to add little else. Rhun wasn't going to have anything much to show Prior Rhys and Gwen when he saw them next. Then he consoled himself with the fact that at least they wouldn't waste their time questioning someone who couldn't help.

"May I go, my lord? I have business to attend to."

Rhun nodded, waving a hand to dismiss the miller. "We know where to find you if we need to speak with you again."

The miller ducked his head and departed.

"My lord!"

Rhun spun around to see Gareth urge his horse off the road and into the clearing in front of the mill. Almost at the same moment, Gwen and Prior Rhys appeared out of the trees and crossed the clearing towards him.

Rhun felt a rush of relief and wasn't ashamed to admit it. Without help, this murder investigation would have had *him* in over his head and drowning.

Gareth dismounted, looking every inch the captain of the guard he was: tall and broad-shouldered with close-cropped dark hair and intelligent blue eyes. He grasped the much smaller Gwen by her upper arms and held her as he looked down into her face. If they weren't in the middle of a murder scene, Rhun would have wagered his best horse that Gareth would have wrapped his wife up in a hug and kissed her. They'd been married for nearly three years, and a blind man could see how much they loved each other.

Rhun wanted that for himself. He hoped that he might find it someday. Maybe even—he allowed himself a sliver of hope and anticipation—with Angharad.

4

Gareth

"We have a murder," Gwen said.

Gareth refrained from wondering aloud how it was that Gwen had managed yet again to be on the scene of a murder before he'd even learned there was a body. Then he looked around the clearing, a feeling of unease rising in him that had nothing to do with the murder. "My lord," he said, turning to Rhun. "Where are your guards?"

"I dismissed them."

"My lord, how could you—"

Rhun raised a hand. "I know, I know. I am a prince of Gwynedd. But this isn't Gwynedd—"

"That's right this isn't Gwynedd!" Gareth said, and then he swallowed, working hard to modulate his tone. "It's Ceredigion, with Normans and spies and common folk who haven't forgiven Cadwaladr for his misuse of them and your father for putting him above them."

Rhun had the grace to look abashed. He bobbed his head in a semblance of a bow, which was more than Gareth deserved for chastising a prince—especially when that prince wasn't even his own master but his lord's brother. "I stand corrected. And before you ask, no—Hywel didn't know that I rode out alone today."

"Why did you?" Gareth said.

Rhun pressed his lips together, such that Gareth thought he wasn't going to answer or had an answer that Gareth wasn't going to like. Maybe he'd been seeing a woman.

At that thought, Gareth put up both hands and took a step back. "Never mind, my lord. Your doings are not my concern."

Rhun gave a short laugh and shook his head. "I'm getting rusty, Gareth. That's all."

"I don't understand."

Prince Rhun's eyes skated to Prior Rhys for a heartbeat and then came back to Gareth. "In Gwynedd, of late the people have been looking to me for leadership. Some have been treating me like I'm already king. It isn't—" the prince paused, thinking, "—good for me."

Gareth took in a deep breath through his nose and let it out, embarrassed at the way he'd dressed Rhun down, even though he was right. He gave Rhun a bow. The prince usually had more sense, but Gareth could understand how stifling it must be to have guards accompany him everywhere he went, and how it might not be good for him to be treated like a prince all the time, even if he was one.

"It won't happen again," Rhun said, "so you don't have to tell my brother."

"Yes, my lord," Gareth said.

"Have you spoken to my brother recently?" Rhun said.

"I was with him for much of the day, but he sent me to the monastery saying he had some business at the castle," Gareth said. "His brow was furrowed as he left."

"He has many concerns, especially since our father should have arrived already and isn't here," Prince Rhun said. "I will find him after we're done here and share the load."

Hywel had acquired a great number of worries since he'd taken over the rule of Ceredigion. Both Prince Rhun and Gareth had spent much of the summer trying to lift some of those burdens, the greatest of which, truth be told, was the festival and of Hywel's own making. Hywel had conceived the idea at the beginning of the summer, and it had consumed him ever since. He wanted it to be perfect; he wanted to impress his father; he wanted to be remembered.

Hywel's other worries—namely the security of Ceredigion and its people—were ongoing. But once he'd opened his heart to his father two years ago and received advice and assistance, much of his anxiety had been lifted from him. Mari's steady influence— and the birth of his son—had gone a long way towards keeping him on an even keel in every other way too.

Gareth bowed again to Rhun and turned back to his wife. "Why don't you talk me through what you know about this death."

Gwen swept aside some stray locks that had come loose from the bindings holding back her hair and gestured to Prior Rhys. "I wasn't the one to find the body. Prior Rhys came to the guest house to find you and got me instead."

Gareth transferred his gaze to Prior Rhys, glad to change the subject back to the task at hand. "So you found the body?"

"No," Prior Rhys said.

"A laborer did," Rhun said. "We have already questioned and dismissed him."

Gareth held back a sarcastic request for *someone* to tell him what was going on before the body in question rotted behind them. Fortunately, it lay in the shade at the water's edge. It wouldn't matter if it took a little more time before they transported it inside.

Gareth tipped his head in Prince Rhun's direction. "My lord, perhaps you could begin by saying how you became involved. Why were you at the mill?" He didn't add *without your guards*, deciding he'd already said enough on that score.

"I was returning to the castle after finishing an errand for my brother—nothing important, just a message to one of his overseers—when a boy raced down the road towards me, waving his arms with a story about finding a body in the millpond. I turned in, of course, and saw Prior Rhys's horse cropping grass by the mill entrance."

"Why were you here, Prior Rhys?" Gareth said.

"I was visiting the mill because the prior of St. Padarn's asked me to inspect it."

"Inspect it? Why is that?" Gareth said.

"While I came to Aberystwyth on behalf of my abbot to confer about a spiritual matter, when Prior Pedr learned that I was the prior of St. Kentigern's, he asked for my advice on the running of St. Padarn's."

The arcane point of doctrine in question was one about which Gareth, fortunately, cared nothing. It didn't appear that Rhys thought it was important either, but he was under orders and was obeying them. Gareth was happy to leave matters of the Church to the Church. And he thought the prior of St. Padarn's was showing remarkably good sense in employing Prior Rhys in more practical matters while he was here.

"It is a rare man who can ask for assistance, and an even rarer one who is as open to new information," Gareth said.

Rhys bowed his head. "Both of which I have found Prior Pedr to be."

Being open to new information was a quality that Prior Rhys had proven himself to possess in large measure, to Gareth's benefit. A former soldier and spy, Prior Rhys had a checkered past which he'd put behind him—mostly successfully—since he'd given his life over to the Church.

"I dismounted and walked to the water," Prince Rhun said, continuing his story, "and there was the body, just as the boy had said."

"Where was it when you saw it, my lord?" Gareth said.

"Bobbing in the shallows on the eastern end of the pond. It had been caught up in an eddy," Rhun said. "While Prior Rhys rode for the monastery to find you, the boy and I rounded up men to retrieve the body from the water. We have so far kept whatever we have learned to ourselves."

Then Prince Rhun related his interview with the miller, and Gwen and Prior Rhys described what they'd found by the edge of the pond. Gareth listened intently to all three before finally crouching beside the body himself. He'd learned over the years that more eyes were better than fewer, and he was glad they'd done what they could to preserve the scene until either he or Hywel could arrive. Gwen knew exactly what to do, of course. He was pleased that Prior Rhys and Prince Rhun had learned as well.

With a wave of his hand, Gareth suggested that the two monks wait in a cooler spot under a tree, and then he looked at the prince. "I appreciate your discretion, my lord. The fewer people who know the details of an investigation, the better."

"That is as Gwen said," Rhun said. "Your thanks should be given to her and to Prior Rhys."

"Don't listen to him, Gareth," Gwen said. "The prince has been nothing but helpful."

Rhun ignored the accolade. "What do you see?"

Gareth surveyed the body, pleased that Gwen had gotten it right again. Not only was it clear the man didn't drown, but the stab wound that Gwen had pointed out was unmistakable. He raised the hem of the dead man's shirt to examine it, but what he saw had him tsking through his teeth. "He knew his killer."

"I agree. When we find out the man's name," Gwen said, "we should be able to limit the suspects to those he knew."

Prince Rhun bent forward, his hands on his knees. "Why are you so sure of that? In the dark, two strangers might speak to one another and stand close enough for one to stab the other."

"That might be true in a crowd," Gareth said, "but would it be true when they're beside the millpond in the dark of night?"

Gwen swung her hands in a two-foot circle around her body. "How often do you allow someone to move into this space, my lord?"

Prince Rhun frowned. "I would allow a woman to come that close."

"But a man?" Gwen said.

"Other than my brother, only when I greet him," Rhun said.

"For which you use your right hand." Gwen pointed at the wound. "No man could die from that wound while greeting another. The angle is impossible if struck with the knife in the left hand."

"Besides which," Prior Rhys said, "if one stranger intends to kill another, he would know that he would find it hard to get close. He would have sprung upon him, surprising him if he could."

Rhun sucked on his teeth. "All right. You've convinced me. He knew his killer."

Gareth laughed. "We'd better be correct about this, Gwen, or we'll never live it down."

Gwen crouched beside Gareth, laughing under her breath too. Having his wife so close jumbled Gareth's thoughts for a moment. Almost absently, he traced the wound with one finger. Then, in a rush, what he was seeing came into focus. His brow furrowed. "That looks similar to—" He leaned in to examine the wound more closely and found Gwen gripping his wrist. He glanced at her, and she shook her head almost imperceptibly.

He sat back, a chill running up and down his spine.

5

Gareth

Gareth stood, and as he helped Gwen to her feet, his
fingers entwined with hers, both of them holding on
tight.

"We should move the body inside." Gareth turned to Prior
Rhys. "Is it customary here to place a body in the chapel or
somewhere else?"

"They have a small room off the nave set aside for it," Rhys
said.

"Good," Gareth said. "It will be far cooler inside than out
here. As it is, he'll have to be put in the ground by the end of the
day tomorrow at the very latest. It's just too hot."

"Probably before," Gwen said.

"Hopefully, we'll know his name before then," Prince Rhun
said.

"We'll do our best," Gwen said.

"Surely someone will have missed him," Gareth said, "but
at the very least, I can draw his face."

"That's a good idea." Gwen nodded approvingly. "Any loved one will find him unpleasant to look upon as he is now. Better to show them the image instead."

Gareth went to his saddlebag and removed paper and charcoal. With quick movements, he sketched a rough image of the dead man's face, trying to draw him as he would have been in life, not bloodless and cold from the water as he was now.

Meanwhile, Prior Rhys beckoned the two monks out of the shade. With Prior Rhys and Prince Rhun assisting, they loaded the body into the largest of the handcarts waiting by the entrance to the mill. Gareth finished his drawing and returned to Gwen's side.

After the men heaved the body into the cart, Gwen pointed to the man's face. Despite the movement required to lift and load him, no pink foam trickled out of the corner of his mouth. "He really was dead when he went into the water."

"You thought you'd made a mistake?" Gareth said.

Gwen shrugged. "Sometimes it feels like all we have are guesses. I'm comforted when they appear to be good ones."

"What are you talking about?" Rhun said, ever curious.

"When a man drowns, he spits up the water he took into his lungs, even after death," Gwen said. "This man is missing that telltale sign, once again confirming our initial supposition."

While Gareth stowed the picture of the dead man in the bag with his paper and charcoal, Gwen said, "Give me a moment," and hurried away towards the mill, disappearing inside.

Everyone stopped, looking after her and uncertain as to what she was doing. Then she returned with a bundle of cloth in her arms, which turned out to be several large bags used for carrying grain.

"None of us wore cloaks today so we have nothing to cover him with, but we don't want him on display as we travel down the road," she said.

"That was thoughtful of you," Prior Rhys said. "Thank you." And between the two of them, they laid the sacks over the body to cover it completely.

Gareth signaled to the monks to start pulling the cart. Prince Rhun and Prior Rhys tugged on the bridles of their horses, but like Gareth, neither man mounted, choosing to walk behind the cart with Gwen. The monks got the cart rolling, and the companions began the half-mile walk back to the monastery.

As they walked, Gareth could just hear the sound of music coming up from the festival grounds on the other side of the river. Music came more clearly from travelers moving along the road, whether from a bard warming up his voice and his fingers on his instrument, or spectators singing the latest ballad they'd heard. Regardless, each person turned his or her head as the cart passed, peering curiously into the bed to see what had prompted such a somber walk by three monks, a knight and his lady, and a prince.

Most of the looks—and many bows—were directed at Rhun, who acknowledged them without fanfare.

"Gwen, it might be a good idea not to discuss any of this with Mari," Gareth said.

Gwen and Mari had rooms in the guest house because Mari's quarters at the castle, approximately a mile and a half away from the monastery as the crow flies, were less than adequate to her current needs. She was pregnant again and sicker even than with her first child. Six months after Tangwen's birth, Mari had been delivered of a healthy boy whom she and Hywel had named Gruffydd after Hywel's grandfather. Thankfully—and despite the difficult pregnancy—Gruffydd had been born without complications and was now a very active one year old.

But Mari's pregnancy meant that she could bear neither the press of humanity at the castle nor the smell. The latrine, in particular, wasn't functioning as it should, and Mari had found the stench unbearable every time she walked outside, prompting her to lose whatever was in her stomach. Prince Hywel had arranged for Gwen to stay with her at the monastery guest house until the heat wave passed, the festival was over, the latrine was redesigned and fixed, and/or Mari managed to get her pregnancy sickness under control.

It would have been more appropriate for Mari to stay at the local convent, but that was no longer possible. Although Alice, Prince Cadwaladr's wife, had given birth to their daughter there three years ago, it had been in serious decline since before the 1136 war and had failed the previous year. None of the interventions implemented by either Cadwaladr or Hywel—or the sisters' order—had managed to turn the tide, and the last nun had died last Christmas feast. With Hywel's permission, the monks had taken over the lands the convent had controlled, including the mill and pond on the Rheidol River.

"Oh, I know," Gwen said. "I wish I could do something for her other than hold the basin and look after Gruffydd. At least we have her eating on a regular schedule now. I'm hoping that the worst of her sickness will soon be over."

"Speaking of Gruffydd, where's Tangwen?" Gareth said, trying to make the question sound casual. He would not want to imply, even obliquely, that she'd mislaid their daughter.

Gwen smiled. "She fell asleep moments before Prior Rhys arrived." Gwen checked the position of the sun in the sky. "I would hope she might still be asleep, but you know Tangwen."

Gareth did. He adored their daughter, but she had never been an easy sleeper and fought it at every turn, as if by sleeping she might miss something important. If her desire to stay awake left her cheerful instead of petulant, they could have let her be. As it was, some days Gareth might pace in circles with Tangwen for an hour to get her to sleep, only to have her wake the moment he laid her on her pallet.

The first time he'd seen Mari set Gruffydd on the bed and tuck a blanket around him, Gareth had laughed at the absurdity of her expectation that the boy would close his eyes and fall asleep on his own. But then he had. If Gareth hadn't seen it with his own eyes he wouldn't have believed it possible.

And sure enough, as they turned in to pass through the monastery gatehouse, Elspeth was just coming out of the guesthouse with Tangwen on her hip. The daughter of Gareth's steward, Elspeth was buxom and blonde, and if she wasn't currently living in a monastery, she would have had men circling her constantly to court her. Her father hoped that a year or two as Tangwen's nanny, under Gwen's sober influence, might steady her and prepare her for adult life. Gareth didn't have much hope of that and might have picked out a man for her to marry already if he didn't selfishly want her to continue as Tangwen's nanny for a little while longer at least.

Elspeth set the child down, and Tangwen dashed across the courtyard towards Gwen, who moved forward to intercept her. With a mop of curly brown hair and brown eyes, Tangwen was the most beautiful little girl in Wales. She was also only eighteen months old, and Gareth was glad when Gwen scooped her up before she reached the cart. She was a little young to be introduced to her first murdered man.

Tangwen waved to him over her mother's shoulder, and Gareth called to her from across the courtyard. "*Cariad,* Papa has work to do. I will find you later."

That seemed to mollify Tangwen, though sending up a wail of frustration would have been equally usual for her. As it was, she had no choice but to go with her mother, who carried her around the corner of the guesthouse a moment later.

Sion, the gatekeeper, had come out of the gatehouse to see who'd entered, and Prior Rhys hustled forward to meet the hosteler, who'd poked his head out of the chapter house. He'd probably been watching for guests to come through the gatehouse, not for a cart with a body in it. Several carts already parked in the courtyard implied that even more travelers had arrived for the festival. Gareth had no idea where they were going to put them all, but no matter the press of people, presumably the chapel would remain free of guests.

He had been hoping to take Tangwen to see some of the performances this afternoon, and Prince Hywel himself would perform tomorrow night. The whole event would conclude the day after that with performances by the finalists and the presentation of awards and prizes.

The festival was taking place in and around a large pavilion in the field below the castle. A small fair and market had grown up beside it. Gareth had counted no fewer than four dressmakers present, one of whom he hoped he could arrange for Gwen to visit. He'd like to commission a new dress as a gift to her.

Various contests were also occurring on the many stages set up around the field. In addition to musicians of every type (among them genuine bards like Meilyr, Gwen's father), dancers, jugglers, and actors had come to perform.

"Is that-is that him?" The hosteler gaped at the shrouded body in the back of the cart.

Gareth took the hosteler's words to mean that their arrival wasn't as unexpected as he'd originally thought. Sion bent to whisper in the man's ear, and he ran off.

"What did you say to him?" Prince Rhun said.

"I told him to stop gawking and fetch the prior," Sion said.

The two monks had disappeared into the stable immediately upon putting down the arms of the cart. They came back with a board on which to carry the dead man, which would provide a more dignified means to bring him into the chapel than to carry him sagging between them. Gareth and Prior Rhys helped them load the body onto it, with Sion carefully replacing the burlap sacks over his body. Then he went back to his watch while Rhun, Gareth, and the two monks each took a corner in order to move the body into the chapel. Prior Rhys walked at the front to lead the way.

The doors to the stone chapel had remained closed all day, keeping the natural coolness of the stones inside. The contrast between the heat outside and the darkened interior was so great Gareth shivered, feeling the sweat cool instantly on his skin. Prior Rhys directed them across the nave towards one of the side wings, through a small doorway, and into a vestibule that contained a small altar, two upright chairs, and a six-foot-long table. This was clearly where the dead usually resided until the burial ceremony. With a heave, they settled the dead man on the table, leaving him on the long board rather than shifting him off it.

"Thank you," Prior Rhys said to the monks. Gareth had figured out by now that silence was considered a virtue in this monastery. The two monks hadn't wasted a single word. Or spoken one, for that matter.

But still, he put out an arm to block their immediate departure. "I know that you heard and saw much today. If you have a need to speak of it, please talk to me, Prior Rhys, or your own prior. I would prefer that nothing of what we know or have surmised leaves this room to reach the murderer's ears."

"Do you hear that both of you?" Prior Rhys's warning tone was like a father might use with a son.

The monks nodded.

"If you think of anything else that you haven't told us, even a detail so small you think it couldn't be important, I want to hear it," Gareth said. "We don't know this man's name, and yet, we have to catch his killer."

Both monks nodded again and left. Gareth turned back to Prior Rhys. "It only occurs to me now that I didn't actually ask them if they knew the dead man."

"I asked before I sent them to hunt through the underbrush. They claimed not to," Prior Rhys said.

"Did they actually say that, or did they merely shake their heads?" Prince Rhun said.

Prior Rhys gave a short burst of laughter, which he stifled instantly. "The latter."

Footfalls came from the nave of the church, and a moment later, the hosteler appeared with the prior of the monastery, Pedr. In looks, the prior was the complete opposite of Prior Rhys, who even in middle age was tall and well built, still with the bearing of the soldier he'd been. Pedr had a stooped, slightly rounded figure and had red hair going both gray and bald. From Gareth's few interactions with him so far, however, his intellect was on a level with Rhys's.

Pedr dismissed the hosteler immediately upon seeing the body, and bent his head in a bow to Prince Rhun. "My lord."

Rhun nodded. "Prior."

This little ritual was repeated with Prior Rhys, who returned the bow. "Prior Pedr."

Gareth nodded too, though Prior Pedr hadn't yet looked at him.

"I see we have lost a parishioner," Pedr said.

"It appears so," Prior Rhys said, "though we do not yet have a name for him."

"Brother Adda says he was found in the millpond," Pedr said.

Gareth inferred that Adda was the hosteler who'd just left. "Yes, but he didn't drown."

Pedr look quickly up at Gareth. "He didn't?"

"Prior, what Sir Gareth means to say is that we believe the man to have been murdered before he was put into the millpond, but we would prefer that as few people as possible are aware of that," Prior Rhys said. "So far we have kept it among us few, though the two monks whose help I enlisted to pull the body from the pond also know."

Pedr stayed at the foot of the table, studying the dead man. "It goes without saying that you are sure of this or you wouldn't have declared it, but I have to ask: you have no doubt that he was murdered?"

"He was stabbed with a knife to the chest." Gareth reached for the man's shirt. "If you would like to see—"

Pedr raised a hand. "I acknowledge your superior wisdom in this matter." He took in a breath. "How long ago did he die?"

"Some twelve hours, give or take," Gareth said. "It is my guess that he spent all that time after the moment of death in the water."

"I have little experience with murder, but I have been made aware of some of the activities Prince Hywel requires of you. Do you need—" the prior's lips curled in distaste, "—to look him over?"

"If I may." Although Gareth would have preferred a private room in which to examine the body, if he could keep onlookers out, he could do his work just as well in here. Unlike some who had accused him of profaning the dead, he didn't believe that searching through a murdered man's clothes or examining his body somehow defiled him or was a crime against God. Quite the opposite, he believed it would be the far greater crime to let a murderer walk free.

In this instance, Gareth didn't think that the prior was so much squeamish as personally offended that any man would murder another. Still, Gareth was glad that he was going to be allowed to work, though it might be that he already knew most of what the body could tell him. "I realize that we must bury him quickly, and I would do what needs to be done now and then leave him in peace."

Pedr gave a jerky nod. "I can give you until tomorrow morning. I'm afraid that doesn't give you much time." Then Pedr looked at Prior Rhys. "If you would walk with me, I know the abbot would appreciate a more detailed explanation of what has happened here. I would be most grateful for it as well."

"Of course." Prior Rhys followed Pedr out the door and departed, though not before he raised his eyebrows at Gareth behind Pedr's back in a quick glance of helplessness and amusement.

Gareth was grateful that Rhys was available to act as go-between for the investigation and the abbot. The last time Gareth had been inside an abbot's office, he'd been in the company of a murderer and a traitor, though he hadn't known it at the time.

With the departure of the two priors, Prince Rhun and Gareth were left alone with the body—though once again, it was only for a few heartbeats. More footfalls came from the nave, and this time, it was Prince Hywel who entered the vestibule, accompanied by a young woman.

Slender, of short stature but with a bearing that spoke of privilege, the woman wore a dark brown headdress, which covered all of her hair, and a matching wool dress of a fine weave. She clutched a handkerchief in one hand and dabbed at her eyes with it.

At the sight of the body on the table, she halted abruptly. As she stared at it, the hand holding the handkerchief dropped, revealing her face: clear, pale skin set off by red lips and dark eyes, brows, and lashes, and an upturned nose. In short, she had the most even features Gareth had ever seen on anyone, man or woman, and was, for lack of a better word, beautiful. But then her face crumpled, she gave a sobbing gasp, ran towards the dead man, and threw herself across his body. "Gryff! Oh Gryff!"

Gareth looked at his lord, one of the most handsome men in Gwynedd himself (according to Gwen), with deep blue eyes and a voice that could charm any woman who looked at him. At the moment, his face was showing an expression closer to impatience than sympathy. Prince Rhun moved to his brother's side. "Who's this?"

"I met her at the gatehouse. She claimed to have heard in the village that a body had been found in the millpond. She feared it was her husband and—" Hywel gestured towards the woman still prostrated over the body, "—it seems she was right."

"At least we now have his name." Gareth observed the woman impartially. Instead of abating, her sobs rose in volume. He frowned, deciding that the woman wasn't doing Gryff or herself any good from that position. Gareth gently peeled her off Gryff's body and made her take a few steps back from it. The woman's eyes streamed with tears, but the sobbing reverted to occasional hiccupping gasps.

Gareth patted her back. "I'm sorry for your loss."

The woman didn't seem to hear him, just continued to sob. Then she gave another gasp, said, "I can't bear it!" and then turned on her heel as if preparing to leave.

Hywel was planted in the doorway, however, and she pulled up at the sight of him.

"Please—" she began.

"We really do need to ask you a few questions before you go," he said.

The woman looked at the floor. "If I must."

Hywel took the woman's elbow and guided her to one of the nearby chairs. She sat, and Hywel pulled the second chair close. "I'm sorry you have lost your husband, but I have a few questions before I can leave you to mourn him in peace. Please tell us your name."

"I am Madlen. His name is Gryff." She sobbed into her cloth anew, though even as she did so, her eyes flicked to the prince's face. "Was Gryff."

Gareth felt a smirk forming on his lips. Hywel was so handsome and personable, he could charm a widow at her husband's laying out.

"When did you last see your husband, madam?"

Madlen looked fully into Hywel's face, tears streaming down her cheeks. "Yesterday evening. He had been working at our booth at the fair, which was open late, so I didn't think anything of it when he hadn't returned to our lodgings by the time I went to sleep."

"And this morning?" Hywel said.

"He wasn't next to me, but he often rises before I do. It was only after I went to our booth myself and spoke to my uncle that we realized something was amiss." Madlen's voice gained in strength the more she spoke, and her story became more coherent. "When I asked my uncle when he'd last seen him, he said he'd dismissed Gryff well before midnight and hadn't seen him since then. I didn't know what to do."

She'd finally mastered her tears, which was all to the good as far as Gareth was concerned. When they'd arrived at the chapel with the body, he'd been almost at a loss as to where to begin the search for the man's identity. The population of the region was growing with every hour as travelers continued to stream into

Aberystwyth for the festival. Even with knowing Gryff's name as they now did, sorting through the people to find the murderer was going to be difficult. It would have been far worse without his name, however, and Gareth was grateful to Madlen that she'd come forward so quickly.

"Who is your uncle?" Gareth said.

"Iolo. He has come to the festival to sell his cloth."

"And your husband worked for him?" Gareth said.

"Yes." The word came out a sob as Madlen fell apart again.

Like most types of traders, cloth merchants ran the gamut from very wealthy to little more than peddlers, moving from house to house and village to village, hawking their wares. Gareth had never heard of Iolo, but he was far less familiar with the people of southern Wales than those who lived in the north, and he'd had little interaction with merchants in his time here. Other than his wish to buy Gwen a new dress, he hadn't had a need for fabric for new clothes this summer. He'd have to ask Gwen to have a look at Iolo's wares, however. She would be able to tell him something of the quality and selection.

"We'll have to speak to him," Hywel said.

Madlen had gone back to her weeping, but at Hywel's words, she looked up. "Why?"

"You're husband died at the millpond. We'd like to know how that came about," Hywel said.

"But—" Madlen broke off, looking from Hywel to Gareth and back again. Then she caught sight of Rhun standing in the darkness, out of the candlelight. Her eyes widened, but she said, "I was told he drowned."

Rhun had been leaning against the wall throughout the interview, his arms folded across his chest, but now he stepped forward. "Madlen, allow me find someone to escort you back to your uncle. Let the prince and Sir Gareth take care of Gryff." He held out his elbow to her.

Madlen's shoulders sagged, and she rose to her feet to take the prince's arm. She and Prince Rhun disappeared back into the main part of the chapel.

Hywel raised his eyebrows at Gareth. "I can't leave you alone for an hour without you stumbling across a murder?"

"Was it that obvious?" Gareth said. "I was hoping we were more subtle than that."

"It was obvious only to me, I think," Hywel said.

But Gareth was staring at Gryff's body. Something about it had changed. He hesitated, deciding that he must be mistaken, but then he looked back and realized what he'd noticed. Gryff's purse, which had been suspended from his belt earlier, was gone.

6

Gwen

For all that Tangwen rarely slept, she was otherwise a fairly biddable child. Gwen had a moment's pause at leaving her with Elspeth yet again, but her nanny promised to keep Tangwen from eating the rocks in the monastery garden and allow her to dig in the dirt with a wooden spoon on the edge of one of the gardens. Tangwen would come to dinner filthy from head to toe, but she'd be happy, which made the whole endeavor worthwhile.

When Gwen entered the courtyard, it was empty except for Prince Rhun, who was just entering the chapel through the front door. She followed him, and once inside the chapel, it didn't take much looking to find Gareth. He was standing over the body as she knew he would be. She took in a breath at the sight of him. He'd cut his hair short again for summer and was clean-shaven. He was thirty years old now, seven years older than Gwen, and his broad shoulders bespoke a lifetime of soldiering. He was courageous, strong, and intelligent. Those blue eyes, which at the moment were studying the body before him, had seen right through many a suspect.

And he was *hers*.

Gareth had removed the dead man's shoes and bared him to the waist. His sopping clothes were piled under the table in a heap, which was just like a man to do. Although Rhun had arrived only moments before Gwen, by the time she reached the vestibule, he'd taken up a comfortable position in one corner, propped against the wall and out of Gareth's way. Prince Hywel was there too, taking precious time away from coordinating his festival.

All three men looked up as she stepped into the little room. Gareth gave her a small smile, and the others acknowledged her presence with a raised hand or eyebrow (that was Hywel), but then they returned their attention to the body. While she wasn't particularly sorry that she wasn't examining the dead man herself, the looks of consternation on the men's faces had her hesitating in the doorway. "What is it?"

"We had a visit from the dead man's wife, Madlen," Gareth said. "Prince Rhun has just returned from escorting her out of the monastery."

"Oh good. Do we know his name now?" Gwen said.

"Gryff, apparently," Hywel said.

"Then what's the problem?" Gwen said.

"Madlen took the purse that was tied to his belt—and she did so secretly, making sure we didn't see her do it," Prince Rhun said.

Gwen looked to the dead man's waist and saw that the prince was right. She had examined the contents of the purse right away, and they hadn't told her anything. It was disconcerting to think that she might have missed something, or that Madlen valued the purse so highly as to steal it. "How did she manage to hide her actions from you?" Gwen made sure when she spoke that no tone of accusation crept into her voice. A mourning woman could be a daunting prospect for any man.

"She threw herself across him when she first arrived. Gareth had to pry her off him," Rhun said.

Gwen's brow furrowed. "She threw herself across him?"

Hywel turned to look at her. "That surprises you?"

Well ... yes," Gwen said. "I mean, he spent the day in the water, so he's soaking wet and smelling more than a little ripe." She moved her hand to Gareth's arm. "I love you very much, but I can't see myself doing that."

Hywel's attention remained on Gwen. "You do have a curious way of looking at things."

Gwen shrugged, not entirely sure what Hywel meant by that. It was his fault that she'd developed a suspicious mind, and suspicion was what she felt towards Madlen at present. "I didn't see her, of course. I don't mean to tell you your job."

"She could have feared to leave it," Rhun said. "A man of Gryff's station wouldn't have had much, but what he did have would have been all the more important."

"I would agree, but did you see how well she was dressed?" Hywel said.

Gwen could tell from the look on Rhun's face that he had— and that he was irritated with himself for not noticing earlier what was obvious to him now. From the sheepish expressions on the men's faces, Gwen could tell that Madlen had made quite an impression on all of them. Gwen resolved to meet this woman as soon as possible and judge her for herself.

"So, you're wondering how it was that Gryff could be so poorly dressed and his wife dressed so fine?" Gwen said. "Perhaps he was doing rough labor and wore his worst clothes, and she came to the chapel dressed in her finest."

"Her uncle is a cloth merchant," Hywel said. "Iolo is his name."

"Gryff is no advertisement for his wares though, is he?" Gareth said. "Especially as a member of the family."

"That's something we should ask Madlen about," Gwen said.

"In retrospect, one of many things we should have asked her about while she was here," Gareth said.

"Did you tell her that Gryff was murdered?" Gwen said. "Did she notice the knife wound?"

"Not that she said, and we didn't say," Gareth said. "I think it's good policy to continue as we've started and not tell anyone what we know."

"I agree," Gwen said. "As time goes on, people may well become suspicious that we are putting so much effort into finding out about a man who drowned, but it would be better if that particular rumor didn't fly around immediately."

"Madlen and her uncle will have to be treated carefully." Gareth looked at his lord. "Shall we strike while the iron's hot?"

Hywel made a rueful face. "I can't. I have to see to Mari, and then I must return to the festival grounds. The contest is heating up. I can't avoid my duties as host." His regret was obvious, though less that he was hosting the festival than that he couldn't be in two places at once.

Gareth nodded in acknowledgement. "Then I will question Iolo." He looked at Gwen, seemingly about to speak, and then transferred his gaze to Prince Rhun. "If you'll forgive me, Gwen, I think Prince Rhun should be my other pair of eyes in this."

Gwen wasn't offended. She'd been silently calculating the length of time it would take to ride to the festival grounds, if that was where Iolo was, question him, and return—and if she felt comfortable leaving Tangwen all that time. She'd already decided that she would have to be excused and was trying to figure out how to tell Gareth. "It's a relief, actually. I don't want to go far from Tangwen anyway."

As Gareth moved towards the door, he trailed a hand down Gwen's spine. She looked into his face, and he gave her a brief nod, which she returned. They'd spent too many days apart since they'd found each other again three years ago, but she knew him and he knew her. Their life together had changed after Tangwen had come into it, and Gwen couldn't be as active in these investigations as she used to be, but that didn't mean she couldn't help.

At this moment, Gwen interpreted Gareth's knowing look as a reminder to ask Hywel about the knife, just to get it over with. Since Rhun didn't know the truth about how King Anarawd died, it was better that he departed with Gareth, so that Gwen could speak to Hywel alone.

Hywel had gone back to surveying the body, bringing a candle closer to peer into the eyes, and then he fixed his gaze on the knife wound.

Gwen took in a breath, taking a chance. "What do you see there?"

Hywel scratched his cheek. "The man was stabbed in the chest." He glanced at Gwen. "Is there more that I should be noticing?"

"You tell me." Gwen's tone was a more combative than she intended, and she softened it. "Gareth saw it too, you know."

"Saw what exactly?"

Gwen looked at him through narrowed eyes. "That wound should look familiar to you."

Hywel straightened and took a step back from the body. "You're going to have to explain more clearly what you mean, Gwen, because I don't know what you're talking about."

"My lord, we've stood here before, over a man killed in identical fashion to this man, with an identical wound."

Hywel sucked on his lower lip. "Why would Sioned have killed this man?" Sioned had been one of the culprits back at Aber two years ago during their investigation of the death of Hywel's cousin. She'd killed a man with a knife to the chest.

"Sioned remains in Gwynedd," Gwen said. "My lord, I'm talking about Anarawd."

"What does Anarawd have to do—" Hywel's jaw dropped. "You think *my* knife killed this man? Gwen—"

Gwen kept her eyes on Prince Hywel's face. He stared at her through a few heartbeats. And then he laughed. "Ah, Gwen. I didn't kill Gryff. I am not lying to you."

Gwen let out the breath she'd been holding. "All right."

Hywel's brow furrowed. "All right? That's it? You believe me?"

"Why would you lie to me?" Gwen said. "If you did kill him, it would hardly be something I could openly accuse you of. You are the Lord of Ceredigion and a prince of Gwynedd. But it would mean we could stop investigating this death."

"And you said Gareth noticed the wound too?" Hywel said.

"Yes."

Hywel ran a hand through his dark hair, mussing it so it stood on end. "I suppose I would have been disappointed if he hadn't. His skill in these matters is one reason he leads my men." He gestured to Gryff. "The man didn't drown. It is murder, but not by my hand. You aren't wasting your time looking for the killer, I assure you."

Gwen hadn't realized how tight the muscles in her shoulders had become out of fear of what Hywel might have done until the tension left her. "Do you understand that I had to ask?"

Hywel barked a laugh. "Oh yes. You could do nothing else. But really, Gwen, do you think I'd be fool enough to kill a man with the same knife I used on Anarawd—especially knowing that both you and Gareth would be among those to investigate the death?"

"You could have been too clever for your own good," Gwen said.

Hywel scoffed. "I could have been, but I would have known not to try to get rid of a body in the millpond. Dead bodies float. Drowned bodies sink. The killer didn't know that."

"I know. I know." Gwen was feeling much better. "Please forgive me."

"I most certainly will not," Hywel said. And when Gwen blinked at him, he added, "There would have been something to forgive if you hadn't spoken to me of it—if you and Gareth had looked at me sideways for the next few days, wondering all the while if I'd killed another man in cold blood. I will say again that I did not. Believe me, the next man I want dead in secret will be done very, very far from you or Gareth."

"That's comforting. I think." Then Gwen glared at Hywel as she caught the amusement in his face. "You're mocking me."

"Just a little bit," Hywel said. "And just so you know, the knife is no longer in my possession."

"What do you mean?"

"Before I married Mari, I gave her the knife and told her the truth of what I'd done," Hywel said.

Gwen stared at him. "You did?"

"She needed to know the whole of the man she was marrying," he said. "She understands who I am."

"She forgave you?" Gwen said.

"There was nothing to forgive, Gwen," Hywel said. "I did what I believed I had to do. That is who I am, and it would have been wrong of Mari to marry me in the expectation that I would change into someone else. I needed to tell her for her sake as much as she needed to know for mine."

Gwen gazed down at her feet, shaking her head. She hadn't expected him to tell Mari the truth. And yet, it eased her heart that he had. Mari and Hywel remained well-matched, but it had always niggled at the back of Gwen's mind that she knew Hywel's secrets and Mari did not.

"Is the knife here, in Aberystwyth?" Gwen said.

Hywel pursed his lips. "I don't think so. If it were, it would be in Mari's room. But Gwen—" he gestured to the wound, "—it wouldn't have had to be my blade that did this. It could be any old blade."

"Why do you say that?"

"At the next meal, take the opportunity to study the knives of the diners around you. I predict that a handful of them will have notches in them. People are lazy. They don't sharpen their knives like they should, and they use old ones because they can't be bothered to buy new ones or repair those they have. You'll see."

Gwen didn't know why she hadn't thought of that before. She could have made a study of belt knives over the last three years. She wouldn't have put it past Hywel to have done so himself. He had the air of a man who knew what he was talking about, and Gwen herself knew enough about blades to know that they became brittle with age, especially ones that had been poorly or cheaply made. In addition, a knife could be sharpened only so many times before it failed.

Hywel's easy denial also had her acknowledging that while Hywel knew all about murder, this murder was too sloppy to have been his handiwork. Certainly, he would have been foolish to have used the same knife to kill a peasant as he'd used to murder the king of Deheubarth. Prince Hywel was the Lord of Ceredigion. He had the reach and the resources to end the life of any man in his domain if his desire was great enough, and to do it without murdering him in the dead of night and throwing the body into his own millpond.

And Prince Hywel was anything but a fool.

"Meanwhile, I'll ask Mari about the blade. It may well be safe at home in a trunk at Aber, but if she brought it, I will have her show it to you," Hywel said.

"And if she brought it, and it isn't to be found?" Gwen said.

Hywel raised his eyebrows. "Then we do have a problem." A bell sounded from the tower. "That is the signal for Vespers. I really must go, and you must see to Tangwen. I will ask Prior Pedr for two men to guard the body. I don't know what more we can learn from him, but I don't want another body to go missing."

"We've had far too much of that in the past," Gwen said.

"True," Hywel said. "But more to the point, if any of us think of something in the short time we have left before he's put in the ground, I want him to be where I left him."

"I'll wait here until the guards arrive," Gwen said.

"It'll be only a moment." Hywel disappeared into the nave but returned a heartbeat later, poking his head through the doorway to the vestibule. "On top of all that, I have an alibi for last night."

Gwen found a smile lurking around her lips. "Let's hear it."

"Gryff has been dead some twelve hours, give or take, correct?" Hywel said.

"Something like that. With the water, it's hard to pinpoint as surely as we might like, but he died sometime after midnight. We'll have to learn about his movements yesterday and last night before we know more."

Hywel waved a hand dismissively. "Regardless, I was with Gruffydd all night."

Gwen's brow furrowed. "The baby, you mean?"

"My son, yes. Mari was sleeping solidly for the first time in a week, and I took Gruffydd away to sleep with me in one of the cells that no monk was using. You can ask Prior Pedr. He saw us together when the brothers filed past us for Matins."

That was the prayer vigil the monks kept in the middle of the night. "I don't need to ask," Gwen said. "You would hardly have taken Gruffydd to the millpond after midnight, nor left him alone in a monk's cell while you murdered a man a half-mile away from the monastery."

Hywel saluted her. "Such was my thought. I hope I have put your concerns to rest."

It was with relief that Gwen accepted Hywel's assertion he hadn't killed Gryff. Maybe he was lying to her again, but she didn't think so. They knew each other for who they were by now. Hywel was Lord of Ceredigion. If he wanted a man dead, he could have arranged for it in a hundred better ways. With Hywel cleared, they could begin the real work of finding out who did murder Gryff.

Since Rhun and Gareth had left to track down Gryff's master, Iolo, that left Gwen to explore some questions closer to home, among them this issue of the notched knife. First, however, she needed to find Tangwen and Elspeth and feed them both. After going to her room to collect a clean dress for Tangwen, Gwen made her way back to the gardens. As she had hoped, Tangwen had spent a happy hour covering herself in dirt. Elspeth's pinafore was equally filthy, and Gwen sent the older girl away to change for the evening meal while she saw to Tangwen.

Elspeth seemed to have infinite patience for watching Tangwen. Gwen always felt when she was minding Tangwen that she should be *doing* something in addition to watching her daughter, even if she couldn't take her eye off the baby for a heartbeat in case Tangwen stumbled into the fire, poked herself with a stick, or swallowed something she shouldn't. Since she'd brought Elspeth into her household, Gwen had come to realize that there was nothing like having a fourteen-year-old girl to watch a baby for keeping both mother and baby happy.

"Let's get you cleaned up, shall we?" Gwen helped Tangwen to her feet, brushed her off as best she could, and then carried her towards the brook that ran past the gardens. Tangwen's dirty bare feet instantly marred Gwen's apron, but since Gwen had spent the last few hours with a dead body, she would change into clean garments before dinner too. Gwen hadn't done more than touch

Gryff in a few places, but that contact was enough to make her feel unclean all over.

The first warm day after Gwen and Tangwen had arrived at the monastery, the monk in charge of the gardens had showed her a little pool, separated from the rest of the brook by rocks, where she and Tangwen could wade to cool off. Gwen had brought Tangwen there every warm evening since.

Once at the pool, Gwen sat on a rock, pulled up her skirt, and slipped out of her boots. She stripped off Tangwen's dirty clothes and set them aside, and then, holding Tangwen's hand tightly, she helped her step into the pool. Tangwen squealed at the cold water and splashed her free hand in it in delight. It was shallow enough that Tangwen could sit on the bottom on a flat rock and still keep her head above water, but Gwen still needed to watch her closely, lest she slide under the surface.

"Do you like the water?" Gwen bent to feel it with the fingers of her free hand. Because the shallow pool had sat in the sun all day and the water flowed in and out of it slowly, it was warmer than the brook that ran beside it. "Is it nice?"

"Nice water." Tangwen rarely said more than one word at a time, so using two together today was something of a triumph.

Gwen scooped water up in her cupped her hand and poured it over Tangwen's head, and then she rubbed at her daughter's dirty cheeks and hands with a wet cloth until they were clean.

"Did you hear about the man found in the millpond?"

The words carried to Gwen from her left. She straightened slightly, continuing to hold onto Tangwen's wrist to keep her upright, and peered in the direction of the sound. Two monks of an age with Elspeth were just visible through the trees that grew down to the water's edge. They lifted up their robes and waded in the brook, still talking.

"I saw him!" the second monk said. "Hosteler Adda sent me to bring water to wash him in preparation for burial tomorrow morning. He said the man's wife came to claim his body. Did you see her?" At the other monk's shake of his head, the second continued, "She was beautiful, but ..." He looked down at the water rushing past his feet.

"But what?" The first monk was trying to walk on the rocks into the middle of the brook. He slipped and fell to one knee, soaking the hem of his robe. He cursed in a very unmonklike fashion and rose to his feet again, balancing with his arms outstretched on either side of him.

"When I brought the water, I looked into the dead man's face. I've never seen a drowned man before." The second monk shook his head. "The funny thing is that he looks very much like my cousin's husband. He is named Gryff too. Do you think I ought to tell someone about that?"

The first monk sputtered his surprise at his friend and slipped off his rock.

Gwen swung Tangwen onto her hip and slithered through the mud on the bank to where the two monks had gone into the brook. "I definitely think you need to tell someone about that."

The two boys swung around, gaping at her. The monk who thought he knew Gryff said, "I didn't mean for anyone else to hear."

"Well I did hear, and your instincts are good." Gwen put out a hand to the boys, trying to put them at their ease. "I am Gwen. Sir Gareth is my husband, and he is investigating Gryff's death. Please tell me again what you just said about your cousin's husband."

Both boys were still standing in the water, staring at her, and it occurred to Gwen that they might be worried about a whole host of things that had nothing to do with Gryff: they'd been chatting with each other, the first monk had sworn like a soldier, and very likely they were shirking whatever duties they should be fulfilling. Vespers, for one.

They could also have been staring in horror at Gwen herself, since her hair was askew, she was shoeless, and she had a naked baby girl on her hip. But Gwen waited, and after another pause, the first monk shook himself. "Tell her, Fychan. This really might be important."

Fychan still looked wary, but he took a few steps closer to Gwen. "Gryff is the name of the husband. And this man looked like him." Fychan shrugged. "That's all."

"Could you come with me?" Gwen said. "Other men will want to hear what you have to say."

Fychan blanched. "I really couldn't."

"You really must." Having Tangwen on her hip meant Gwen was somewhat unbalanced, but she took two steps down the bank towards the water.

Her movement seemed to prompt the boy, however, and he nodded, seemingly resigned to his fate. He began to pick his way towards the shore.

"Thank you," Gwen said. "Let me get my things."

Gwen returned to the pool where Tangwen had been bathing, swept up her boots and Tangwen's clothes, and arrived at the path that ran through the gardens at the same time that the two monks appeared at the top of the bank. She took a moment to drop the clean dress over Tangwen's head and put her own boots back on. The hem of Gwen's dress was wet, but she hoped it wasn't too noticeable, and she tried to tame her hair back into its headscarf. The truth was, Prior Pedr intimidated her more than a little. Like Prior Rhys, he seemed to be able to see right through her, but unlike Prior Rhys, they had no shared experience to temper their relationship.

Fychan waited patiently for her to ready herself, and then he followed her back to the cobbled courtyard. Upon reaching it, Gwen hesitated. She didn't see anyone she knew. Another party of guests had just arrived. The guesthouse was already full to bursting, so perhaps these people were sleeping in the stables. Gwen certainly didn't want to disturb them with a discussion of the dead body lying in the vestibule.

She turned to the first monk, who'd come with them but whose name she didn't know. "Can you ask your prior if he will speak to me? It would be better yet if Prior Rhys from St. Kentigern's is with him."

The monk ducked his head in acknowledgement of her request and ran off without arguing or questioning her.

Fychan didn't seem to want to look at her, but by taking a step closer and lowering her voice she forced him to look into her eyes. "If you are right that this is the man you knew, then you have done not only him, but Prince Hywel, a great service."

The boy's head came up at that, and his expression lightened, which was what Gwen had hoped for. "I shouldn't have been at the brook. Dafydd and I missed Vespers."

"I guessed as much." Then Gwen let out a sigh of relief as both priors appeared, stepping out of the doorway to the chapter house. "Hopefully, in a moment, where you were or what you were doing won't matter in the slightest. I'll be sure to put in a good word for you too."

Fychan shook his head. "Thank you, but Prior Pedr never forgets anything. I'll be mucking out the latrine tomorrow, you can be sure."

Gwen hid a smile at the boy's morose expression. "Just tell the truth. What happens after that is out of our hands."

7

Hywel

Hywel had been feeling unsettled all day. Days ago he'd sent a scout up the road to the north to let him know when his father, King Owain, crossed into Ceredigion. That morning, the man had returned to report that Hywel's uncle, Cadwaladr, would be arriving ahead of the king. Earlier, Hywel had dismissed Gareth and returned to the castle in order to determine whether Cadwaladr had arrived. Consequently, he'd missed the initial finding of the body.

Now, as he rode through the gatehouse of his castle, his heart sank to see it full of his uncle's men. Hywel closed his eyes before dismounting, gathering his internal strength and preparing himself to withstand whatever snide comments or outright ugliness his uncle threw at him.

The passion with which he hated his uncle was something that Hywel rarely allowed anyone to see, and it was important that today not be an exception. Nobody could ever know how Hywel felt. They could guess all they wanted, but if he kept those feelings hidden, when the time came for him to bring evidence against his uncle for his next crime, he could claim impartiality. Some would distrust Hywel's motives. Cadwaladr certainly would. But the day would come when Cadwaladr would do something so heinous that his father would have no choice but to cast his uncle out of Gwynedd forever. Hywel was going to make sure that his own emotions didn't stand in the way.

So far, his uncle's most grievous crimes included hiring Danish mercenaries to ambush King Anarawd of Deheubarth and conspiring with the Earl of Chester to overthrow Hywel's father as King of Gwynedd. Beneath those major sins were dozens of minor ones including throwing Gareth out of Ceredigion for disobeying an order. Gareth had refused to cut off a boy's hand for stealing a pig. Given that Gareth had ended up in Hywel's service, with knighthood, land, and honors commensurate with his skills and intelligence, Hywel was willing to give Cadwaladr a pass on that one.

As Hywel strode across the packed earth of the courtyard and up the steps into the keep and the great hall, he endeavored to clear his mind and place a neutral expression on his face. It wouldn't do to focus on Cadwaladr's villainy if he was to greet him cordially.

Aberystwyth Castle was built in wood rather than the stone that was being used in some of the newer Norman castles. The wood construction had facilitated Hywel's burning of it three years ago, but it had also allowed him to rebuild it quickly once he took over Ceredigion from Cadwaladr. Hywel's plan was for a castle larger in scale—larger than most of the Norman stone castles, with a more expansive palisade and many buildings within it. Wood burned, of course, but it was far less expensive than stone. Wood or stone, Hywel intended for this castle to be the pride of all Ceredigion.

Upon entering the hall, Hywel at once spotted his uncle, who (as usual) was impossible to miss. Always the center of attention in every room he entered, he reclined in a chair halfway down the hall, surrounded by other guests. He was holding court as if he owned the castle again, an attitude that burned Hywel's gut and forced him to take in another deep breath to clear his mind. There was no point in avoiding this first meeting, and better that it happen now than when the hall was even more full of guests.

Anyway, if Cadwaladr could come without shame or compunction to Ceredigion, a land he had once ruled through fear and intimidation, Hywel could pretend that all was well too. Striding forward, his arm outstretched in greeting, he said, "Welcome to Aberystwyth, Uncle."

Cadwaladr stood and grasped Hywel's forearm in a strong grip. With a flick of his hand, he dismissed the various hangers-on who'd gathered around him. Hywel wasn't sorry the conversation would be witnessed only from afar, in case his façade of welcome slipped.

"Nephew. I see the rebuilding continues apace."

"Yes." Hywel couldn't quite bring himself to add 'sir' on the end and was glad his father wasn't here to witness this meeting either. All Hywel had done so far was greet his uncle, but he was already teetering on the edge of his hatred, a hair's breadth from falling off the knife edge he walked. He gritted his teeth in the semblance of a smile. "I see you have been given food and drink. Are your quarters satisfactory?"

"Indeed. The room is fine," Cadwaladr said.

"Alice did not come?" Hywel said.

"She is with child again and cannot travel," Cadwaladr said.

Hywel nodded, experiencing an unexpected moment of understanding and accord with his uncle. Mari was pregnant again too. It was inconvenient, but it was the way of marriage. "If you'll excuse me, I must see to the arrangements for tonight's meal." Hywel dipped his head in a bow, congratulating himself on the quickness of their exchange and its cordiality. A small victory.

But with a lifted hand, Cadwaladr stopped Hywel from moving towards the rear door. "I hear a body has been found in the millpond."

Hywel hesitated, half-turned away, cursing the speed at which rumor traveled in a small community. And then he suppressed his irritation as best he could, meeting Cadwaladr's gaze. "That is true."

"Who died?" Cadwaladr said.

Hywel reminded himself yet again that until three years ago, Cadwaladr had been the steward of these lands. Poor ruler or not, he would know many of its inhabitants. "A man named Gryff, an apprentice to a cloth merchant," Hywel said. "Did you know him or know of him?"

Cadwaladr frowned. "No. He drowned?"

Hywel kept his face perfectly composed—or hoped he did. Leave it to his uncle to go straight to the salient point. Everyone else was assuming Gryff had drowned because he was found in the millpond, and neither Gareth nor Hywel had said differently. Hywel supposed he shouldn't have been surprised that his uncle was curious. Men could be thrown into the water after death. Perhaps Cadwaladr had done it himself.

Hywel had no compunction about lying to Cadwaladr, but whatever lie he told needed to be credible, and lies were always better when they contained a grain of truth. "We are in the early hours of making inquiries. It does appear that he drowned."

Cadwaladr's frown deepened. "A bad business. All men should know how to swim."

"My father feels as you do." Hywel made another move towards the door, congratulating himself yet again for getting out of this initial meeting unscathed. He had a vested interest in not humiliating himself. Hywel's father would prefer that Hywel not humiliate Cadwaladr either, and Hywel obeyed his father in all things, even when it grated.

He'd almost reached the exit when footfalls came up behind him, and a hand caught his arm. Hywel hadn't stopped at the sound of his uncle's boots, hoping against hope that Cadwaladr wasn't really coming for him. But now he turned again, resigned to his fate, only to blink and jerk back at finding his uncle's face right in his. Cadwaladr was a few inches taller, which forced Hywel to look up at him. He hated that. "What?" The word came out sharply before he could stop it.

"You're lying. I can see it," Cadwaladr said. "You know something about the way that man died that you aren't saying."

"No," Hywel said. The lie was purely defensive.

Cadwaladr's eyes narrowed. "You're lying now. He was murdered, wasn't he? That's why you were so evasive in your answer to me."

Hywel looked past his uncle to make sure that none of the onlookers were close enough to overhear and took his tenth deep breath since he'd walked into the hall. Then he looked back, his gaze steady on his uncle's face. "We think so."

"Aren't you going to ask me if I had anything to do with the death?"

"No," Hywel said.

Cadwaladr sneered. "Why not?" When Hywel didn't answer, he continued, "You believe I did have something to do with it, don't you? That's why you lied to me. You would have brought it up in some unguarded moment, hoping to catch me out."

Hywel rolled his eyes. "That is not it, Uncle. We are keeping the fact of the murder a secret in order to lull the murderer into a sense of security."

"So you treated me like you would the murderer," Cadwaladr said.

"Why do you twist my words?" Hywel said. "We aren't telling anyone."

"Who do you mean by 'we'? Gareth?" The sneer was fixed to Cadwaladr's face.

"Of course," Hywel said, not backing down. "His skills in these matters are legion."

"Since I'm here, you need to ask me now."

Hywel swallowed down a scoff and decided to do as his uncle asked, despite his determination not to let him get the better of him. He gave his uncle a short bow—in parody of the greeting he'd given him before—straightened, and put his heels together. "Did you have anything to do with Gryff's death?"

"Of course not." Cadwaladr dropped Hywel's arm, reverting without warning to his usual air of unconcern and disdain.

"Than why did you mention it?" Hywel said.

Cadwaladr's nose was in the air. "It was only a matter of time before you came to me for answers. It's a wonder that your father has never seen fit to commission me to investigate these unlawful deaths. I would do it better."

Hywel stared at his uncle, horrified by the vision that rose before his eyes of Cadwaladr stomping through a crime scene and then all over the witnesses. Not to mention, the fact that it would be a travesty to make him the lead investigator in a crime he himself committed. Before he could stop himself, Hywel said, "You take too much on yourself."

"You can never seem to think beyond me."

Hywel straightened his tunic with a jerk. "If you are referring to the several instances in which you have been questioned during an investigation, you might remember that you *were* involved."

"Not the last time."

Hywel gaped at his uncle, incredulous. "You left the body of my cousin on Aber's beach!"

"It was a small matter. A mistake," Cadwaladr said. "In the end you know as well as I that I had nothing to do with her death. It is the same here. I didn't even know the man."

Hywel snorted. "It was you who brought up the death, not I."

Cadwaladr sniffed and turned away. Hywel watched him go, shaking with rage, not only at what his uncle had said, which was bad enough, but that he would confront him in his own hall. Hywel turned away too, knowing that he should leave before he said or did anything more rash.

Before he exited by a rear door, however, he shot a look over his shoulder at his uncle. Cadwaladr had returned to his chair, kicking it back and putting his feet on a nearby table. With his hands clasped behind his head, he was the very picture of a calm and collected lord of his domain.

He hoped Cadwaladr's outward expression was a front for inner turmoil, because after that exchange, Hywel was anything but calm and collected. Then again, his uncle may have been plotting that ambush for weeks and had merely used Gryff's murder as a means for getting it done. Cadwaladr wasn't unintelligent (regretfully), just unwise.

Before Hywel returned to the festival grounds below the castle, he sought out his steward, a man named Morgan. His father's steward, Taran, had recommended Morgan for the position, and Hywel had found nothing in their two-year association to make him regret that choice. The man was built like a boar—apparently Morgan was the champion arm wrestler among Hywel's soldiers—but he had never used his strength in battle, having learned to read, write, and account as a youth before his physical prowess became clear. As Hywel thought about it, Morgan rather looked like a boar too, with curly brown hair from the top of his head to the tops of his feet. His brown eyes were the one exception, looking at everyone and everything around him with dry amusement.

Hywel found Morgan supervising the turning of the spit upon which a sheep was roasting. With a jerk of his head, Hywel pulled him aside. "Thank you for seeing to my uncle's wellbeing."

Morgan looked at him gravely, bushy eyebrows raised. "It was my duty."

"I will speak to Gareth about setting a man to watch him," Hywel said, "but I would ask you as well to inform me if my uncle meets with anyone unusual—or does anything unusual."

"Can you define unusual, my lord?"

Hywel found his teeth grinding together—not at Morgan's request for clarification but at having this conversation at all. "My uncle, as you know, has conspired with many of my father's foes over the years. He hasn't come to Ceredigion because he loves music. He is here for something else. I want to know what it is."

"Does this have to do with the death of that merchant, Gryff?" Morgan said, showing that his usual astuteness hadn't deserted him.

"I do not know. My uncle claims not."

"As one might expect," Morgan said.

Hywel eyed his steward. "You should know that we believe Gryff was murdered."

Morgan didn't even blink. "How?"

"A stab to the chest," Hywel said. "All the more reason to wonder at my uncle's interest in it."

"Do you believe his assertion that he wasn't involved?"

"It is not what I believe or don't believe at present. I have no reason to suspect him other than that I always suspect him. But no, Gryff's death seems far below the doings of my uncle."

Morgan gazed past Hywel, looking towards the entrance to the great hall. "He brought many men, your uncle. Did you know?"

Hywel's eyes narrowed. "How many?"

"Twenty came with him to the castle, but I have been informed that he left some fifty more outside Aberystwyth."

"What?" Hywel said. "Fifty cavalry?"

"Yes."

"Can you tell me where exactly?" Hywel said.

"In the woods about two miles to the northeast of St. Padarn's," Morgan said. "I only learned of this moments ago when one of the farm boys came in and spoke of it. He was riding in the back of his father's hay cart when he saw them setting up camp near St. Dafydd's chapel."

Hywel was aghast at the news. "Your network of spies appears to be better than mine."

"I'm sorry, my lord, I—"

Hywel waved a hand. "Please know that I am in no way angry about that. I'm impressed and grateful."

"I'm a Ceredigion man, born and bred," Morgan said. "I regret to say that the men of Gwynedd remain newcomers and are often ill-trusted."

"For good reason," Hywel said, "thanks to my uncle."

"You are not painted with the same brush," Morgan said.

Hywel almost laughed. He had tried to be fair, ruling with a firm but just hand. But when a man didn't get what he wanted, or was punished, it often didn't matter to him or his family that his sentence had been just.

"You are vulnerable, however," Morgan said. "It isn't that the people are tinder, just waiting to be lit, but they distrust. King Cadell of Deheubarth should arrive at any moment and those two—Cadell and Cadwaladr—are as the two faces of a coin. Both want to rule Ceredigion, and neither is to be trusted."

Hywel already knew that, but it was good to hear Morgan articulate it. "Again, thank you. Please let me or Gareth know if you see or hear anything more about these men of my uncle's or have further thoughts on the matter."

Morgan bowed. "Of course, my lord."

Hywel headed for his horse, which had been fed and watered in his absence, and found Evan, Gareth's second-in-command, holding his bridle.

"Do you have orders for me, my lord?" he said.

"Yes, I do." Hywel would have sent Gareth to investigate if he were not inconveniently busy with the murder. Evan would do in his stead. Hywel mounted his horse and turned its head. His uncle might not be involved in this murder, but as surely as the sun would rise tomorrow, he was involved in something.

8

Gareth

It was different having Prince Rhun for company instead of Hywel. Gareth didn't dislike his presence. It was simply new to him, and like any new thing, it would take some getting used to. Prince Rhun was closer to Gareth's age than Hywel was and, quite honestly, probably closer in natural temperament to Gareth, too.

As they strode across the monastery courtyard to the stables, Rhun glanced at Gareth. "Is something the matter?"

"Not at all." Gareth hastily rearranged his expression, smoothing his furrowed brow. "I was merely thinking about the murder, and what we might discover when we speak to Iolo."

"Have you encountered a cloth merchant by that name before, here in Ceredigion?" Rhun said.

"No. Not that I remember. He must have come for the festival. Madlen implied as much." They entered the darkness of the stable where their horses were being kept. Two boys came out of the depths of the stalls to greet them, but Gareth didn't need a guide to find his horse. Braith whickered at his approach, snuffling at Gareth's hand for the apple he knew would be there.

The boy who led out Gareth's horse was almost too small to lift the saddle, so Gareth helped him throw it onto Braith's back and cinch the buckles tight. Then they walked him back into the hot sunshine of the late August afternoon.

"I keep thinking back over that interview with Madlen," Rhun said as he mounted his horse. "I'm not used to being fooled in this way, if she was fooling us at all. Perhaps there is an innocent explanation for why she took the purse."

"Even if there isn't, I imagine we'll be given one," Gareth said.

Rhun released a surprised laugh. "You distrust everyone's motives, don't you?"

"In a murder investigation, I have learned to," Gareth said without apology.

"Do you think it is human nature to trust or distrust?" Rhun said.

Gareth's brow furrowed in thought. Rhun's mind worked differently from that of his brother. Hywel viewed the world through cynical eyes. Rhun was more open and unjudgementally curious, which was what Gareth was feeling from him now.

"Think of a child like Tangwen," Gareth said.

They left the monastery and were riding through the village of Llanbadarn Fawr, which had grown up around St. Padarn's. Aberystwyth, a slightly larger village, was located one mile to the west on the seaside. Hywel's castle, their destination, was a mile and a half to the south of both villages, sited on a hill overlooking the sea. The festival pavilions and tents were set up on the flood plain below the castle in the curve of the river Ystwyth.

"She neither trusts all nor distrusts all, but she trusts and distrusts based on instinct. A child's instincts are often better than those of an adult, who trusts or mistrusts based upon experience."

"And sometimes those experiences play a man false." Rhun nodded. "I see what you're saying."

"Now, sometimes a child's instinct can play her false too," Gareth said. "Tangwen has been known to favor people who speak to her in a soft voice, and a man who understands how a child's mind works can manipulate her into trusting where she shouldn't."

"A frightening idea," Rhun said.

This conversation had carried them down the road from St. Padarn's and across the Rheidol River to the ford of the Ystwyth River below Hywel's castle. In the last few days, the number of tents and flags had grown from a mere handful to more than fifty. The market fair was in full swing.

Welsh society as a whole was based upon kinship and land ownership. Hywel, as lord of the land, ruled Ceredigion, and each of his lesser lords tithed to him. In turn, the people of Wales, whether they farmed, fished, or herded, owed tithes to their lord. At one time the majority of the Welsh people had been, while not slaves, not exactly free either. But over time that had changed such that each man had been given responsibility for himself. He controlled his own flocks and the product of his labors, even if he continued to tithe to lord and Church. At one time, true slavery had been common too, though that practice was disappearing. More often than not, it was the Welsh who'd been enslaved by invading hordes.

Since the Normans had come, small villages had sprung up across the land, and with them came established merchants, traders, and craftsmen. They traveled all around Wales and into the March, just as bard's had always done. As the child of a bard, Gwen had sung up and down the length of Wales before her father, Meilyr, returned to Gwynedd to sing for King Owain as his court bard. Gwen's father had served two kings of Gwynedd in his time—King Owain and his father, Gruffydd, before him—and Gwen's brother, Gwalchmai, looked to do the same.

Gareth hadn't realized until this moment what an accomplishment this festival was for Hywel. That so many people had come—high and low alike—showed the respect they had for him and for music—and possibly for *his* music. As the son of the King of Gwynedd, Hywel wasn't a bard the way Gwen's father and brother were. But he'd been trained by Meilyr, and his voice possessed a clarity that Gareth had never heard in another singer.

Hywel's stature—both as a prince and as a musician—meant that when he personally invited the premier bards of Wales to come to Ceredigion, they had accepted. The King of Gwynedd was entertained by his bard at Aber—and occasionally by Hywel—on an almost daily basis. But music of the quality they could produce was far less commonplace in the little villages, hamlets, and homesteads spread across the rest of Wales.

In fact, for some, hearing music like that found at this festival was the chance of a lifetime.

Rhun and Gareth dismounted at the entrance to the tent fair. To cut down on thievery, Gareth—who'd been in charge of such details—had fenced the market to allow only two entrances to the grounds, both guarded by Hywel's men. The two on guard at the moment, Goch and Rhodri, happened to be two of the more sensible soldiers in the garrison.

They saluted Gareth and bowed to Rhun at their approach. Goch and Rhodri were accompanied by Hywel's scribe, Barri. The name derived from the Welsh word for mountain, but the man was a hillock compared to the much larger soldiers beside him. Goch, with his flaming red hair, was dwarfed only by Rhodri with his enormous feet.

"How goes it, Rhodri?" Gareth said.

"Well enough, my lord," Rhodri said.

"I was hoping that you would have a list of all the craftsmen and traders who have set up their tents here," Gareth said. "In particular, we are looking for one Iolo, a cloth merchant."

Rhodri turned to Barri, who consulted a paper with a long list of text down one side. "Iolo ap Llywelyn that would be?"

"That's the one," Gareth said.

"Third row, ninth stall down. One of three cloth merchants we have here today," Barri said, proving that size had nothing to do with intelligence. Hywel had chosen well when he asked the scribe to take time from his regular duties to help maintain order at the fair.

"Excellent," Gareth said. "Thank you."

Prince Rhun took a step into the fairgrounds, but Goch stopped Gareth before he could follow. Rhun returned to the entrance, having realized that Gareth wasn't with him.

"Is there something amiss, my lord?" Goch said. "Something we should know about? I hear there's been a death."

Gareth scratched his cheek. "Yes. A man was found dead in the millpond. You already heard this?"

Both guards nodded.

Gareth wasn't surprised. The rumor mill was working better than the watermill today—perhaps more quickly than usual *because* there were so many more people available to spread the news. Their walk from the mill to the monastery with the body in the cart would have been easily enough to start tongues wagging. Gareth hadn't even tried to restrain Teilo from talking. At least Gareth could count on the monks for discretion with outsiders, though by now the entire monastery had to be aware of what had happened.

"We have learned little more than that, my lord," Rhodri said. "I am sure that most of the details are likely to be wrong. You know how it goes."

"I do." Gareth jerked his head, indicating that Rhodri should step to one side. Barri and Goch were attending to a man with gear over his shoulder who was asking for tent space.

"I will tell you as soon as we have information I need you to know," Gareth said. "For now, the name of the dead man appears to be Gryff. And yes, he was found dead in the millpond."

Rhodri opened his mouth to speak but then closed it.

"What is it?" Gareth said sharply.

Rhodri cleared his throat. "One of the rumors we heard was that Prince Rhun saw the man drowning in the millpond and swam out to save him."

Rhun let out a *whoosh* of surprised laughter. "I suppose that's better than if the word had been that I'd killed him. But no, I was one of the first on the scene. That is all." He eyed the soldier. "You should know that we are here asking questions because the man didn't drown."

"Murder?" Rhodri's eyes widened.

"That is for the ears of you and Goch only," Gareth said. "I mean it. Everyone is assuming he drowned, and we want to keep it that way until we know more."

Rhodri nodded fervently. "We will tell no one."

Gareth supposed that if he was going to enlist members of the guard to help in the investigation, they had to know they were dealing with murder, but he wished Prince Rhun had asked him first before announcing it to Rhodri. Then again, Rhun was a prince. He wasn't accustomed to asking permission to do anything.

"Beyond this, we know little else and are in the first hours of our investigation," Gareth said. "It's probably fruitless to try to stem the tide of rumors, but at least you know the truth."

Rhodri pressed his lips together in a look of satisfaction, and Gareth felt better about sharing this bit of information. He might need quick action from both guards if all didn't go as he expected in the next hour. At the very least, as soldiers, it was their job to keep an eye on the comings and goings of everyone in the fairgrounds. With a murderer on the loose, they needed to stay alert.

While he'd been talking to Rhodri, the number of festival-goers had continued to swell. Afternoon had given way to evening, and people were shopping before returning to the music program in the next field over. Leaving the two guards to their duties, Gareth and Rhun moved quickly through the crowds. They turned down the aisle Barri had mentioned and started counting stalls.

"There he is." Rhun put a hand on Gareth's arm.

"Which booth?" Gareth said.

Rhun pointed with his chin to a stall twenty feet away. A man with close-cropped dark hair and a bushy mustache was adjusting his wares on a table, while speaking to a large man wearing a too-warm coat and a hat pulled low over his eyes. He looked like he ought to be a patron, since he had a hole in the knee of his breeches. Where the hat didn't cover him, his blond hair and bushy beard stuck out all around.

Then Madlen set a stack of many-colored fabrics on the table beside her uncle and ducked back into the tent behind the stall, one wall of which was completely open. A canopy extended from the tent to cover the wares, protecting them and the customers from the elements, which today consisted only of bright sunlight.

Gareth felt like saying, "Ah ha!" but restrained himself. He was glad to be able to talk to both uncle and niece without having to track Madlen down somewhere else.

"She seems remarkably composed for a woman who just lost her husband," Rhun said.

"You read my thoughts, my lord," Gareth said.

But then, as they made their way forward, a cry followed by a wrenching sob came from the recesses of the tent. Rhun shot Gareth an apologetic look. The blond patron glanced around. Noticing Gareth and Rhun, he bent his head briefly in acknowledgement of their evident station, which was far above his, and disappeared into the crowd. Together, Gareth and Rhun approached the cloth merchant.

Iolo looked up, his expression questioning. He thought they were customers.

"I am sorry for your loss," Gareth said.

Iolo's mouth turned down. "And you are?"

Prince Rhun eyed Iolo, not taking offense, but he didn't answer him either. Gareth suspected that Rhun would happily claim to be someone else entirely if Gareth let him, just for fun. So Gareth spoke for both of them, "I am Sir Gareth, the captain of Prince Hywel's *teulu*, and this is Prince Rhun of Gwynedd."

The man's face paled, as it should have, and he bent fully at the waist in a bow. "My apologies, my lord. I am not from around these parts. I did not know."

Rhun dipped his chin slightly in acknowledgement and moved a hand to indicate that the man could straighten. "We are here about the death of your niece's husband, Gryff."

Iolo stared at them for a count of five, to the point that Gareth was wondering if Rhun should repeat what he'd said. Then Iolo said, "I see." He turned to look into the recesses of the tent behind him. "As you can see, Madlen is distraught."

"I can only imagine what she must be feeling," Rhun said.

Gareth took the picture he'd sketched of Gryff and handed it to Iolo. "Just to be clear, this is Gryff?"

Iolo took the paper. "That is well done! Yes, that is Gryff."

"What was Gryff's relationship to you?" Rhun said.

Gareth was happy to let the prince keep speaking. He was good with people and had made Iolo feel at ease with grace, especially given that they'd gotten off on the wrong foot at the start.

Iolo's brows drew together. "Is there some purpose to these questions, my lord? Gryff is dead. What more is there to say?"

"We're just following up. A man died," Prince Rhun said. "We want to be thorough."

Iolo continued to look puzzled. "I thought Gryff drowned in the millpond?"

Gareth grunted. He didn't like to lie outright to anyone, even suspects in a murder investigation. Lying was for criminals, and if Gareth lied to them, pretty soon it might be hard to tell who was who. "Any time a man dies prematurely, questions must be asked. The monks, for example, are concerned about the nature of his death."

Iolo had a naturally ruddy complexion, and with this comment, some of the color left his face. "Are they wondering how Gryff got there? Do you think he might have—" Iolo swallowed hard, "—done himself in?"

That wasn't what Gareth had been thinking at all. He'd just been trying to deflect Iolo's queries, but his question gave Gareth a moment's pause. Since he had known it was murder from the start, he hadn't considered the various reasons a man might die if it wasn't, and the specifics of what people might think. "We are pursuing every line of inquiry."

"How else does a man end up dead in a millpond in the middle of the night?" Rhun said, taking up the questioning again.

"Slipped, perhaps," Iolo said. "Gryff often drank more than was good for him."

"While the idea that Gryff took his own life surprises you, the idea Gryff might have died because he was too drunk to save himself would not?" Rhun said.

Iolo shrugged and began rearranging the piles of cloth in front of him. It was as if he'd lost interest in the conversation, but his hands shook before he clenched them into fists and stilled them. "It isn't as if he could swim, and a drunk man, as we all know, has little control over his limbs."

"Do you have any idea what he might have been doing at the millpond in the early hours of the morning?" Rhun said.

"The pond is on the road between here and Aberystwyth village, is it not?" Iolo said. "Maybe he got lost on the way to our lodgings from the fair."

"Maybe," Rhun said.

"I'm sure you know your business, my lord," Iolo said, suddenly turning affable. It was the third persona he'd put on in what was still a relatively short conversation. "Gryff was a dreamer. Why he did or did not do anything has never been clear to me."

"Yet you kept him on," Rhun said. "He married your niece. So we ask again, what was his relationship to you?"

"He was my apprentice—" Iolo waggled his head, his eyes turned upward for a moment, "—well, my journeyman. I had hope that he would take on more and more of the duties of a master draper, but—"

Rhun tipped his head. "He was not doing so?"

"He never proved as capable as I would have liked," Iolo said.

Silence fell for a moment, punctuated by Madlen's sobs, still ongoing in the background. Gareth could see her, hunched over on a stool with her face in her hands. Prince Rhun had done an excellent job questioning Iolo so far, but when after another pause he didn't have another question on the tip of his tongue, Gareth said, "You had hopes of something different from Gryff at one time?"

"I brought him into my business after a chance meeting on the road. He was looking for a trade, and I had need of an apprentice. One thing led to another. I took him on permanently."

"When did he and Madlen marry?" Gareth said.

At first Gareth wasn't sure Iolo had heard the question, since he didn't respond right away, but then he said, "They weren't together long, a few months only."

"Please describe exactly how you and Gryff met," Gareth said.

"My cart was stuck in the mud," Iolo said. "Gryff helped me to become unstuck, stayed around to help that day and the next, and then stayed permanently. His circumstances had taken a turn for the worse after he'd had a falling out in his previous situation."

It was a common story, even up to the part where Iolo and Gryff had met by chance. Two strangers could strike up a friendship or form a business relationship if they journeyed together. A trader such as Iolo, who might return to his home village once every few months, would have long experience turning strangers into friends, and for Madlen to marry Gryff made sense, since they were together all day every day.

"I see," Gareth said. "When did you last see Gryff?"

"Last night before I retired," Iolo said promptly. "We had a great deal to do and a short amount of time to do it in. As you can see, Madlen and I are run off our feet. Gryff was supposed to have arranged the fabrics last night, not to mention that he should have slept in the stall to guard it." Iolo put out a hand to Gareth. "Not that I am in any way criticizing the watchfulness of your men, my lord. But a man has to protect what little he owns."

"We understand," Rhun said. "What happened next?"

"I went to the latrine and returned to find him gone. I didn't see Gryff again."

"When did you arrive in Aberystwyth?" Rhun said.

"We've been in the area for two weeks. We arrived in Aberystwyth three days ago to set up the stall." Iolo leaned forward, looking at Rhun. "My lord—all these questions—what is this really about?"

"As I said," Prince Rhun said, "we have questions about how Gryff came to be in the millpond. That is all."

Iolo glanced at Gareth before looking back to the prince. It occurred to Gareth all of a sudden that Iolo had been speaking so openly to Rhun not out of respect but because he thought him a soft touch. Iolo seemed more wary of Gareth, never mind that so far they had no indication he'd done anything wrong.

"We are simply making inquiries. Thank you for your time," Gareth said.

"Please let me know when the body is set to be buried and where." Iolo gestured to where Madlen sat sobbing. "Madlen is suffering in this matter."

"That reminds me—" Gareth had been saving the questioning of Madlen until the end, "—we need Madlen to return Gryff's purse to us, or at least allow us to view its contents."

Madlen's sobs ceased in mid-breath, proving that she'd been listening to every word that had passed between her uncle and Gareth and Rhun.

Iolo said, "What?"

"Before Madlen arrived at the chapel where Gryff's body lay," Gareth said, "Gryff had a small purse at his waist. After she left, it was gone."

Iolo's cheeks grew ruddy, his initial surprise turning to anger. He glared at his niece. "Is this true?"

Madlen gaped at the men, all of whom were looking at her. Tears were still wet on her cheeks but no new ones fell. Her hand went to her heart, and her breathing quickened. "I don't-I don't know—"

Rhun made a gesture to indicate that he would like to come around the table and enter the tent. "If I may?"

Iolo shrugged. "Of course, my lord." His voice was calm again, and Gareth might have thought him composed except for the way one hand fidgeted with the hem of his tunic. Soon he might wear a hole in the fabric. Then Iolo saw Gareth looking, and he hurriedly clasped his hands behind his back.

Meanwhile, Rhun entered the tent. Madlen hid her face in her apron, as if that would somehow stop her from having to answer any more questions.

Rhun crouched before her. "Madlen."

As with Hywel, Madlen couldn't ignore the prince. The tears for Gryff may well have been genuine, but she didn't seem to be able to resist the attentions of a handsome man, and today she'd been graced by two powerful and charismatic princes.

Gareth looked down at the picture he'd sketched. In life, Gryff may well have been handsome too. And in fact, if he were handsome, that would explain a great deal—in particular, how he could win a place beside Iolo when he seemed to lack any of the skills required, and win Madlen's heart, she who was beautiful, wealthy, and more well-bred than he appeared to be.

"Madlen," Rhun said, "I imagine you want us to discover the circumstances surrounding your husband's death?"

After a moment of hesitation, she nodded.

"We'd like to know why Gryff was at the millpond, if he was with someone at the time, and how it was that he ended up in it. Don't you want to know that too?" Rhun said.

Madlen nodded again.

"So, we need you to show us the purse you took from Gryff's body this morning and tell us why you took it." Rhun was speaking to Madlen as if she were only a little older than Tangwen, each word simple and clear in its meaning. As with the earlier questioning of Iolo, Rhun's instincts were good, and Gareth was glad he'd come along. His ability to woo women was an unexpected bonus.

Usually, everyone thought of Hywel as the brother who was able to turn the head of every woman he met. In fact, before his marriage, he *had* turned every woman's head, whether he intended to or not, and coaxed any woman he wanted into his bed simply by smiling at them. Rhun had always had more restraint than Hywel, though Gareth was realizing only now that he had the same skill.

After another long pause, Madlen turned on her stool and felt inside a sewn leather bag set on the ground behind her. She pulled out the small leather purse Gareth had seen at Gryff's waist earlier that afternoon and handed it to Rhun. "He owned very little, you know. I didn't want to leave what he did have in the chapel overnight in case someone took it."

Gareth thought Prior Pedr might have something to say about her distrust, but Rhun nodded. "I understand, Madlen, but you should have asked us first." Rhun stood and handed the purse over the table of fabrics to Gareth, who took it.

Madlen's face crumpled, threatening tears again. "I wasn't thinking clearly."

Finally, in the first sign of sympathy he'd shown her, Iolo went to his niece and patted her on the shoulder. Rhun left the tent through the open flap, and Gareth untied the strings on the purse. The contents were unchanged from what Gwen had described, and despite Madlen's concerns about theft, few would have bothered with what Gryff possessed.

Gareth showed the items to Rhun, whose upper lip lifted in something of a sneer. He opened his mouth to speak, glanced at Madlen and Iolo, and then closed it. Gareth nodded and said in an undertone, "We'll speak of this later, my lord." Then he tied up the purse again. "Thank you. She can keep this now if she wants." He held the purse out to Iolo.

He took it, and the action seemed to decide something for him because he clenched it in one hand and lowered his voice so it wouldn't carry. "Please forgive my niece. She isn't herself."

"We understand," Gareth said. "Grief can do strange things to people."

"We will take our leave," Rhun said.

Iolo bowed. Gareth and Rhun departed, though Gareth glanced back as they were leaving and caught a glimpse of the blond man who'd been speaking to Iolo earlier. He approached Iolo's stall, as if he'd been waiting for Gareth and Rhun to leave, but when Iolo looked up, he frowned, clearly not happy to see him. Gareth stopped before he turned the corner, his hand going to Rhun's arm. "Wait, my lord."

Gareth peered through the crowd, but a half-dozen people filled the aisle, blocking his view of the stall. He took a step to one side, hoping to get a better view, but the blond man had already gone.

"What is it, Gareth?"

"Nothing, apparently." Gareth shook himself and continued walking towards the entrance to the fair. "What were you going to say about the purse, my lord?"

"Its contents hardly could be viewed as worth stealing, no matter how poor the thief."

"I thought the same," Gareth said.

"Something isn't right. I'd like to know what." Rhun wrinkled up his nose as though he'd caught a whiff of a foul substance.

Gareth gave a laugh. "You sound like Hywel."

"Good. I'll take that as a compliment." Rhun gave Gareth a quick smile.

"Do you have any other thoughts about the interview?" Gareth said.

"I have many, but only one that might be important." Rhun said. "Did you notice that Iolo isn't doing much grieving?"

9

Gwen

When the two priors reached Gwen, she asked the young monk, Fychan, to tell them what he knew of Gryff and this other wife. Elspeth came out of the guesthouse at the tail end of Fychan's explanation, her eyes widening even at the little bit she heard. Gwen moved closer to Elspeth, passing Tangwen off to her as she did so.

"What's going on?" Elspeth had changed into a thin blue dress, which matched the color of her eyes, and a clean white overtunic. Fortunately, it wasn't as hot on the cobbles as it had been earlier, especially in the long shadow cast by the guesthouse across the monastery courtyard.

"It has to do with the dead man," Gwen said. "I'd prefer Tangwen stayed well out of it."

"Gryff had two wives?" Elspeth said. "Can a man do that?"

Gwen laughed. "No, he can't. Don't worry. Gareth and I will get to the bottom of whatever is going on here."

Elspeth nodded, her eyes still wide. "I'll take Tangwen to dinner, shall I?"

"I would be grateful," Gwen said.

Then Elspeth showed a toothy grin—one that Gwen hoped she wasn't turning on any of the monks lest it tempt them to forsake their vows—and said, "I want to hear about it afterwards."

Gwen shook her head. "Only if Gareth agrees."

Elspeth pouted, and Gwen reminded herself to speak to Gareth before the girl turned her wiles on him. He would resist them, but it would be easier to do so if he knew in advance that Elspeth was going to direct them at him.

Gwen returned to the two priors and Fychan, and the four of them trooped back into the chapel so Fychan could give Gryff's face more than a passing glance. Before they reached him, Gwen put out a warning hand. "This won't be easy to see."

The boy sighed. "I've seen dead people before. I saw Gryff's body before."

No child reached the age of fourteen without encountering a dead loved one, whether parent, grandparent, sibling, or friend, so Gwen let him go. As Fychan approached the head of the table, Prior Rhys peeled back the cloth that covered Gryff's face.

Fychan nodded. "I swear it's him."

"Thank you, Fychan," Gwen said.

"Who's 'him'?"

Relief swept through Gwen to hear Gareth's voice, and she intercepted him a foot from the table on which Gryff's body lay. He'd come through the doorway of the chapel alone, and Gwen asked, "Where is Prince Rhun?"

"He went back to the castle to speak Hywel and aid him in his time of need," Gareth said.

Gwen smirked. Hywel was being run off his feet, even with a competent steward and many underlings to serve him. He wanted the festival to be perfect. More to the point, he wanted his father to be proud of him. Sometimes it was hard for a son to see what was in his father's eyes when he looked at him. In Gwen's opinion, too often he mistook concern for disappointment. Gwen listened to the tones in King Owain's voice when he spoke of Hywel, and she knew, even if Hywel didn't, that King Owain was already proud of his second son.

Gwen was looking forward to the arrival of King Owain's entourage for another reason: he would be bringing her father and brother. Gwalchmai would soon be fifteen. His voice had started changing within a few days of Tangwen's birth. Her father had spent many months on pins and needles, terrified that it would change into a disappointing baritone, but the pure tenor that had emerged six months ago was all that anyone could have hoped for. As when Hywel's voice had changed, Meilyr had continued to work with Gwalchmai daily, falling back on the long years of training to ease him through the worst of it.

Gwen put a hand on Gareth's chest to stop him from moving and lowered her voice so as to avoid disturbing the conversation Fychan was having with the two priors. "First, did you discover anything interesting?" She wanted him to tell her his news first because the moment he found out about the two wives, that knowledge would drive out all other concerns.

Gareth raised one shoulder in a half-shrug. "I can't say that I found out very much or am any closer to discovering who murdered Gryff. Rhun and I had a discussion with Iolo and Madlen, but it left me with more questions than answers. We can pick it apart later." He pointed with his chin to Gryff. "What's going on here?"

Prior Pedr overheard his question. He steepled his fingers in front of his lips, and said, "It seems that we have a slight wrinkle in our understanding of who Gryff was. Fychan here—" he gestured to the young monk, who turned bright red as everyone's gaze fell on him, "—believes this Gryff to be the same as the one who married his cousin, a woman named Carys."

There were few occasions that could flummox Gareth, but this appeared to be one of them. He looked at the body and then back to Fychan. Then he pulled out a piece of paper from his pocket and showed it to the boy. "When he was alive, did he look something like this?"

The boy stared at the paper. "Yes! Yes! That's exactly him."

Gwen never grew tired of watching Gareth's skill with a piece of charcoal. He collected scraps of discarded paper and parchment wherever he could and would draw anything: her or Tangwen, his horse, a castle, or the sea outside their house on Anglesey. The looks of surprise on the faces of those who had never seen him draw before always warmed her heart. Too often people assumed they knew him. As with his ability to read, which wasn't common in knights, he had hidden depths of which most people were unaware.

Prior Rhys was not among those who underestimated Gareth, however. He rubbed at his chin. "What do you want to do?"

"We have to find her," Gareth said, "and bring her here if we can."

Gwen looked at Fychan. "Do you know where she might be living?"

"Yes," he said, but then he paused, looking back into Gryff's face. "At least, I know where they used to live. It isn't far, some five miles to the east, in the village of Goginan."

Prior Pedr nodded. "I know of it."

"Might I borrow Fychan, then?" Gareth said. "We have to pursue this matter of Gryff's death beyond the usual, and if Carys can help—" He broke off, suddenly wary, and Gwen knew why. So far, the only people who knew that Gryff hadn't drowned were Gwen and Gareth, Rhun and Hywel, and a small group of monks. If they expanded that circle beyond these few, they faced the real danger of all Aberystwyth knowing the truth by morning.

Prior Pedr seemed to understand what Gareth had been going to say without him saying it, because he nodded. "He must be buried tomorrow morning. Anything else would be unacceptable. You should go now."

Nobody argued with that. By dawn, the man would have been dead for more than a full day. Another day of heat like they'd had today and nobody would be able to enter the chapel because of the stench. It would be bad enough by tomorrow morning.

"I will endeavor to return with her before the ceremony," Gareth said. "If it's only five miles to Goginan. We can reach it before full dark if we hurry." They were two months past the solstice, but the sun still set well past dinnertime and many hours later than it would come December.

Prior Pedr gave a slight bow. "As you wish."

Everyone but the two monks who'd been guarding the body before they entered—and who would continue to do so after they left—filed out of the chapel. Against all expectations, given where she'd just spent the last half hour, Gwen's stomach growled. She was well on her way to having missed dinner. Gareth hadn't eaten either, and he also looked with regret towards the dining hall. "I have an apple in my saddle bag. Perhaps this second widow will offer me some bread and cheese."

Gwen looked up into Gareth's face. The strong summer sun had bronzed his skin—where it had brought out the freckles across her cheeks. She stepped closer, putting both hands on his chest. "You take care."

Gareth nodded. "I will. But I have some concern for you." He swung around, spying Prior Rhys conversing with Pedr in the shade of the chapel. He lifted a hand to him. Rhys acknowledged his signal with a raised hand of his own, finished his conversation with Pedr, and came over to them.

"What can I do?" Prior Rhys said.

"I would ask for the loan of your horse for Fychan to ride," Gareth said. "The monastery nags are too slow."

"Done."

With a wave of his hand, Rhys sent Fychan to the stable to retrieve the horse and then turned back to Gareth. "What else? I would be happy to come with you. The abbot has relieved me of all duties until this matter is resolved. He agrees that bringing Gryff's murderer to justice takes priority over everything else."

Gareth shook his head. "While I value your company and perhaps could use another pair of eyes, there's a murderer on the loose. We have no leads to his identity, no notion as to his whereabouts, nor any clue as to why Gryff was murdered. Gwen, however, was one of the first to see the body, and I am concerned for her safety. She has already been hurt too many times. I won't allow it to happen again."

Prior Rhys frowned. "The monastery is not defensible. Nor is it meant to be. Perhaps she should move to the castle?"

If it had been only for herself, Gwen might have protested that she didn't need anyone to watch over her. Two years ago, she would have asked to travel to Goginan with Gareth. But Tangwen's birth had changed everything. As when she'd been pregnant, Gwen agreed that she must restrict her investigating to places closer to home. But moving to the castle wasn't the answer either. "All the beds at the castle are full. I'd be sleeping with Tangwen on the floor of the hall. Surely sleeping among so many strangers cannot be safer than the guesthouse."

Gareth rubbed at his forehead, studying her.

"It isn't that I'm so brave," Gwen said. "I would never do anything to endanger Tangwen. You know that."

"I do," Gareth said, "but too many times you have become the point of interest to a culprit who thinks you have learned something, or know something, and acts before he thinks things through."

"These murderers have a habit of giving me too much credit," Gwen said, trying to lighten the mood.

It didn't work. Gareth didn't even twitch a smile. "It is my job to protect you."

Prior Rhys cleared his throat. "I admit that I have failed you in the past, but if you entrust your wife and daughter to my keeping, I will see to their safety in your absence."

Gareth let out a breath. "I confess that is as I hoped. And Newcastle wasn't a failure. You had no idea of the threat we were facing. None of us did. But there are few arms I would trust more than yours."

"I have only a knife," Prior Rhys said.

"Are you telling me that wouldn't be enough?" Gareth said.

The two men held each other's gaze through several heartbeats. Prior Rhys had been a spy for Empress Maud before giving up that life for the Church. That didn't mean he'd locked himself away from the world or forgotten all his skills.

"It will be enough," Rhys said.

"I do feel better knowing you're here, Prior Rhys," Gwen said.

Prior Rhys bowed. "I'm glad to be of service."

Gareth pulled Gwen to him and kissed her temple. "Kiss Tangwen for me and tell her I will see her tomorrow morning."

"I will," Gwen said.

Gareth reached into his pocket and pulled out the sketch of Gryff.

Gwen took it, her brow furrowed. "Don't you need this?"

"I drew more." He glanced up at the sky. The sun was heading into the sea. "It's too late today to canvas the village or the festival grounds to discover Gryff's movements on the day he died. We'll start that tomorrow, but you could show the picture around the monastery if you get the chance."

Gwen nodded.

Gareth put a hand to her cheek. "If Tangwen lets you, that is. If not, don't worry about it. There is always tomorrow, and I will return with Carys and—hopefully—some answers."

Prior Rhys caught Braith's bridle as Gareth mounted, and Fychan pulled up beside him on Rhys's horse. "I will send word of your absence to the castle," Rhys said. "Prince Hywel might see fit to increase the guards around the monastery. His wife and son are here too, after all."

"I should have thought of that." Gareth reached down and clasped Rhys's forearm. "If you would send the message, I can leave with a lighter heart."

"I will do so immediately," Rhys said.

Gareth departed with Fychan, and the prior turned to Gwen. "I must arrange for word of our need to be sent to the castle. What is next for you?"

- 116 -

"Food first," Gwen said, "questions later. Gareth suggested that I show the picture around the monastery. Do you think it would be possible to speak to some of the brothers?"

Prior Rhys plucked at his lower lip. "It's irregular, but the abbot did emphasize how important this investigation was and assured me of the cooperation of everyone in the monastery."

Gwen acknowledged that the abbot probably didn't want her speaking to any of the monks alone, even though she was married. She found the monastery a strange sort of place. It functioned much like a castle, with a lord (the abbot), a steward (the prior) and many underlings, all with specific tasks. Except that there were no soldiers and no women. It seemed to her an unnatural way to live.

10

Gwen

Gwen joined Elspeth and Tangwen in the dining hall, where the guests had been lingering over their food and mead. With more than twenty-five people seated around the table, every room in the house had to be full to bursting.

Before he'd left earlier, Hywel had convinced Mari to join them for the meal, and she was making a brave attempt to do so. Gruffydd and his nanny, Bronwen, were present too. The girl was of an age with Elspeth, though the similarities ended there. Bronwen was quiet and shy, dark where Elspeth was blonde. Both were reliable nannies, however, and despite their differences, the two girls seemed to get along well, perhaps even more so because of their contrasting natures. Hafwen, Mari's patient maid, stood behind her mistress's chair, prepared to meet Mari's every need.

Mari was as pale as ever, her blue eyes, dark brows and lashes, and red lips standing out in her white face, but her voice was stronger than it had been yesterday. From the remains of the food on her trencher, it appeared that she'd managed to eat a little this evening too—if not yet a normal amount, at least not so little as to invite comment.

They had found seats at the end of the long wooden table. Mari sat in a cushioned upright chair on the end, while Elspeth and Tangwen sat on the bench to her right, and Gruffydd and Bronwen sat to Mari's left.

Gwen plopped down on the end of the bench next to Tangwen. "My lady."

Mari took a tentative sip of her heated wine. "Hywel tells me there's been a murder and that you briefly suspected him."

Gwen glanced down the table. Mari had kept her voice low, but this really wasn't something Gwen wanted anyone else to overhear. Fortunately, their fellow diners were too busy with the remains of their meal to pay attention to her, and the family of four to Gwen's right included a five-year-old son who was refusing to sit quietly and kept shrieking at his mother. Gwen was somewhat surprised Mari would bring up Hywel's possible role in the murder in a public setting, but Mari obviously thought the notion was so unlikely as to border on the absurd—and not something she needed to keep quiet about.

Mari noticed her furtive movements and raised her eyebrows. "What's wrong? Surely you don't still suspect him?"

Gwen leaned closer to her friend. "No. It isn't that. It's just that we hope to keep the knowledge that Gryff was murdered to ourselves for now. We want to lull whoever did kill him into a false sense of security."

"Oh. I'm sorry. I didn't know." Mari tipped her head. "And Hywel?"

Gwen shot her a rueful look. "I didn't want to suspect him, but the wound is similar to the one he gave Anarawd."

Mari managed a sardonic smile. "I realize that his suspicious nature has rubbed off onto you, but you should have known better. Hywel is smarter than to have used the same knife in two murders."

"As he himself told me." Gwen hesitated. "Do you have the knife with you here at Aberystwyth?"

"I left it in a trunk at Aber." Now Mari gave Gwen a broad smile. "If someone else found it, carried it all the way to Aberystwyth, and used it to murder that poor man, it isn't my fault—or Hywel's."

Gwen smiled too. "I believed your husband as soon as he said he didn't do it. Gareth and I are already tugging on other threads."

"Speaking of which—" Mari elbowed Gwen in the ribs and leaned in even closer to whisper in her ear, "Do you see that man's knife? It's old and notched in two places."

The man in question, dark-haired, of medium height with a short v-shaped beard, was dressed, despite the heat, in a fine green wool coat with embroidery on his sleeves. Gwen had learned when she'd been introduced to him yesterday that he was a minor landowner from lands south of Aberystwyth. He sat two seats down from Bronwen, beside his wife, who was dressed in an equally fine dress of deep red.

Mari spoke the truth, and as Gwen looked more closely at the knife, she realized that her conversation with Hywel was yet more evidence of how much he trusted her. Three years ago when she'd confronted him with Anarawd's death, Hywel could have foisted her off with a lie or distracted her with a survey of notched knives at Aber. Instead, he'd told her the truth of his involvement in it.

A cup clattered on the table in front of Gwen—fortunately it was empty—and Gwen used one hand to set it upright and the other to catch her daughter around the waist. Tangwen had been entertaining Gruffydd by making faces at him across the table. She'd learned it from Dai, who made faces at her to make her laugh or stop whatever fit she happened to be throwing. Tangwen missed the boys even more than Gwen did.

Tonight, however, Gruffydd was making up for their absence. Though only a year old, he was fully walking and speaking single words, much to the astonishment of everyone around him. Together, Tangwen and Gruffydd had managed to smear their faces with honey, knock over Bronwen's cup of mead, and nearly fall off their benches, just in the short time since Gwen had joined the meal. She would have preferred to plop them both on the floor and let them eat their dinner from there, but the other diners would have looked askance at that, so she'd resisted the impulse.

"Lady Mari." The minor landowner with the questionable knife had set down his mutton, and now he bent his neck in a bow to Mari. "Let me say for all of us that we are honored to have you at our table."

"Thank you." Mari inclined her head regally. She'd become very good at it since she'd married Hywel.

"It is comforting to us that you are here, my lady," he said. "We all feel safer."

"Is there some reason you might feel unsafe?" Gwen said.

"It is my understanding that a dead man lies in the chapel," he said.

"Yes, one does," Mari said.

"He drowned, they say," the landowner said.

"Indeed." Mari really was playing her part well.

"And yet, I have noticed the comings and goings of many soldiers today," the man said. "The word is that the man drowned, and yet Prince Hywel has sent men to investigate the death?"

Gwen looked down at her plate. This landowner was annoyingly perceptive.

But Mari was ready with an answer. "Any time a man dies of unnatural causes, my lord is concerned. He wants everyone to feel safe, particularly with so many people here for the festival."

"I heard he killed himself." One of the women down the table from Gwen was chewing rapidly on her food and speaking around it. She was tiny, maybe reaching only as high as Gwen's shoulder, but her voice projected over the general babble in the room.

"Then why would they allow him to lie in the chapel?" said a merchant's wife, who was wearing a full wimple. "I don't like it. It isn't right."

Her husband—a tall, thin man with wispy, balding hair, sitting beside her—put what looked like a warning hand on her arm. "I'm sure that's not the case, dear. Because you're right. He wouldn't be allowed to lie in the chapel if the abbot believed he took his own life."

The tiny woman looked down the table at Gwen. "Your husband is involved isn't he? What does he say?"

"It is too soon to say much of anything," Gwen said, "but no, he doesn't believe the man took his own life."

"So he drowned." The merchant frowned. "Does he believe the drowning wasn't an accident?"

Everyone at the table was listening avidly now, looking from the merchant to Gwen and back again. Gwen swallowed hard, made uncomfortable by all the attention. "As Lady Mari said, any unexplained death requires attention. There are enough questions with this one to warrant an investigation of how it came about."

"Thus the extra measure taken for your security, Lady Mari." The landowner smiled in satisfaction. He seemed to have decided that foul play was involved. Gwen supposed there was no help for it. People were going to jump to their own conclusions, and it was hard to fault them for jumping to the right one. Still, she consoled herself with the knowledge that nobody knew about the stab wound. "Though I would hope your lord husband doesn't believe you to be in danger here?"

"My lord does not believe any of us have any reason to be concerned—unless you had something to do with the man's death, of course." Mari passed this last addition off with a laugh, which everyone around the table joined in with except Gwen, who was watching the expressions on the diners' faces. The only furtive look so far had been her own.

Gwen spoke up. "As a precaution, you're right that the prince will augment the guard around the monastery tonight. We don't want anyone to feel unsettled, and if you are concerned about your safety, you are free to move your lodgings to the castle or elsewhere."

A burly man with a patchy beard, sitting at the far end of the table, snorted into his cup. "Not likely to find any place with room to spare at this hour, are we?" Then he gestured expansively to the room at large. "Besides, where better to stay than in the same place as the Lady of Ceredigion?"

He rose to his feet, his movements awkward since the bench he was sitting on was occupied by five other people. He bowed at the waist to Mari and sat again. Mari nodded her head and smiled, though she, like everyone else in the room, was quite sure the man had drunk far more mead than was good for him.

"Speaking of the poor man's death, we are trying to discover exactly who he is and what he was doing at the millpond so late at night. We hope to notify whomever of his kin we can find." Gwen pulled the sketch that Gareth had given her from her pocket and handed it to the landowner. "Do any of you recognize him? He may have gone by the name of Gryff."

The landowner looked at the sketch and then passed it to his wife. The sketch went all the way around the table to a general shaking of heads. It had been a long shot that any of them might have known him. Gwen had hoped that because these visitors were from other parts of Wales, and Iolo was a merchant who traveled far and wide throughout the country, someone might have seen Gryff before somewhere else.

Then one of the women seated down the table from Gwen leaned forward. Up until now she'd remained silent, and Gwen had barely noticed her. Closer inspection revealed pretty brown eyes ringed with dark lashes and brown hair that perfectly matched her eyes. She also had pox scars on her forehead, cheeks, and chin, marring her loveliness. "I saw him yesterday."

Gwen leaned forward too to look past Elspeth and Tangwen, who was currently standing on the bench to eat and jumping up and down at the same time. "You did?"

"Yes. We had just arrived, and I saw him speaking to the gatekeeper as we waited on the cobbles for the hosteler to come for us. They spoke briefly, and then he went away." She handed the sketch down the table to Gwen.

"Had you ever see him before?" Gwen said.

The woman shook her head. "Nor again. I only noticed him that one time because he seemed to be anxious. I'm sorry he's dead."

"Thank you." Gwen spoke fervently. "Thank you so much."

Mari put a hand on Gwen's arm. "You should speak to the gatekeeper. The girls and I will look after Tangwen."

"I will be back as soon as I can." Gwen kissed Tangwen's plump cheek, patted Elspeth's hand, and bid goodbye to the other guests. "Thank you."

As she headed for the door, a buzz of conversation rose behind her. She knew it had to do with the speed of her departure from dinner, but she also knew that even if she'd waited an hour to act on the woman's information, they still would have talked among themselves when she left. That made her stop and return briefly to Mari's side, bending to whisper in her friend's ear. "Let me know if you learn anything else, will you?"

"Of course," Mari said. "They'll have this investigation wrapped up by bedtime."

Gwen gave a low laugh. "Except they'll have decided the cook did it because he's stealing supplies from the monastery to sell for his own enrichment."

Mari laughed too, but then she sobered, looking up at her friend. "You know, it could be something like that."

Gwen shook her head, still laughing, and this time went through the door. Within a few moments, she was hastening across the cobbles towards the gate. The sun had all but set, and the courtyard was in full shade. Sweat had trickled down her back all through dinner, and the slight breeze that came in from the gardens came as a relief. The wet fabric on her back cooled instantly, and she stood for a moment in the center of the empty courtyard, her arms outstretched, trying to catch more of it.

The gatekeeper stayed in a little room adjacent to the gate, in order to watch it at all times. In the winter, he was allowed a brazier to warm himself, but today his door stood open to allow that same breeze that stirred the air in the courtyard to reach him. While the warmth of the day had dissipated, it could hardly be called cool.

Gwen was pleased that it was the same gatekeeper who guarded the door most days. Several of the older monks took turns with the duty, because the gate had to be manned through the night as well as the day, but Sion was the monk most often present. White-haired and crotchety on the surface, he'd fallen in love with Tangwen from the moment he'd laid eyes on her. To his mind, she could do no wrong. Fortunately, he included Gwen in his adoration.

"My dear," he said as she appeared.

"Brother Sion," Gwen said. "Are you well?"

"I am. Thank you for asking. This weather agrees with these old bones." Sion squinted at her. "But you aren't here about my health. I see urgency in you. What is it? Is Tangwen—"

Gwen put out a hand to the old man. "She is well. Covered in honey, but well."

Sion smiled, as Gwen hoped he would. Some men went through life with an edge to them, just waiting for someone to cross them, and some couldn't help but see the best in people. Sion might have affected a gruff exterior, but from his reaction to Tangwen, there was no doubt in Gwen's mind that he was of the latter type.

Then Gwen went on. "Yesterday afternoon, you spoke with a young man. One of the guests saw him come and leave. Do you remember him?" Yet again, Gwen brought out the sketch of Gryff.

Squinting down at the image, which he brought to within a few inches of his face, Sion frowned. "I do remember him. We've had many comings and goings these last few days, you know, but I remember this man in particular. Anxious fellow. He wouldn't give me his name or tell me what he wanted except that he was looking for the prince. He'd already been to the castle without any luck."

"Did he know Lady Mari was here?" Gwen said.

"He seemed to. Certainly he hoped to find Prince Hywel with her."

"When you said that the prince wasn't here, what did he say?" Gwen said.

"He sounded near to tears, to tell you the truth." Sion peered closer at her. "Why are you asking all this?"

"Sion, the young man in question lies dead in your chapel."

"Oh!" Sion sat back on his stool.

"Did you not see him when they carried him into the monastery?" Gwen said.

Sion looked at Gwen warily, and then he leaned forward again, motioning conspiratorially for her to do the same. Gwen did as he asked, putting her own face closer to his than would normally have felt comfortable.

"My eyes are such that I can't make out faces from any distance."

"It is a common problem," Gwen said.

"Especially in a man with my years," Sion said. "Can you tell me the poor man's name?"

"His name was Gryff. I am among those charged with discovering his movements in the hours before he died."

"I'm afraid I never saw him again beyond that afternoon," Sion said. "I will pray for him."

"I wish we knew what he wanted Prince Hywel for," Gwen said.

"It must have been something important for him to have ended up dead by morning," Sion said, and then his eyes widened. "That means—that means his death wasn't an accident!"

Gwen didn't begrudge Sion his conclusion, since he'd brought her the first piece of information that indicated Gryff *might* have had a secret worth killing him over. He seemed to have married two different women, which could have been reason enough to murder him, but only if one of the women herself had done it. Gwen hadn't yet met either woman, but she was struggling to picture one of them stabbing Gryff in the middle of the night and throwing him into the millpond. Still, stranger things had happened.

Gwen made a shushing motion with her hand and moved even closer to the old monk. "Please keep this quiet. If you would say nothing to anyone about what you told me, I would be grateful. Only a very few know that we suspect Gryff's death wasn't an accident."

"Why shouldn't I tell—" Sion's voice broke off as understanding spread across his face. "You don't want the killer knowing you suspect murder. Very clever, my dear." Then his eyes narrowed. "I assume the abbot knows?"

"Your abbot and your prior, and the two monks who took him from the millpond." Gwen made a rueful face. "And maybe all the diners in the hall, though they're still guessing."

"A secret stops being a secret when two people know about it," Sion said.

"This has reached the ears of far more than two," Gwen said, "but we can still try."

Sion bent at the waist. "I will say nothing to anyone else until you give me leave."

"Thank you," Gwen said. "May I ask if Gryff said anything else to you or did anything else while he was here? Anything at all, no matter how unimportant it might have seemed at the time?"

"Nothing."

"So, you're saying he came, he asked for Prince Hywel, and he left," Gwen said.

Sion's brow furrowed. "Well, not exactly. He did do one thing. As it was near the dinner hour, he asked if he could bring my meal to me. Of course I was grateful, and I said so."

Gwen contemplated the gatekeeper, wondering if Gryff's action could have been a kindness only, or if his offer had been rooted in another purpose. "That was kind of him." She wished Gareth were here because he might have seen what she was missing.

"He appeared to be a thoughtful young man. He would have made a fine monk," Sion said.

Gwen smiled gently. "He was married."

He shrugged. "In the old days that didn't matter."

Sion couldn't possibly have remembered those 'old days', back before the Normans came to Britain, but Gwen wasn't going to argue with him. And maybe Gryff would have made a good monk—if he hadn't been married to two women. She didn't tell Sion that. He'd learn it soon enough.

"And then what did Gryff do?"

"After he delivered the food, he left. I never saw him again." Sion shook his head sadly. "Such a nice young man to be so troubled."

Gwen looked towards the chapel where Gryff lay. "Troubled appears to be one word to describe him. Clearly there was more to him than we have discovered so far."

11

Rhun

Rhun returned to the castle to find that not only had his
Uncle Cadwaladr arrived, but so had King Cadell of
Deheubarth with his niece Angharad, coming to the
festival a day late, along with all their retainers and household
staff. While King Cadell had brought his own tents and pavilions
rather than try to squeeze into the already overfull castle, both he
and Cadwaladr had deigned to dine with Hywel in the hall for the
evening meal, which was just getting underway when Rhun
arrived. Hywel had left both front and back doors open to catch
whatever breeze might pass through the hall.

Hywel had also saved a place for him next to Angharad,
whose shy smile at Rhun's approach made his heart thump
uncomfortably in his chest. Maiden that she was, she wore her
long, dark hair down her back and held away from her face by a
blue mantle the same color as her eyes. Her long lashes pointed
demurely downwards as he found a seat beside her. But then he
caught a flash from her eyes—something along the lines of
assessment and curiosity—and he suppressed a smile. Cadell was

dangling her in front of him like bait for a particularly large fish, but he was already well and truly hooked.

"Prince Rhun," Cadell said from his prime seat to the right of Hywel. Cadwaladr sat on Hywel's other side, making this dinner one of the most awkward occasions in living memory. "Prince Hywel tells me that a man has been found dead in the millpond?"

Rhun checked Angharad's face, which turned to meet his, her curiosity openly evident now, and then he looked past her to meet Cadell's gaze. "Yes, my lord."

"And you are assisting in the investigation as to how he arrived there?"

"Yes."

"Is that usual?" Cadell said.

Rhun caught the look Hywel shot him from beyond Cadell. Unfortunately, Rhun wasn't sure how he was supposed to interpret it—as discouraging or encouraging—so he soldiered on as best he could. "Thankfully, I can't say that men die in such a fashion very often in my brother's domain."

"Surely the death of a peasant is hardly the concern of the Lord of Ceredigion," Cadell said.

Angharad stiffened beside him and looked down at her trencher. She didn't say anything, however, and it was as if she'd withdrawn inside herself.

"I would disagree, my lord." Rhun glanced at Angharad again before looking to the King of Deheubarth. "If a lord believes the death of any of his people—man, woman, or child—is beneath his concern, by what right does he call himself a lord?"

Cadell looked gravely at Rhun for a moment and then reached for his goblet. "Well said, Prince Rhun."

Rhun's face reddened, first at Cadell's suggestion that Gryff's death was of no consequence, and then at the realization that the king didn't agree with what he'd just said. Cadell had been testing him. Rhun didn't think he'd been found wanting, but rather that Cadell thought him soft with honor.

Hywel's hand had been resting on the table by his cup, and he clenched it into a fist before removing it to his lap. "When we have been visited in the past by curious events, my brother has been helpful in unearthing the truth. My father trusts him in all things."

"That is good to know," Cadell said.

With something akin to horror, Rhun realized that Hywel and Cadell weren't talking about this current death, but about the death three years ago of Cadell's brother, Anarawd. It was a wonder that Cadell could remain in his seat, knowing that Cadwaladr, the man who'd ordered the ambush of Anarawd and all his men, sat on the other side of Hywel, chewing unconcernedly on a piece of mutton.

Only now did Rhun understand the look Hywel had given him. It had said, *tread carefully.* "With the festival underway and many strangers in Aberystwyth, it seems particularly important that the matter of this man's death be laid to rest quickly," Rhun said into the silence that had fallen on the high table.

Hywel shot him a quick smile. Rhun had finally said something right. At the same time, Rhun felt awkward about taking even a thimbleful of credit for Hywel's accomplishments. His brother didn't appear to want Cadell to know of his own role in their father's affairs. Rhun would have to corner him about that later, but in the meantime, it wasn't a lie to say that he had *helped* Hywel in the past. Since the finding of Gryff's body, he'd certainly received an education from Gwen and Gareth.

"My brother, of course, assists my father in Gwynedd's affairs at all levels," Hywel said. "He came to Ceredigion because I had need of his wisdom in various matters, and it's a lucky accident that he's here to assist me in this too."

Now Hywel was stretching the truth. "Nonsense, Hywel has—" Rhun stopped at the look of horror on Hywel's face, one Rhun hoped only he had seen. He coughed, took a drink of mead, and waved a hand dismissively. "Ah ... nothing."

That wasn't what he'd been about to say, of course. He'd been about to say, *Hywel doesn't need me and has both Ceredigion, and this investigation, well in hand.* Which was stupid of him. It wasn't as if he'd forgotten who he was talking to or about Anarawd's death. But this was the King of Deheubarth, the domains of which had once stretched as far as this very castle. His discontent was usually masked, but it was nonetheless well known.

Regardless of the polite face he showed Hywel and King Owain, everyone knew that Cadell deeply resented Gwynedd's annexation of Ceredigion. After the 1136 war King Gruffydd, Rhun's grandfather, had given it to Cadwaladr, but he'd mismanaged it so badly that Hywel was still cleaning up after him three years on. After Cadwaladr arranged for Anarawd's death, Cadell had argued that Ceredigion should return to him. Instead, Rhun's father had given it to Hywel.

Some had whispered that Cadell might have colluded with Cadwaladr to bring about Anarawd's murder, though Cadwaladr had never gone so far as to sell out Cadell to save his own skin. Which would have been very like him. To Rhun's mind, there could be only two reasons for this: one, Cadell hadn't been involved; or two, he had been involved, and three years ago Cadwaladr had valued their future relationship over forcing Cadell to take some of the blame. Cadwaladr had been interested— forever and always— only in helping himself.

Rhun decided it was time to change the subject. "What news from the south? I congratulate you on your conquests of Carmarthen and Llanstephan."

Cadell bent his neck graciously. "It has been a good summer. Before long, we will drive the Normans from our land once and for all."

That was going to be quite a task, though one everyone at the table was heartily in favor of. It was easier said than done, however. It had been eighty years since the Normans first landed on the shores of England. They had launched their invasion of Wales almost immediately thereafter, supposedly provoked by attacks by Gruffydd ap Llywelyn. He'd been a ruler of all Wales, though hated by Rhun and the people of Gwynedd for usurping the throne from the House of Aberffraw, Rhun's ancestors.

Still, the truth then had been the same as now: Norman lords chipped away at Welsh territory whenever they could. They'd gained almost the whole of it during the lifetime of Rhun's grandfather, only to have the Welsh rise up and beat them back again. King Owain, Rhun's father, was the strongest king among all the kingdoms of Wales, and he kept a constant and watchful eye on his eastern border. Every victory against the Normans—even by a somewhat distrusted ally such as Cadell—was a cause for celebration.

"King Cadell and I have been discussing the wars in the east as well," Hywel said. "Earl Ranulf of Chester remains a prisoner of the king, but it seems that negotiations are underway for his release."

"That man has switched sides so many times, it's a wonder that any side in this quarrel might trust him again," Rhun said.

The quarrel in question was between Stephen, the dead King Henry's nephew, and King Henry's daughter, Maud. Although King Henry had secured the promise of all his barons to support Maud's claim to the throne, upon Henry's death, Stephen had crossed the English Channel and been crowned king before Maud had set foot in England. It helped that one of Stephen's brothers was the Bishop of Winchester and had been the one to do the crowning.

England had been at war ever since, a prize half torn apart by the maneuvering of these two Norman rulers. What the Saxons, the conquered inhabitants of England, actually thought of who ruled them, Rhun didn't know. The Welsh had never minded when a man married a foreigner. Rhun's own mother was Irish. But Rhun felt himself to be wholly Welsh, and to his mind, any Welshman who tolerated Norman rule was not a man at all.

"Agreed. But if Earl Ranulf goes free, he will still be powerful," Hywel said. "Both sides will want him on their side, though we all know that the only side he truly cares for is his own."

Since Rhun had last spoken with Earl Ranulf two years ago, the earl had abandoned Empress Maud for King Stephen, and then almost immediately quarreled with Stephen's supporters, who'd accused him of plotting against the king's life. Stephen had subsequently thrown Ranulf into prison, where he rotted to this day. No matter what promises he made to Stephen in order to secure his release, he would remain a threat—possibly to both sides.

"That is all one has to remember about Ranulf," King Cadell said. "King Stephen will release him, but if he does, he should watch his back. Ranulf will renew his allegiance to Maud, and the fighting will start yet again. Mark my words."

"I mark them." Rhun raised his goblet to King Cadell. "Before Stephen imprisoned him, Ranulf was planning a campaign against my father and trying to gather support from the other Norman barons for the campaign. Once free, I have no doubt he will look to our borders, with or without the support of Earl Robert of Gloucester." Earl Robert, the bastard son of King Henry, was Maud's half-brother and her chief supporter and general in this war.

"I will be interested to hear how it goes for your father in the east in the coming months," Cadell said.

Rhun set down his goblet, taking care not to upset it. It was a move matched by Hywel. While Cadell returned to his meal, seemingly unaware—or feigning unawareness—of the significance of what he'd just said, Rhun could not dismiss the words so easily. Cadell was telling Rhun and Hywel that if Ranulf made war on Gwynedd, he would sit to one side and watch. He would not come if King Owain called him. Gwynedd and Deheubarth were still ostensibly allied, but Cadell was stating clearly that war on Gwynedd's borders was of no concern to him.

Rhun and Hywel looked at each other. It was as if the lines between them and Cadell had been drawn in the air around them. With Cadwaladr still sitting beyond Hywel at the table, they were literally surrounded by enemies.

Angharad made a slight movement under the table with her hand, almost touching Rhun's leg but drawing back at the last instant. Rhun caught the motion out of the corner of his eye. If he hadn't been so finely tuned to his surroundings, taking in every cleared throat, every ducked head, he might have missed it. He reached out and caught her hand instead.

They sat together through a dozen heartbeats as the tension at the table eased, and everyone started breathing again. Neither Rhun nor Angharad acknowledged the other or the fact that Rhun still held her hand under the table. Then, finally, Angharad turned her head slightly towards Rhun and spoke in a low voice. "Do not think I share my uncle's hatred of all things Gwynedd."

Rhun glanced past her to Cadell to see if he was paying attention to his niece, but at that moment he pushed back his chair to stand and move down to the far end of the table to speak to another of Hywel's guests. Rhun's eyes narrowed to see it, thinking of all the ways the evening could play out because of what Cadell had said. Rhun's mind didn't often contemplate plots and subterfuge, but he knew betrayal was of constant concern to his father—and for good reason.

He turned to look fully at Angharad. "Do you not?"

"Cadell has no sons." Her eyes moved to her plate, and she looked very hard at it rather than at him.

"You mean he has no one to watch his back as Hywel and I watch our father's," Rhun said. She might also be telling him that if he married her, he might have a claim to the throne of Deheubarth. But to think that was definitely getting ahead of himself.

"My uncle is following a dangerous path. When he took Llanstephan, he challenged his own uncle, Maurice, who held the castle for King Stephen. Uncle Cadell is not in as secure a position as he would have you believe." Angharad was telling Rhun what he needed to hear. "The truth is, he cannot afford to help your father hold off the Earl of Chester. He cannot leave the south, even for a good cause."

Hywel might have said that anytime anyone promised the truth, very often what came out was anything but the truth. But

Angharad's assertions coincided with Rhun's own assessment of Cadell's situation. Rather than confess his weakness in order to use it as an excuse (and a legitimate one) not to fight, Cadell had chosen to brazen it out, knowing that Hywel would never dream to challenge a guest, no matter how bold the provocation.

Rhun put his head close to hers. "Be very careful, Angharad. I would not have you speak so plainly if it means rousing your uncle's ire." He squeezed Angharad's hand and let it go.

"You need to know what he plans," Angharad said. "He wants Ceredigion."

"We have known that for some time. Don't trouble yourself over the matter."

"He doesn't care how he gets it." Angharad's attention was still mostly on her plate, but she shot him another look, and this time he saw fear in her eyes. "He has brought men with him."

Rhun's stomach clenched. "What?"

Angharad's mouth barely moved as she spoke. "He has another fifty cavalry, in addition to those who camp with us on the festival grounds. He left them off the road to the south of Aberystwyth."

Rhun felt again for her hand. "If you need anything— anything at all—you come to me. I can keep you safe."

Angharad eased out a breath. "Thank you."

Rhun would have given anything to take Angharad out of the hall immediately. He could have housed her with Gwen and

Mari at the monastery. But such an act, more than anything else he could have done short of pulling out his sword right there and then and challenging Cadell directly, would have violated the pledge of hospitality Hywel had given Cadell. It would also have been tantamount to eloping with her. On the whole, Rhun wasn't opposed to the idea, but he hadn't discussed marriage with her yet, and a few squeezed hands did not amount to a lifelong promise. Hywel might think nothing of sneaking around with whomever caught his eye, but if any conversation should be plainly spoken, it was when a man asked a woman to marry him.

Still, elopement was not without precedent between Gwynedd and Deheubarth. For a moment, Rhun amused himself contemplating the parallels and possibilities. When Rhun's aunt Gwenllian was fifteen years old, she eloped with King Cadell's father, Gruffydd. Anarawd and Cadell were the sons of a previous marriage, so there was no blood relationship between Rhun and Cadell, but custom called them cousins.

It was Gwenllian's death, in fact, that had prompted Gwynedd to get involved in Deheubarth in the first place. The Normans had hung Gwenllian from the battlements when she'd defended her castle in her husband's absence. Ironically, Gruffydd had been in Gwynedd, arranging for Rhun's father and Cadwaladr to come to Deheubarth to help him defend Ceredigion.

Besides, it wasn't so much propriety that demanded Rhun sit on his hands, but a desire not to ruin Hywel's festival. Cadell might have fifty hidden men, but he hadn't turned them on Hywel, and now that Rhun knew about them, he and Hywel could devise a strategy for addressing the problem.

Rhun also didn't have any indication that Angharad was, in fact, in danger from her uncle. And within a few moments of the end of their conversation, her chaperone signaled that Angharad should retire with her women to her tent, leaving her uncle to continue his revelry. The longer Rhun spent with King Cadell, the more the king's manner irritated him. It seemed to Rhun that he kept looking around the hall, measuring it with his eyes as if he was evaluating where he'd put his tapestries when he moved in.

Hywel, as host, was required to maintain his seat for far longer than he otherwise might have. Fortunately, an hour after sunset, Hywel's steward appeared in the rear doorway to the hall and sent a boy to Hywel's side. At the message, Hywel rose from his seat, and Rhun rose to go to the door with him. By then, the formal aspect of the feast had broken up and most of the seats at the high table were empty, as their various occupants had moved to other locations in the hall. Most of the women had left.

The steward was waiting for them in the courtyard of the castle. With the sun finally having set into the sea, a cooler breeze wafted past Rhun. The hall had been stifling in comparison, but such were the high spirits of most everybody involved that nobody minded. Rhun was also pleased to see that the problem with the latrines had been sufficiently addressed. He could smell sea air, wood smoke, and the verdant scents of a warm August evening.

"What is it?" Hywel said to his steward, a capable man named Morgan whom Taran had found for him.

"I didn't want to interrupt your meal, but a messenger has come from Prior Rhys asking for more men to guard the monastery. He also sent this for your eyes only." Morgan handed a piece of paper to Hywel. "I already sent the men."

Rhun peered over his brother's shoulder to read the letter, understanding immediately why the prior had written down what he wanted to say to Hywel rather than trusting the whole of the message to another man to relay verbally. The letter told of a possible other wife for Gryff, and that Gareth had gone to fetch her. Prior Rhys also explained why Gareth was concerned for the safety of Mari and Gwen.

"Thank you for sending the guards," Hywel said. "I myself will go now to inspect the grounds and speak to my wife."

"Could there be some trouble along the lines of which we spoke earlier—" Morgan hesitated.

"Not yet. Not here, but I understand Prior Rhys's concern." Hywel turned to Rhun. "Will you come?"

"Of course." Then Rhun scowled at his brother. "You really shouldn't have exaggerated my past role in your investigations to Cadell. I have been of very little use, and you know it."

"You sell yourself short. I rely on you." Hywel turned back to Morgan. "More people have come to the festival than I anticipated, and I am wary about having Cadwaladr and Cadell in the same hall. I need you to watch them more closely than ever."

"Yes, my lord."

"You weren't there in the hall to hear Cadell speak." Hywel related the conversation with Cadell to Morgan, whose expression grew even more concerned.

"It wasn't a declaration of war, but Cadell certainly resents Gwynedd," Rhun said.

"We also need to be more careful about our guests," Hywel said. "I'm not suggesting that anyone be searched or made aware of my concerns, but even the kitchen staff need to be on their guard for suspicious behavior. One murder is quite enough for the week."

"I will see to it," Morgan said.

"Meanwhile, Rhun and I need our horses saddled. We'll ride to the monastery now."

"And then to the northeast?" Morgan said.

"Indeed," Hywel said.

"Northeast?" Rhun said as Morgan turned away.

"Cadwaladr brought more men with him," Hywel said. "Fifty cavalry. I want to see them with my own eyes."

Rhun stared at his brother. "I was going to tell you at the first opportunity that Cadell left fifty men hidden in the woods to the south of Aberystwyth."

It was Hywel's turn to stare at Rhun. "Who told you that? Angharad?"

Rhun nodded.

"So we're surrounded, though not by numbers I would normally fear."

"I share your puzzlement," Rhun said.

"I need Gareth back, except something tells me this murder can't wait either." Hywel sighed and looked down at the ground. "I must have been mad to think this festival was a good idea."

"It was a good idea," Rhun said immediately. "It still is."

Hywel shook his head, but Rhun cut him off before he could speak again. "At the very least, you can view it as a chance to flush out your enemies."

Hywel's head came up at that.

Rhun nodded to see it. "Don't you think King Cadell sees this week as an opportunity? He isn't here for the music, I can assure you. He's here to evaluate the state of your domain, the nature of your rule, and to assess your defenses."

Hywel was nodding slowly. "Already we have learned that Cadwaladr and Cadell brought small armies with them. I haven't forced them to act, but they have acted anyway."

"Now, the question before us is if they are working together," Rhun said.

"I shudder to think." For the first time in a week, Hywel genuinely smiled. He clapped a hand on Rhun's shoulder. "You have brought me back to myself. A spy I am and always will be. I was a fool to ever forget it."

"What's astonishing to me is that I've been thinking like you," Rhun said. "As I sat at the table tonight, looking around the room and contemplating what I'd learned today, I realized that I was distrusting the motives of every single person I'd met."

"Except for Angharad," Hywel said.

"Except—" Rhun broke off, gazing into his brother's face and reviewing Angharad's words to him in his head. He had to acknowledge that it wouldn't be outside the realm of possibility for Cadell and Angharad to be working together. Cadell could have meant to incite anger in Hywel and Rhun so that Angharad could come in as a balm to assuage Rhun's fears. Or, at the very least, to imply—as she had done—that she could be trusted where her uncle could not.

Hywel smirked at the look of surprise on Rhun's face. "You really are beginning to learn, brother."

12

Gareth

Fychan was not a talkative traveling companion. In fact, the boy seemed to regret having opened his mouth in the first place and was now making up for his lapse by a studied muteness. Even so, five miles wasn't far to travel on a fresh and rested horse—even mostly uphill, since Goginan lay at the base of the mountains and was the site of a silver and lead mine, an important source of income for Hywel.

Because of the trade to and from Aberystwyth, the road upon which they traveled was well maintained, and as Gareth had hoped, they reached the village while it was still twilight. Fychan guided them to the home of Gryff's (other) wife, Carys. As Gareth dismounted, she was sitting on a stool outside her house, watching two small children playing in the dirt. One was the age of Tangwen, and the second was a year or two older.

At the sight of Gareth and Fychan coming towards her, Carys stood, her brow furrowing. Recognizing Gareth's station by his sword, gear, and fine horse, she bobbed a curtsey. "What brings you to Goginan, my lord?" Then before Gareth could answer, Carys looked past him to Fychan, and her eyes widened. "Fychan! You were a boy last I saw you! Look how you've grown."

Fychan smiled sheepishly and turned bright red. "Cousin Carys."

Carys put her hands on his upper arms and kissed each of his cheeks in turn. "I heard you'd turned to the Church."

"Yes, Cousin." Fychan managed to disentangle himself from Carys, and he gestured to Gareth. "This is Sir Gareth, captain of Prince Hywel's *teulu*. We have come—" Fychan broke off at the raised eyebrow from Gareth, flushing again. The boy really didn't want to be the one to send this pleasant conversation into the terrible turn it was about to take.

Gareth took a step towards Carys, one of the sketches he'd made in his hand. "May I ask, is this your husband?" He tried to keep his face calm and his demeanor unthreatening. He wanted a truthful answer from Carys, given without fear of what might come next.

Carys took the paper, her eyes widening again as she examined the picture. "Yes! Yes, that's my Gryff." She looked up. It was only then that the muscles around her lips tightened as she realized that something might be amiss—that this might be more than a pleasant social call. "Why are you asking me this?"

Gareth tipped his head to Fychan, pointing towards the two small children. Fychan understood instantly what Gareth needed from him. He swooped down upon the children, tickling them and herding them a dozen yards farther away from their mother. Then Gareth took in a quick breath and let it out, bracing himself for the task that had brought him all this way. "I'm sorry to tell you, Carys, but this man, if he is your husband, is dead."

Carys gasped, put her hand to her mouth, and staggered a few steps back. She would have fallen if Gareth hadn't caught her. "No! No!" She shook her head back and forth rhythmically.

This initial moment when a loved one learned about a death was always the worst part for Gareth. He tried not to rush it, to be gentle in the telling, and when he'd managed to get the words out, he always felt as if a burden had been lifted from his shoulders. For the person being told, however, it was only the beginning of the hard times.

"Sit here while I get you some water." Gareth guided Carys back to her stool and then disappeared inside the darkened house. He was looking for the cup and the pitcher of water. It was resting on the sideboard, as it must be in every Welsh house he had ever entered, ready for the refreshment of a guest. He poured water into the cup and brought it back to Carys. "Drink."

She took a sip, and Gareth crouched in front of her. "Do you think you could answer a few questions?"

Carys nodded, hiccupping a little and wiping at the tears on her cheeks with the back of her free hand. Her blond hair was pulled away from her face, though tendrils had come loose and framed it. Far more than before he'd told her of Gryff's death, she looked very young—no more than eighteen to Gareth's eyes. Too young to have suffered this loss.

"I'm sorry to have to ask this, but when did you last see your husband?"

Carys took another sip from the cup. Her attention was fixed on a patch of dirt somewhere to the right of Gareth's foot. "Days ago," she said, and now her voice came out dull and lifeless. The reality of her future was beginning to set in. "He was supposed to visit this coming Sunday."

That was in three days' time.

"Why was it that Gryff was absent? He was employed by ..." Gareth left the question hanging on purpose, hoping Carys would finish it. Given her present state, he needed to lead her along, but he didn't want to supply her with the actual answers.

"By that cloth trader he met," Carys said. "He could never settle on any one thing, could my Gryff, but he always worked. We always had food to eat." Tears leaked out of her eyes and spilled down her cheeks.

Gareth glanced beside the cottage, where an extensive garden lay. It faced southwest, where it would be warmed by every ray of sun it could soak up. He suspected that the garden was her doing, and a large part of the food they ate came from her efforts, even with two small children to raise.

"Did the cloth trader pay Gryff well?" Gareth said.

"He paid better than any work Gryff had ever done," Carys said. "Gryff worked in the silver mine until he hurt his back. Then he did odd jobs for the blacksmith. He was herding sheep for my brother when he encountered the trader—Iolo was his name—stuck in the mud. He helped him out, and then one thing led to another." Carys put her head into her hands. "I can't believe he's dead!"

She wept, and Gareth allowed her to do so. He rose to his feet and stretched his back, waiting for her tears to slow and considering what question he should ask her next, if he was going to be able to ask her any more questions at all. Her grief seemed genuine. When he'd told her of Gryff's death, she'd responded in a way that looked completely natural to Gareth—and he had experience in such matters. He'd told more wives than he liked to recall that they'd become widows. He found it hard to believe that Carys had murdered her husband, though he reminded himself to keep an open mind. There was no telling the lengths to which a betrayed woman might go to get her revenge.

Then Carys cut herself off abruptly and looked up from her hands. Since Gareth was now standing, she had to look up a little higher than she had before, and he took a step back so she didn't have to crane her neck. "How did Gryff die?"

Gareth had been wondering when they'd get to that. "He was found in the millpond not far from the monastery at Llanbadarn Fawr."

Carys blinked back a fresh onslaught of tears, her eyes wide as she gaped at him. "What? You mean he drowned? My Gryff? No." She was back to the rhythmic headshaking. "That's not possible. Not my Gryff."

"It could have happened if he'd drunk too much," Gareth said, trying out Iolo's suggestion. "If he couldn't swim—"

"He could swim!" Carys glared at Gareth.

Gareth looked carefully at her. "You're sure?"

"Of course I'm sure. He taught me." She gestured to her children. "My older boy is only three, and he already swims like a fish. Gryff believed it was never too early to teach a child who lived by a river to swim."

Gareth didn't disagree, and her certainty made up his mind for him. "If we could beg lodging from you tonight, would you come with me in the morning to Aberystwyth? At the very least, I am sure you would like to see your husband into his grave."

Carys sobbed aloud at the mention of Gryff's funeral, her momentary anger forgotten and her grief renewed. But she nodded her agreement as well.

"Is there someone close by who can watch the children in your absence?" Gareth said.

"My sis-sister-in-law," Carys said, gasping out a sob in the middle of the word. Then she moaned. "I must speak to my brother. He never liked Gryff."

Gareth filed that piece of information away for future examination and bit his lip. He had more to tell Carys, and it wasn't going to be pleasant for her to hear. It wouldn't be worse than the news of her husband's death, but it would add insult to the injury. "I regret to say that I have more news that you won't want to hear, but I think it's better to tell you all of it now than for you to discover it tomorrow."

At first he didn't think Carys had heard him because she continued to weep, hunched over with her face in her hands. Then she quieted, and although she didn't look up, her voice came sharply. "What is it?"

He cleared his throat, finding it awkward to speak to the top of her head. "Another woman has come forward claiming to be Gryff's wife."

Carys jerked, almost falling off her stool. "What?"

"I'm sorry." He must have apologized to Carys six times already and might have to do it six more. "That's how we learned his name. The woman came into the chapel where he had been laid out and told us she was his wife. We discovered that you were his wife too only because Fychan is a brother at St. Padarn's and recognized Gryff's face when they brought him in."

Carys had been pale from weeping, but now the rest of the color drained from her face, leaving it pasty and drawn. "Who-who is this woman?"

"Her name is Madlen. She is Iolo's niece."

"No!" Carys stood up so suddenly that she startled Gareth, who took a surprised step backwards. Carys brushed past him without another word and set off down the hill towards a cluster of houses below hers that lay nearer to the river.

Gareth went after her. She was distraught, and he was worried about what she might do. She said she could swim, but she wouldn't be the first widow who tried to drown the pain that she couldn't master. Because his legs were longer and he wasn't crying, Gareth caught up with her after fifty feet or so. He tugged on her arm for her to stop and came around in front so she couldn't keep walking. "Where are you going?"

"To see my brother!" Carys wrenched away from Gareth, shoving at him with both her hands to his chest, and took off again.

She didn't hurt him, of course, being half his size, but she was quicker than he expected, and she got away from him. At least he knew now that she wasn't heading for the river but for the closest house. It was larger and sturdier than hers, with a new roof and possibly three rooms inside.

"Alun! Alun!" Carys wailed the name as she approached the house.

The front door was on the other side of the building, facing south and away from Gareth, so he didn't see the man until he came around the side of his house. He caught Carys in his arms as she barreled into him. "What is it, Carys?"

Before she could answer through her sobs, Alun looked past her to Gareth, standing on the pathway that led up to Carys's house. "What have you done?"

Gareth put up both hands in what he hoped was an unthreatening manner and began to walk towards the pair. Gareth was a knight and could fight if he had to, but he had no interest in pulling out his sword to protect himself from a grieving widow and her brother. Alun, if Gareth had heard the name right, was the size of an ox with a neck at least as thick as Gareth's thigh. "I am the bearer of bad news, that is all."

"What bad news?" Alun looked down to the top of Carys's head.

"Gryff is dead!" Carys said between sobs. "He was found in the millpond in Llanbadarn Fawr."

Alun's face turned deep red. "I'll—" But whatever he was going to say or do was lost in the outpouring of tears coming from Carys and the army of children who surged around the corner of Alun's house, engulfing him and Carys and moving on up the hill. Gareth turned to see Fychan standing at the top with Carys's two little ones, who would now be growing up without their father.

Fychan looked helplessly down at Gareth and the sobbing Carys. "What do you want me to do?"

"Carry on minding the children. We're not finished here." Gareth waved a hand at Fychan, who bowed his acceptance, and then Gareth walked the rest of the way down the hill to where Carys and her brother stood.

Alun glowered at Gareth. "Who are you?"

"Gareth ap Rhys." Gareth kept his expression calm, and as he came closer, Alun's expression faltered. For the first time, Gareth's general appearance seemed to register.

Alun swallowed back whatever insult or (more likely) threat he'd been about to throw at Gareth and gave him a stiff bow instead. "My lord. I'm sorry. I didn't realize who you were."

"I am the captain of Prince Hywel's guard," Gareth said. "I have done nothing to your sister but tell her what has occurred."

Alun seemed to be struggling with himself. "Can you explain, my lord?"

Gareth raised his chin, realizing what he was seeing: Alun was used to browbeating everyone he encountered, though the way he was holding Carys suggested that he genuinely cared for her. It had probably been a long time since Alun had asked anyone a polite question as he had Gareth just now.

Not one to hold a grudge, Gareth related to Alun the essential details of the finding of Gryff's body, without mentioning the stab wound. He was still keeping that in reserve. He didn't know how long he was going to be able to do that, or if it would help them find the murderer, but it was all he had.

Towards the end of the telling, Carys's sister-in-law came out of the house and wrapped her arms around Carys. The two women sobbed together, and then the sister held Carys at arm's length and looked into her face. "You always have a place with us. Isn't that right, Alun?"

"Of course," Alun said. Not every man would relish taking on three more mouths to feed, but to Alun's credit, he welcomed his sister without hesitation.

"Come inside." The woman put her arm around Carys and guided her around the hut towards the door.

Alun put his hands around his mouth and bellowed up the hill for Fychan to bring the children, which after a moment he did, having scooped up the youngest in his arms in his haste to answer the summons.

Fychan skidded to a halt at the bottom of the hill. "What is it?"

"Send the children inside," Alun said.

Fychan obediently put the child down, and Alun urged all of them towards the house. They went willingly enough, and when they too had disappeared, Alun turned back to Fychan. "You saw Gryff's body?"

Fychan nodded, shifting nervously from foot to foot.

"You're sure it was Gryff?"

Again the nod.

"So he's really dead, eh?" Alun stroked his chin and continued before Gareth had to answer that question. "I always knew he'd come to a bad end."

"Why is that?" Gareth said.

Alun dropped his hand. "He was a layabout, that's why."

Gareth's conversations with most everyone had given him that impression, first from Iolo's disappointment in his associate, then from Carys, and finally from Alun, who proceeded to lay out Gryff's failings more fully: he would always arrive later than he said he would; he would fail to complete an assignment by the end of the day or simply wander off halfway through; or he'd forget the details of what he'd been asked to do to the point that he became useless and it became quicker just to do the work oneself. Only Madlen hadn't seen him as others did, and that difference made Gareth wonder yet again why Iolo had kept Gryff on and if it had been only for Madlen's sake.

"His only value, as far as I could see," Alun said, "was his ability to deliver messages. He would remember what had been said after hearing it once, and repeat it word for word at the other end, regardless of how much time had passed."

"That is a useful skill," Gareth said. "Could he be trusted not to repeat what he'd said to another?"

"As far as I could tell, he forgot the message the instant he delivered it," Alun said. "Money meant nothing to him. A good day's work meant nothing."

"That makes him a difficult man to have for a brother-in-law," Gareth said. "You must have worried a great deal about your sister."

"He could have been a bard, you know," Alun said. "But he threw that away too."

"A bard? Nobody mentioned that he could sing," Gareth said, thinking of the festival and wondering if Gryff had meant to participate.

"He could sing anything," Alun said, "but no bard would take him on as an apprentice because he was so unreliable."

"But you would think that he could memorize any song," Gareth said.

"And forget it again by the next day," Alun said, "once he'd sung it once."

That kind of behavior was reminiscent of a man Gareth had encountered during the time he'd protected a community of nuns in Powys. One of the laborers who worked in their fields had been dropped on his head as a small child. He could be trusted with menial tasks, but spoke slowly, shied away from contact with people, and often listened without comprehension. But he had a head for numbers that defied all logic and expectation.

"I gather Gryff also drank too much?" Gareth said.

"Who told you that?" Again, Alun started talking before Gareth could answer. "The man had a hollow leg. He could drink me under the table and walk home in a straight line afterwards. I've never seen a man who could hold his mead like Gryff could."

Iolo had implied exactly the opposite, but all Gareth did was make a note of that in his head and continue his questioning. "How did Gryff and Carys meet?"

"Oh," Alun waved a hand, "he has cousins around here. He married Carys after she conceived his child. My father regretted the match, but at that point, he felt it was better that they were wed. Gryff had been working in the mine, but he hurt his back." Alun shrugged. "I was there when the accident happened and it was genuine, but it wasn't as if he'd ever been a hard worker in the first place."

"When was this?" Gareth said.

"Some three years ago." Alun screwed up his face for an instant. "It did give Gryff a fiery hatred of Prince Cadwaladr, Lord Hywel's uncle." Alun added this last bit of information as if Cadwaladr might be someone Gareth didn't know.

"Really?" Gareth said. "Why is that?"

"He was working the men too hard, trying to extract ore too quickly," Alun said. "He needed money and didn't care what it took to get it."

Gareth felt his face fall blank. He knew why Cadwaladr had needed money three years ago: He'd first needed to pay a retainer fee to the Danish mercenaries he'd hired to murder King Anarawd and his men, and then he'd needed to pay them off.

Alun didn't seem to notice Gareth's change in demeanor and continued, saying, "Gryff did odd jobs after that and was herding my sheep when he encountered the cloth trader, Iolo."

"What did you think of his new employment?" Gareth said.

"To tell you the truth, I was relieved," Alun said. "Gryff was a dreamer. Even herding sheep, which requires only the intelligence of a sheep half the time, was too much for him some days."

Alun seemed genuinely upset at the loss of Gryff for Carys's sake, but more regretful than angry or grieving on Gryff's behalf. If grief was a reflection of love, neither Iolo nor Alun had loved Gryff. Neither man gave any indication they knew Gryff had been murdered either. Gareth wanted to see Alun's face when he was finally told. Perhaps that moment ought to come soon.

But not yet.

"When did you last see Gryff?" Gareth said.

"Oh—" Alun tapped his chin as he thought. "It must have been the Sunday before last. He tried to visit Carys and the children when he could. The trader let him off on Sunday, and he would come if he could walk from wherever he was staying at the time."

"Did you know he was in Aberystwyth?" Gareth said.

"I knew he was coming for the festival. He suggested we all come down for it, but—" Alun gestured helplessly around him. "I try not to leave my herds for more than half a day."

"Aren't you a miner too?" Gareth said.

- 161 -

"Not every day," Alun said. "I sometimes pick up work when they need an extra hand."

Gareth knew a little of silver mining. The work took place underground in open shafts, and workers made their way down steep tunnels to where the silver was found. Usually, silver and lead were extracted together, and they had to be separated in a furnace to release the silver. It was hard work, hot and dangerous at times, and a life Gareth could be thankful every day he wasn't born to.

Still, it was lucrative since miners were often paid in ore, which explained the size of Alun's house and the extent of his herds. It was hard to think what Alun might have gained from Gryff's death, especially if Gryff had finally been able to support Carys without help.

"Was Gryff usually staying in a place close enough to Goginan to walk home?" Gareth said.

"Not often," Alun said, "Iolo ranged all through Deheubarth and Ceredigion, into Powys, and all the way to Shrewsbury. Gryff came when he could."

"What about Carys? Would she have been willing to bring the children to Aberystwyth, even if you didn't come with her? Surely Iolo would have allowed them to sleep wherever Gryff was staying?" Though as Gareth asked that, he realized that he hadn't yet told Alun about Madlen. Gareth could see why Gryff would have been loath to suggest such an arrangement.

"If Carys discussed it with him, I never heard of it," Alun said.

"Excuse me, Cousin." Fychan stepped forward. He'd been so quiet Gareth had all but forgotten the boy was there. "Didn't I see you a couple of days ago near St. Padarn's monastery?"

Alun's brow furrowed. "Did you?"

Gareth raised his eyebrows. Fychan was a sharp-eyed boy. He'd been right about Gryff, and Gareth was inclined to believe him in this too. "Were you in Aberystwyth two days ago? Did you see Gryff?"

The big man's face grew red. Then the color seemed to take over his whole body to the point that he bore a striking resemblance to the silver furnace he occasionally worked. Gareth imagined him breathing fire. But then Alun took a deep breath, striving to calm himself. He might be a big man in Goginan, but Gareth was of a far higher rank as a knight. And they both served Prince Hywel one way or another.

"Fychan speaks the truth. I visited Aberystwyth for a few hours two days ago," Alun said.

Two days ago Gryff was still alive. "Did you see Gryff?" Gareth said.

"I did."

Gareth raised his eyebrows. "Why didn't you mention it when I asked when you'd last seen him?" Gareth didn't want to antagonize the big man, but this was a piece of information that should have come out far earlier in their conversation. Keeping secrets was the first indication of a guilty conscience.

"I forgot about it until Fychan said something. Earlier, I thought you were asking about when he'd last come here."

"How did you get to Aberystwyth?" Gareth said. "Did you walk?"

"I have a cart and horse," Alun said.

"You traveled two hours there and back to see Gryff?" Gareth said. "Why?"

Alun scoffed. "I didn't travel to Aberystwyth to see Gryff. I had other business in the village. I ran into Gryff by chance. I hadn't known he'd arrived yet or that his master had lodgings in the town."

"What did you two talk about?" Gareth said.

"Nothing of importance, though—" Alun's brow furrowed, "—he didn't seem right to me. As I said, Gryff was always a dreamer, but that day he was tense, anxious even. It was noticeable enough that I asked him if he was well, but all he said was that Iolo was working him hard at the festival. He was in a hurry and didn't want to talk."

"What kind of hard work does a cloth merchant do?" Gareth was genuinely curious. As far as he could tell, a cloth merchant bought cloth and then sold it. He wasn't sure where the apprentice came in, especially since Iolo had Madlen to help him.

Alun waved a hand. "Gryff did all the physical work: he put up the tent; he cared for the cart and horse; he even dug a latrine in the evening if they miscalculated how long a journey might take and had to make camp in a remote place."

"That doesn't sound like the work of a layabout," Gareth said.

"It does if it took him three times longer than the average man to do the work." Alun snorted. "I'd wager the only reason Iolo kept him on was so he didn't have to do the work himself."

Gareth grunted his acceptance of Alun's reasoning. That might be a wager he would win. "What of Madlen?"

"What of her?" Alun said. "She's Iolo's niece, isn't she?"

"Did Gryff ever speak of her?" Gareth said.

Alun pursed his lips. "Not that I remember, or not with any significance. She looked down on him, and such an attitude grows old after a while, even for one as easygoing as Gryff."

Gareth swallowed, bracing himself for the wrath that he knew would come the moment he opened his mouth again. "She came to the chapel at St. Padarn's saying she was Gryff's wife."

But instead of becoming angry, Alun simply gaped at him. "What? That's absurd."

"I tell you it's true," Gareth said. "We wouldn't even have known that he had a wife in Carys—and had children too—if Fychan hadn't come forward—" And then Gareth broke off as he carried that sentence to its logical conclusion in his mind: if Fychan hadn't come forward, they would have buried Gryff's body. If not for the murder investigation, that would have been the end of it. Carys would never have known what had happened to her husband.

Alun was too caught up in the news to wonder at Gareth's unfinished sentence. He turned to Fychan, his face questioning.

Fychan bobbed a nod without needing Alun to actually ask him anything. "Sir Gareth speaks the truth."

"That is utterly mad. Why would she say such a thing?" Alun said.

"Our assumption was that she believed herself to be Gryff's wife," Gareth said.

"That isn't possible." Alun's voice was full of certainty.

"You don't believe that Gryff would have led Madlen on?" Gareth said. "That he might not have told her of his wife and children?"

Alun shook his head. "No, I don't. At the very least, if Madlen was under the protection of her uncle—as we know her to be—he would never have consented to the match without meeting his family. Besides, I just told you that Gryff asked us to come to Aberystwyth for the festival. Why would he have asked us if he was betraying Carys with Madlen?"

"I don't know," Gareth said, thinking of his own marriage to Gwen, which had united his family with hers, though at the time, his family consisted only of himself. "I gather you yourself have never personally met Iolo?"

Alun frowned. "Come to think on it, I haven't. I suppose if I'd gone to the festival as Gryff had asked I finally would have."

"Didn't you find it odd that you never had met him before?" Gareth said.

Alun shrugged. "It was typical Gryff. Or so I thought then. But I'm starting to wonder if I knew the man as well as I thought I did."

13

Hywel

Hywel and Rhun went first to the monastery to see to the wellbeing of Gwen, Mari, and the children. When they reached it, the women were sitting on a bench near the guesthouse with Tangwen and Gruffydd. Hywel came to a halt in front of them, crouching low to examine the stones the children had piled in the dirt.

"That has kept them occupied for the last hour," Gwen said.

"I see that." His fingers were itching to pick up his son, but he knew better than to disturb him when he was happy.

"How goes it with you?" Mari said.

Hywel straightened and kissed her temple. "Well enough. Though Cadwaladr sat beside me tonight."

Mari drew in a breath. "Cadwaladr has arrived?"

Rhun laughed. "He was surrounded by enemies because Cadell is here too."

"Neither can mean me immediate harm. Not today, anyway." Hywel sat on the bench beside his wife and took her hand. "This is nothing for you to worry about."

Mari gave him an exasperated look. "If you didn't want me to worry, you shouldn't have said anything."

Hywel knew that was true, but he found it impossible to keep secrets from her. He saw Gwen studying them from Mari's other side. "What have you discovered that I don't know about?" he said to her.

Gwen dipped her head. "I appreciate your confidence that I would have discovered anything."

Mari elbowed Gwen in the ribs. "It seems Gryff came to the monastery on the afternoon he died."

Hywel's eyes lit. "He did? Why? What did he do?"

"He was looking for you, actually," Gwen said.

Hywel's expression turned wary. "For me?"

"Yes. We don't know why—or rather, the gatekeeper to whom he spoke doesn't know why or what he wanted you for."

Hywel and Rhun exchanged a glance. "You can't go back to that day." Rhun said, correctly interpreting the regret on Hywel's face. "What's done is done, and you weren't here."

"Gryff offered to bring the gatekeeper his dinner, and then he left, without having found you of course." Gwen clenched a hand into a fist and dropped it onto her thigh. "I wish we knew what he wanted."

Hywel rubbed his chin. "That is truly the question of the hour. You learned this from the gatekeeper?"

"I did," Gwen said. "I even questioned the cook afterwards. He remembered only that Gryff had come into the kitchen, requested the meal for Sion, waited until it was ready, and departed."

Mari looked concerned. "Are we thinking that Gryff might have wanted access to the kitchen for some reason?"

Gwen shrugged. "In past investigations, we might have worried about poison, but we have no reason to suspect him of doing anything wrong. Gryff is the victim here."

"Or so we have assumed, since he was the one who was stabbed," Hywel said, "but what if the man who killed him did so in self-defense? We could be looking at this the wrong way around."

They all thought about that for a moment. "He did marry two women," Rhun said. "That is not the act of a righteous man."

Gwen shook her head. "We need more information than we have. Perhaps when Gareth returns, he'll be able to shed some light on these events."

"Speaking of Gareth," Hywel said, "I need to speak to him the moment he returns."

"Oh no," Gwen said. "What's happened? Not another murder?"

"Barring the ones I committed in my head at the feast?" Hywel said, only half-jesting. "No. But Rhun and I have discovered that my treacherous uncle and King Cadell have each brought fifty cavalry with them to Ceredigion and hidden them in the woods around Aberystwyth."

"What?" Gwen and Mari said together, looking from Rhun to Hywel.

Tangwen had looked up at her mother's shocked voice, and Gwen put out a hand to her, bending forward and saying, "It's all right, *cariad*." Tangwen returned to her play, and Gwen straightened. "Where?"

"Evan found Cadwaladr's force near St. Dafydd's chapel." Hywel motioned with his head to indicate where Evan stood with their horses. As Gareth's second-in-command, Evan was standing in for him until he returned. Rhun had left his captain, Gruffydd, to stay with Morgan and keep an eye on the goings on at the castle. "It lies to the northeast of here. Cadell's fifty cavalry are to the southeast. I sent men to scout his encampment as soon as I heard of it from Rhun."

Gwen looked inquiringly at Rhun, who nodded. "Angharad told me of it."

Gwen didn't quite hide her knowing smile, but she managed to look down at her toes before it became too obvious. "I don't expect Gareth to return tonight, my lord."

"I know," Hywel said. "We'll have a look tonight without him."

Prior Rhys came around the chapel and hastened across the courtyard towards them. "You received my message, my lord?" he said when he reached them.

"We did," Hywel said. "Thank you for the information. We have doubled the guard around the monastery."

Prior Rhys jerked his head in a nod. "I would hope that you are looking to your own back as well. An errant knife in the hands of a determined man can do a great deal of damage, as we saw with Gryff."

"Rhun and I are both taking extra care," Hywel said. "Thank you for staying here with Gwen and Mari."

Prior Rhys bowed. "I am honored to have been so trusted."

Hywel and Rhun, with Evan and a handful of men, rode northeast from St. Padarn's. They rode without torches, but the moon was up in the starlit sky, illuminating the road to St. Dafydd's Chapel. The road rose to several hundred feet above the monastery, and then fell again as they dropped into the adjacent valley, which like most of the area surrounding Aberystwyth consisted of green fields and stands of trees. This was rich land. Hywel was determined to keep it out of his uncle's—or Cadell's—hands.

At the point where Evan told them they needed to walk, they pulled their horses off the road and into a patch of woods that hadn't been cleared for farmland. As he tied his horse to an oak tree, Hywel could hear a brook gurgling to the north of their position. And then he heard the unmistakable clip-clop of horses along the road they'd just come down.

All the men froze, with their hands over their horses' noses to silence them. From the calls and shouts coming from the road, the riders were making no attempt to keep quiet.

Rhun stepped close to Hywel and said, "I count a dozen at least."

"Cadwaladr's men. That's the approximate number he brought to the castle tonight." Hywel pointed with his chin to Evan. "How close are we?"

"It's a short walk to the camp," Evan said, "a quarter of a mile, no more."

"We should hurry." Hywel gestured to the road along which the riders had now passed. "They're making so much noise, we could walk openly and they'd never notice, but I want to be in position before Cadwaladr gets there."

Rhun looked at Evan. "I assume they've posted sentries."

"Not deep into the woods when I was here the first time," Evan said, "just around the camp's perimeter."

"Cadwaladr doesn't fear attack," Hywel said.

"He has no reason to," Rhun said.

They started forward, Evan in the lead.

"What's he thinking, bringing so many men to Ceredigion?" Rhun said, articulating what was going on in Hywel's own head. "How could he imagine you wouldn't notice fifty men?"

"Perhaps he doesn't care, or he actually wants me to know," Hywel said.

"Why?" Rhun said.

"Because he is looking to get the better of me, to make me squirm," Hywel said. "He believes I would never challenge him while he is my guest. You know how his mind works. Cadwaladr sees what is right in front of him, and if he thinks it's good for him, he never thinks of the consequences."

"Such has been his downfall up until now," Rhun said.

- 172 -

"Do we have any reason to believe he has changed?" Hywel said.

"I fear the day that we don't discover what he is up to until it is too late," Rhun said.

"I don't. I look forward to it." Hywel pushed aside a tree branch and held it for Rhun. This time of year, the branches were fully leafed, green and glossy, though he couldn't see their color in the darkness. "For then Father will be forced to banish him from Gwynedd forever."

Rhun stopped beside Hywel. "You don't want that, brother. You think you do now, but you don't. Cadwaladr has the power to wreak a kind of havoc on us that even he doesn't appreciate. Right now, he is containable. But the moment he commits himself to betraying Father completely, or you, there's no telling what he might do."

Hywel didn't answer. It wasn't that he didn't believe what Rhun was saying, but when it came to Cadwaladr, Hywel was incapable of reasoned thought. He couldn't see how Cadwaladr banished from Wales forever could be worse than Cadwaladr sitting beside his father's chair in Aber.

Rhun put his hand on Hywel's elbow to emphasize his point. "Have you truly encompassed the worst of what Cadwaladr could do? What if his plan is to attack the festival in conjunction with Cadell?"

"Cadell doesn't want to openly attack me," Hywel said, "not with Father arriving at any moment and war on his southern flank."

"What if his plan is to murder Father?"

Hywel stared at his brother, whose face was just visible in the bit of moonlight that filtered through the tree branches.

"What if he were to succeed?" Rhun urged. "We would retaliate, chase him from Wales, and kill him if we could, but would Father's death be worth that bit of revenge?"

"Of course not," Hywel said.

"Then be careful what you wish for." Rhun dropped Hywel's elbow and continued walking.

"I'm sorry, Rhun." Hywel hustled after him. "I didn't think of that."

"I know. And that's the danger we all face. We have grown so used to hating Cadwaladr that we cannot see him clearly. Even Father has allowed the sickness to infect him. Hate blinds you to what is before you in favor of what you want to see—or hope to see—or perhaps even need to see."

Hywel studied Rhun's back as they strode onward. This summer had changed his brother, or perhaps Hywel was just noticing the change that had been taking place gradually over the last few years. When he was younger, he'd dismissed Rhun's open demeanor as innocence. He'd looked down on him for it—Hywel could admit that now—and he could also admit that he'd been wrong to do so.

"You are right, of course," Hywel said.

"We need to discover what he's up to and stop him before he starts." Rhun's long legs caught up to Evan, whom they'd allowed to get ahead of them, though the rest of their men had stopped when they had, protecting their rear.

Hywel was glad that Cristina, his father's wife, was not accompanying King Owain to Ceredigion. She whispered into the king's ear and often told him things that weren't true. Cristina was already campaigning for Owain to favor her sons over any of his other sons. That couldn't be allowed to happen, not just for Hywel's own sake, but for Rhun's.

Among the Welsh, illegitimate and legitimate sons inherited equally. Dafydd and Rhodri, Cristina's two boys, were far down the hierarchy of Owain's sons. First, of course, were, Rhun and Hywel. They were the children of King Owain's first love whom he never married. Then came Cynan, Cadell, and Madoc, ranging in age from twenty-three to eighteen. Only after various of his women had given birth to these five had Owain fathered legitimate sons by Gwladys, his first wife: Iorwerth, just of age now at fourteen, and Maelgwn, his younger brother.

It occurred to Hywel only now that all the while he'd been playing his games—with his women, spies, and intrigue—Rhun had been keeping the kingdom together for their father in ways Hywel hadn't appreciated except in that he hadn't had to do it himself.

Rhun had been learning about people, about the way they thought and acted, and noting the difference between what they said and what they did. Hywel had said for years how glad he was to be the second son, that it was going to be Rhun rather than he who would some day become King of Gwynedd. He'd always meant it. But this was the first time he'd admitted to himself that Rhun really might make a *better* one.

"Well, well. What have we here?" Hywel crouched beside his brother behind a holly bush.

Evan stood against a pine tree, blending in against the dark bark in his brown cloak and plain tunic. He didn't need to say anything because they all could see what Cadwaladr had brought: a small army. Men talked around three fires. One tent only had been put up towards the north end of the camp. The weather was clear and warm, and whatever warmth or protection from the elements anyone needed could be provided by the fire and the surrounding trees.

"He isn't trying to hide that they're here," Rhun said.

Hywel shook his head. He couldn't make sense of what he was seeing. "If Cadwaladr means to bring this force to bear on Aberystwyth, he would hardly have left it in plain sight. But he didn't bring these men into the village for the festival, nor inform me of their existence, as simple courtesy demands."

"Maybe it isn't you Cadwaladr doesn't want knowing about them," Rhun said.

That set Hywel back on his heels. "Not me?"

"What if his true enemy is Cadell, for instance?" Rhun said.

"You mean they've had a falling out?" Hywel laughed low and mocking. His uncle had hired men to kill Cadell's brother. The idea of them working as allies, in the past, present, or future, was almost obscene.

But Rhun's suspicions had already gone there. "Or he is bringing these men across Ceredigion to the other side for some purpose of his own. It could be the opposite: he and Cadell, as allies, could be planning a campaign he doesn't want you—or Father—to know about."

"My lords." Evan murmured the words, drawing their attention back to the camp. Cadwaladr himself had just ridden in with his guard. Hywel was relieved to know that his uncle was out of the castle, even if his absence meant he was plotting some new intrigue.

The sanctity of hospitality forbade aggression, either on the part of the host or the guest, and not for the first time Hywel understood why. To invite a man to dinner and then murder him as he ate was a crime beyond any other. Few would attempt it because in order to live afterwards, a man had to be so powerful that his enemies would continue to treat with him, despite their fear and hatred.

Cadwaladr dismounted and—almost as if he knew where Hywel and Rhun were hiding—strode towards their section of the woods. He didn't come all the way, thankfully, but stopped at the fire pit nearest to Hywel's hiding place. A man stood to greet him, bowing.

"What news, Erik?"

Only great effort stopped Hywel's jaw from dropping.

"Nothing yet, my lord. The death of that man in the millpond is on everyone's tongue. Nothing else." The man spoke with a faint Dublin accent. Even without it, Hywel could have guessed who he was from his large stature and blond hair—blonder even than Rhun's.

Rhun whispered low in Hywel's ear. "I saw that man speaking to Iolo at his stall today."

Hywel waved a hand at his brother, shushing him. He wanted to know what Rhun knew, but Cadwaladr was still talking to Erik.

"And my nephew?"

The big Dane gave a half-shrug. "I found few who consented to speak ill of him. And even those men were only discontented because Hywel had denied their claims to land or a cow in a dispute with a neighbor. He hasn't put a foot wrong since he arrived."

Hywel raised his eyebrows, glad to hear it but surprised too. He had felt he'd been misstepping right and left for three years. Cadwaladr gazed past Erik towards the trees, tapping on his thigh with his fist. Hywel could feel his uncle's eyes burrowing into him, even though he knew Cadwaladr couldn't see him. Still, he hardly dared breathe. Rhun held his breath as well.

"Try harder," Cadwaladr said. "I must have something I can bring before my brother when he arrives."

"Yes, my lord," Erik said.

"What of this death? Is it murder?"

"I have no word on that, my lord."

Cadwaladr grunted. "It must be. I haven't seen that bastard Gareth around, and that means he's out spying and asking questions about things he shouldn't."

"My lord—"

"Find him. I want to know what Gareth is doing, what he knows, and if we can turn this man's death to our advantage," Cadwaladr said. "If a murderer is walking free, I need to know it."

"Yes, my lord."

With another grunt, Cadwaladr turned away from Erik and strode back towards his horse. One by one, his men bobbed to their feet in order to bow as he passed. He mounted and rode out of the clearing without looking back, surrounded by the men he'd ridden in with. Gradually, the men around the fires returned to what they'd been doing before their lord's arrival, and Hywel began to breathe again.

Rhun let out a burst of air. "Well."

All of a sudden, Hywel found himself surprisingly cheerful. "We don't know why he brought all these men, but we've solved one mystery, anyway."

"What mystery is that?"

"Did you hear what Cadwaladr called that man? It's Erik, Godfrid's missing guard from two years ago," Hywel said.

Rhun stared at Hywel and then turned to look where Erik sat on a log before the fire, contemplating the flames and drinking from a flask. "He's been working for Cadwaladr all this time?"

"It seems so."

"The Book of Kells is long gone, though," Rhun said. "We returned it to Ireland two years ago. What could have kept Erik beside Cadwaladr all this time?"

"Money," Hywel said. "He couldn't return to Godfrid after he ran away, could he?"

"My lords, should we send word to Gareth of the threat against him?" Evan said.

Hywel tapped his brother's shoulder, and they both retreated with Evan deeper into the woods, back towards Aberystwyth. Hywel's men formed a perimeter around them as they slunk away.

"How many know that Gareth rode to Goginan this evening?" Rhun said.

"A handful only. The connection is through the monastery." Hywel looked back to the camp. They'd come far enough now that trees hid it from view, though he could smell the wood smoke.

Rhun nodded. "Sending a man might only call attention to his whereabouts."

Hywel agreed. "Gareth, of all of us, seems safe enough until morning. Now, shall we see what Cadell's men are up to?"

14

Gwen

Gwen was sitting at the entrance to the guesthouse as Gareth and Fychan rode through the gatehouse the next morning. They were followed by a large man driving a cart with a woman on the seat beside him.

Tangwen had been toddling back and forth in the courtyard since breakfast, picking up stones and dropping them again. Gwen hadn't managed to coax Mari downstairs yet today, but Gruffydd was walking across the cobbles holding onto Bronwen's thumbs. At the sight of the horses and cart, Bronwen scooped the baby up and retreated with him out of the way of any hooves.

Gwen stood, her eyes on the woman on the cart seat. From her blotchy face—and the resigned look on the face of the man beside her—she'd been crying for much of the journey. Gareth dismounted and bent to Tangwen, picking her up and kissing her. "Were you a good girl while I was gone?"

Tangwen squealed as he tickled her. Since he didn't need an answer, Gareth set Tangwen down and motioned to Elspeth and Bronwen that they should take both babies away. The two girls and their charges disappeared into the monastery gardens. Gwen watched them go and turned back as the man helped the woman down from the cart.

With the arrival of the cart, the stable boy appeared out of the stables, and the abbot, Prior Rhys, and Prior Pedr came through the open door from the monks' dining hall. The abbot and Prior Pedr strode towards the woman, but Prior Rhys headed to where Gareth and Gwen stood, interrupting Gareth's brief summary of his visit to Goginan.

"I see you found her," Prior Rhys said.

"I did. Carys is her name, and that's her brother, Alun." Gareth gestured towards the pair, who were bowing before the abbot. "Carys is distraught at Gryff's death. Alun is a bit more philosophical. Neither confess to any knowledge of his relationship with Madlen."

"Then this may start to get interesting."

The voice came from behind her, and Gwen turned to see Hywel stepping through the guesthouse door. Sometimes she wondered if he waited around doorframes and in corridors for instances like this, just so he could say something witty while making his entrance. He was tightening the bracer on his left arm.

"When did you arrive?" she said.

He raised his eyebrows at her surprise. "Late last night. Rhun and I had an adventurous evening." He looked at Gareth. "We have much to discuss."

"Yes, my lord."

Hywel looked back to Gwen. "Where's Gruffydd?"

"With his nanny," Gwen said. "How's Mari?"

Hywel made a rueful face. "Sleeping. I don't think this is going to be a good day."

Gwen missed her friend but accepted the realities of marriage and child bearing. Hopefully Mari would give Hywel many sons, and not all of them would be as difficult to produce as these first two.

Prior Rhys pointed with his chin towards the gatehouse where a man and a woman had just entered. "Your wish may have come true already, my lord."

"Is that—?" Gwen looked at Gareth.

"Madlen and Iolo," Gareth said. "Does Madlen know about Carys?"

"Not unless someone else told her," Gwen said. "I haven't even been introduced to her yet." Before they knew for certain that Gryff had another wife, Prior Pedr had sent word to Iolo as to when he and Madlen should arrive at the monastery this morning for Gryff's funeral. For her part, Gwen hadn't had any contact with the pair at all.

"Good," Gareth said. "Go to her. She's going to notice that Carys is weeping over Gryff's body and wonder at it. I want you to be there when she asks who Carys is. I want you to be the one to tell her."

"Me?" Gwen shook her head. "You are a bad man, Gareth ap Rhys." But Gwen squeezed his hand and walked to intercept Madlen and Iolo before they came any farther into the monastery courtyard. Gareth had described Madlen's clothes from yesterday, and what she wore today was equally fine. Sewn from the finest wool, Madlen's deep blue dress, the same color as Iolo's tunic, wouldn't have looked out of place at the high table in Hywel's hall.

Madlen's long hair was braided into many separate strands, in the old tradition for a widow at her husband's funeral. Carys hadn't done anything to hers but put it into a chignon at the back of her head and cover it with a scarf. After a five-mile cart ride, wisps of hair had come loose and framed her face. She must have been at least twenty, but today she looked no more than fourteen.

When Gwen reached Madlen and Iolo, she introduced herself. Neither looked happy to meet her, though they were polite enough. Madlen barely looked at her, instead standing on her tiptoes to look past Gwen to the cluster of people in the central area of the courtyard. Without explaining who they were, Gwen gently guided the pair to one side, out from underneath the gatehouse as well as out of the path that the monks carrying Gryff's body would follow. "The funeral procession should begin soon. You're just in time."

Madlen's brows drew together. "Who is the abbot talking to?"

The abbot had been talking to Carys and Alun, and now he gestured that they should follow him into the chapel, Carys continuing to sob all the while. Prince Hywel had already left to return to the festival. Not only should his father be arriving today, but Hywel himself would be performing that evening.

Gwen had been going over in her mind how to broach the subject of Madlen's status. As the woman Gryff married first, clearly Carys should have pride of place, and regardless of what had been written in the contract, Madlen's marriage was invalid—in the sight of both God and man. "I'm sorry to tell you this, Madlen, but that woman is Gryff's wife and the mother of his two children."

"What are you saying?" All color leached from Madlen's face as she stared at Gwen. "No."

"I am sorry, Madlen," Gwen repeated, "but he had a wife before you. If you believed yourself married to Gryff, your relationship was in no way legal." Gwen didn't say that because Madlen hadn't given him a son, she wasn't entitled to any inheritance either.

Iolo rubbed his chin. "You're saying that Gryff deceived us?"

"That does appear to be the obvious conclusion," Gwen said, without adding the possibility that they had some responsibility for what had happened as well. Particularly Iolo, as Madlen's guardian, should have done some more checking. "My lord husband is in no doubt that Gryff was married to Carys long before he met Madlen. They never divorced, and she bore him two children."

Madlen was standing with her hand over her mouth. Then she dropped her hand, looking wildly around in a manner that had Gwen thinking she was looking to run. Iolo must have thought the same thing because he caught Madlen's arm. "Don't. You're here now. You made your bed. Now lie in it."

Gwen frowned at the harshness of his tone. She cleared her throat, having more questions, but nonetheless feeling awkward about asking them. "Did you not wonder at his absences?"

"He said he had a sick grandmother he needed to visit," Iolo said. "He would leave us every so often to do so."

"Oh!" Madlen's eyes widened. "He was seeing his wife! All this time he was seeing his wife instead!"

"It seems so." Gwen found herself feeling sorry for Madlen. From Gareth's description of her and what she'd done in the chapel, Gwen hadn't felt drawn to her or even very sympathetic. But this was a different girl, not weeping like Carys, but shocked, her life without Gryff stretching before her.

Six monks appeared at the entrance to the chapel, carrying the body in its coffin on their shoulders. The circular graveyard lay adjacent to the monastery. It had its own small chapel and priest, and it was he who ministered to the villagers of Llanbadarn Fawr, who didn't normally worship in the monastery chapel. Though the procession could have gone through the gardens and didn't have to leave by the gatehouse, tradition demanded it. The monks paced towards the road and out onto it, turning north to walk with solemnity down the narrow road until they reached the gravesite, which had been dug earlier that morning.

Carys and Alun followed immediately after the abbot and Prior Pedr, and then two dozen monks fell into place behind them. Madlen held back. Even after Iolo urged her forward, her feet seemed to move reluctantly. "He's really dead," Madlen said, low enough so that only Gwen could hear her, since Iolo had lost patience and was striding to catch up to the last of the monks. "He's really dead."

"I'm sorry for your loss," Gwen said.

Her mind shied away from putting herself in Madlen's place. Someday, she might be the one following behind her husband's coffin to see him into his grave. Gareth had faced death in the past at Hywel's side and would again. It was the reality of being married to a soldier. It was the reality of being married.

Gwen still fought through sleepless nights when she lay awake for hours, her stomach in knots as she worried for him. Having Tangwen helped to distract her, but every night Gareth lay beside her in bed was one to be thankful for. She'd missed Gareth last night and had woken every few hours to reach out a hand to him, only to find that he wasn't there. That would be Madlen's fate for every night from now on.

Madlen's face twisted into a grimace. "I saw that woman here in Aberystwyth on the day Gryff died, you know."

"What woman?" Gwen said.

Madlen gestured ahead of her. "That woman. His *wife.*" The last word came out with an added sneer, for which Gwen couldn't blame her.

"You saw Carys the day Gryff died? When and where?" Gwen said.

"She was near our lodgings in Aberystwyth," Madlen said. "We always stay with a tavern keeper we know. She was outside the tavern. Watching it."

Gwen looked ahead through the undyed robes and bowed shoulders of the monks between them to where Carys walked, herself with a bowed head. "Are you sure it was she?"

"Most definitely." Madlen gritted her teeth. "She must have found out that Gryff loved me instead of her. She drove him to his death!"

Madlen's sudden adamancy and anger were somewhat alarming.

"What do you mean, 'drove him to his death?'" Gwen said. "Do you know something about Gryff's death that you need to tell me?"

Madlen's eyes widened as she realized she'd gone too far in making an unfounded accusation. "What? No! No, I didn't mean— I didn't mean anything by it. Don't listen to me." She put her face in her hands and sobbed.

Gwen would have to check with Gareth, but with two small children at home, it would have been quite a feat for Carys to be gone all day to Aberystwyth, murder her husband in the early hours of the morning, and then return to Goginan. On top of which, Carys could have directed the same accusation at Madlen: Madlen had discovered Carys's existence and murdered Gryff in a moment of passionate anger. Though, given Madlen's emotional theatrics, the more likely scenario would have been for Madlen to murder *Carys*, not Gryff.

Gwen eyed the grieving girl, wondering if Madlen was such a good actor as to be able to deceive them all with her tears and regrets, and that she really did know something about Gryff's death that she wasn't telling. Honestly, Gwen couldn't tell. She'd been lied to before and not known it, and she'd disbelieved another's words and found them later to be true. People lied. It was the one and only thing Hywel and Gareth would have her assume.

Upon arriving at the gravesite to witness the funeral, Gwen was glad she'd arranged in advance for Elspeth to keep Tangwen inside the monastery grounds. Emotions were running high between the two grieving widows, and the difficulty of the situation would only have been compounded by Gwen's chattering daughter, who wouldn't have understood the gravity of the occasion.

Still, it was a beautiful spot in which to be buried. Gwen hoped the peacefulness here, aided by the scents of the late summer flowers and the leaves twirling in the breeze above their heads, would ease the hearts of the two women Gryff had loved. The heat of the day hadn't yet risen, and as the priest began to read the words of the Latin prayer at the gravesite, Gwen closed her eyes and allowed the warm sun to bathe her face.

The mourners stood with bowed heads around the grave until after the priest finished and the gravediggers began shoveling the dirt over the top of Gryff. Carys and Alun turned away with the abbot, who had invited them to break their fast with him. Poor

Madlen, as the second woman in Gryff's life, received no such recognition.

So as the small group dispersed, only Madlen, Iolo, Gareth, and Gwen remained to watch the final stages of Gryff's burial. Madlen stepped forward and tossed a handful of dirt into the grave, and then dropped a lavender blossom after it. "My life is over."

"Don't be ridiculous." Iolo put an arm around Madlen's shoulder, the first real sign of comfort Gwen had seen him give her today. "The world is full of men."

That was a singularly unhelpful comment, and Iolo should have known better. Of course, Gwen's own father had said the exact same words to her once upon a time. She'd been sixteen and had to watch Gareth ride out of her life after being banished from Ceredigion by Cadwaladr, who'd been his lord at the time.

Gareth had been standing on the other side of the grave from Gwen, and she glanced up to meet his eyes, which flashed with something akin to amusement before turning serious again. "If you can think of anything else that could tell us why Gryff was by the millpond that night," he said to Madlen, "please contact me at the castle or here at the monastery."

Iolo sighed. "I heard we have you and Prince Hywel to thank for keeping Gryff out of a suicide's grave."

Gareth nodded in brief acknowledgment of the truth. "I don't believe Gryff killed himself."

"Obviously, your word was enough for the abbot." Still with his arm around Madlen, Iolo turned away. "Come, girl. We have work to do."

Sniffing and dabbing at her eyes, Madlen went with her uncle. Their stall at the market fair needed manning.

Gareth watched them go, his hands on his hips.

"What are you thinking?" Gwen said.

Without answering, Gareth held out his hand to Gwen. She took it, and they started walking back to the monastery. "I'm thinking that before we go any further, we need to clarify our timeline. I want to make sure we haven't missed anything."

Gwen nodded. When an investigation had this many moving parts, it was always important to reassess with each new snippet of information. Sometimes Gareth sketched out a chart on one of his pieces of paper so he could keep it straight in his mind.

"Well," Gwen said, "the first thing anyone has admitted— though whether or not it's true is based only on Iolo's word—was that Iolo, Madlen, and Gryff have been in the vicinity of Aberystwyth for two weeks, though they only reached the town four days ago."

Gareth opened a narrow wooden gate in the hedge that surrounded the monastery gardens and led Gwen through it. She could hear Tangwen and Gruffydd shouting somewhere in the distance. Gareth heard their voices too and picked up the pace, heading in their general direction. "The next day," he said, "Alun came to here and spoke to Gryff, though he claims they spoke about nothing out of the ordinary. Before Alun saw Gryff in the street, he hadn't realized he was even in Aberystwyth."

"The following day," Gwen said, "Madlen says she saw Carys outside their lodgings. We have no evidence for that either save Madlen's word."

Gareth stopped in the middle of the path. "Madlen saw Carys outside their lodgings?"

"So she told me just now," Gwen said.

Gareth rubbed his chin. "Carys could have learned of where he was staying from Alun."

"If Madlen isn't lying," Gwen said. "Regardless, later that afternoon, Gryff sought out Prince Hywel, spoke to the gatekeeper, and went away disappointed. He was murdered in the early hours of the following morning. We still have no idea why he wanted to speak to Prince Hywel or why he was murdered."

"That single incident—that he wanted to speak to Prince Hywel about something—raises my hackles," Gareth said.

"Mine too," Gwen said.

"It's our only indication of any motive for murder other than the surprising fact of having two wives," Gareth said.

Gwen sighed. "It isn't much to go on, is it? Both sides say he didn't have an impressive intellect, or at the very least he was a dreamer. He doesn't sound like a master manipulator who could have maintained such an elaborate deception for so long, much less become involved in something bigger that got him killed."

"Looks can be deceiving," Gareth said. "We know that if we know anything."

"Then I am well and truly deceived," Gwen said.

Gareth started walking again. "He knew his killer."

Gwen nodded. "That seems clear because of the knife to the chest. His death looks like a confrontation gone wrong more than a sneak thief."

"Gryff had nothing worth stealing," Gareth said.

"That we know of," Gwen said, "though if he did have something worth stealing, the murderer would have taken it, don't you think?"

"I suppose so," Gareth said, "and until we find our killer, we won't know what that was."

Just then, Tangwen came around from behind a large lavender bush—of the same color flower as the one Madlen left on Gryff's grave—and held out her arms to Gwen. Gwen picked her up and carried her towards the herbalist's hut, which had a bench resting against the south facing wall. Most of the bench lay in the full sun, since it was now mid-morning, and the sun was well up above the trees.

Gwen sat on the end that was still shaded by the eave of the roof and adjusted Tangwen in her lap so she could nurse her.

Gareth sat beside them and put a finger through one of Tangwen's brown curls, letting it curl around it. Elspeth appeared briefly, checking on her charge, but Gareth waved her away. Tangwen would nurse for a while, possibly falling asleep in the process, and they didn't want to discuss their investigation in front of her nanny.

Gwen's brow furrowed in thought as she cradled her daughter. "We need to talk to Carys about her whereabouts on the day Gryff died. Could we be wrong about the time that he died?"

"The gatekeeper saw Gryff towards the dinner hour. He was alive then," Gareth said. "Iolo and Madlen saw him later in the evening. Did Carys stay in Aberystwyth until nightfall?"

"Maybe somebody saw her," Gwen said. "You can sketch her too and ask around. What about Alun?"

"Are you thinking that Alun could have lured Gryff to the millpond?" Gareth said.

"I imagine it wouldn't have taken much luring," Gwen said. "Carys and Gryff were married. She was the mother of his children. To me, it's a matter of *why* either of them would have wanted Gryff dead. By all appearances, he hadn't been good for much before this, and now he had enough money to support Carys. Why kill him?"

"Jealousy," Gareth said.

"That applies to Carys, but not to Alun," Gwen said. "And even if Carys was jealous, killing Gryff wouldn't have solved her problem. Better to have killed Madlen."

Gareth tugged on his ear. "That's a difference between a man's response to being cuckolded and a woman's: a man is more likely to murder his wife, while a woman is more likely to murder the object of her husband's attention."

"I'm not sure what that says about us women that our anger is directed at the other woman, rather than the cheating, lying husband."

Gareth put up both his hands, laughing at Gwen's vehemence. "I know where my loyalties lie, my dear."

Gwen laughed too. "That still leaves hate as the motive, however, which implies a crime of passion. I don't like it. Meeting by the millpond like Gryff did with his killer couldn't have been a spur of the moment thing."

"Unless Gryff went there for reasons of his own and the murderer—who admittedly he knew—followed him. They argued, and Gryff died." Gareth looked towards the courtyard, a corner of which they could see from where they sat in the garden. Alun had appeared beside his cart. "Maybe we can get some of these questions answered. I'll send Alun and Carys to you."

"Where are you going?" Gwen said.

"I think it's time I used the resources I have to my advantage." Gareth grinned. "I have several dozen men at my disposal. Even leaving many on guard duty and others asleep, we can cover a great deal of ground. Let's see who else saw Gryff that day."

As he promised, Gareth sent Carys and Alun over to Gwen, who remained sitting on the bench. Tangwen had fallen asleep, and Gwen tucked her against her chest, watching the pair walk towards her. She scooted over slightly so Carys could sit down in the shade without sitting as closely to her as Gareth had been, and so that as Tangwen slept, she wouldn't kick Carys.

Carys, however, reached out a hand to Tangwen's bare foot, rubbing at her smooth baby skin with her thumb. "So sweet. I have one this age."

"Where is he now?" Gwen said.

"He's with Alun's wife," Carys said.

"Did you leave him with your sister-in-law two days ago when you came to Aberystwyth?" Gwen took advantage of the opening, which had come far sooner than she'd hoped.

"What did you say?" Carys said.

"I assume you saw the other woman, Madlen, at the gravesite?" Gwen said.

Carys blinked, threatening to dissolve in tears again, but she managed to beat them back. "I saw her."

"She said that she saw you in Aberystwyth the afternoon before Gryff died. You were standing outside their lodgings," Gwen said.

Carys's mouth fell open. "She lies."

"Does she?" Gwen turned her head to look at Alun, who had taken up a position under the eaves (and thus out of the sun) with his shoulder braced against the wall of the hut and his arms folded across his chest. His expression remained completely blank. Something was going on here.

Alun licked his lips. "It's an absurd accusation."

"Would you be willing to tell me what you and Gryff discussed when you saw him the day before he died?" Gwen said.

Alun gestured impatiently with one hand. "I already told your husband. We talked of nothing of importance. He was planning to visit Carys on Sunday. I offered to fetch him, but he said he would start early and was happy to walk. That is all."

"He didn't say anything else? The next day he came looking for Prince Hywel, very upset. He didn't mention any concerns to you?"

"No," Alun said.

"Is there anything at all that was unusual about that conversation? Did he perhaps give you something?" Gwen knew she was grasping at straws, but the investigation would stall out without new information.

"No," Carys said.

"Yes, he did." Alun uncrossed his arms, and for the first time, his expression was clear of tension. "He gave the cross to me to give to you, Carys."

"A cross?" Gwen said.

With obvious reluctance, Carys pulled out a small gold cross that had lain hidden underneath the bodice of her dress. It looked very much like the one Gwen herself wore that Gareth had given to her.

Gwen leaned closer to examine it. The cross was finely worked, with the letters C and G interwoven together. "C.G.," Gwen said. "What does that stand for?"

"C is for Carys," Carys said, "and G is for Gryff, of course."

Gwen looked back to Alun. "What did Gryff say when he gave it to you?"

Alun shrugged. "Not much, which is why I forgot about it until you asked. He wanted me to give it to her."

Alun seemed to forget events easily. Gwen turned back to Carys. "Did he say where he got it? Did he have it made especially for you?"

Again Carys looked to Alun. "He didn't say."

Gwen thought it was a spectacular gift to say so little about. "Weren't you curious?"

Alun snorted his disgust and uncrossed his arms. "I thought it was a waste of money. You can't eat a cross." He gestured towards Carys. "Though you can't tell a woman that."

"Carys, why do you think he didn't wait to give it to you himself?" Gwen said. "It's beautiful."

"I don't know, but I am so glad he sent it when he did." Carys clutched the cross, and now the tears spilled down her cheeks again. "It's something of him." Then her look turned fierce. "If he hadn't given it to Alun, I would never have known about it. That whore would have kept it for herself."

"Carys!" Alun spoke sharply to his sister.

"She has no right! No right to his things or anything about him." And with that, Carys leapt to her feet and ran off down the path, heading away from the monastery.

Alun and Gwen looked after her, and then they looked at each other. "It's a hard thing." Alun shook his head. "I never understood why Carys loved Gryff so much, but she did."

15

Gareth

Before the funeral, after Gareth sent Gwen to speak to Iolo and Madlen, Hywel pulled him aside and laid out what he'd learned of Cadwaladr's and Cadell's doings the previous evening while Gareth had been tracking down Carys. Hywel also told him of the personal animosity Cadwaladr still seemed to hold towards Gareth himself and the threat against him.

"We already knew he hated me," Gareth said.

But Hywel shook his head. "This seems to be more intense than before—and even less rational than usual. You need to watch your back. In fact, I'm going to detail men to watch it for you."

Gareth gave a tsk of disgust. "Having guards around me all the time will limit my activities."

Hywel's eyes lit at that. "Such do I live all the time."

"You're Lord of Ceredig—"

Hywel openly laughed.

"What?"

"Who would have thought eight years ago when Cadwaladr sent you away in disgrace from this very spot that it would be his disgrace which would become paramount, while you are a trusted companion of the Lord of Ceredigion and the King of Gwynedd?"

Gareth looked down at his feet and shook his head. The odd thing was that while his circumstances had changed—and without a doubt his life was better for it, from his service to Hywel to his marriage to Gwen—he was the same man he'd been then. In fact, it was that decision that had made him the man he was today.

When Gareth had disobeyed Cadwaladr, he'd done so because he could no longer stomach his orders. For months he'd been wavering on the edge of a cliff. A little push and he could have fallen into dishonor. He could have obeyed Cadwaladr and remained in Ceredigion. Even in his defiance, he hadn't consciously valued that sense of honor as he did now, but he thanked God that he'd had enough of it to do what he'd done. That decision had been the turning point in his life.

Hywel stepped closer, his voice low and urgent. "I don't need to tell you that it is because you have the strength to choose what is right over what is easy that you hold the position you do. I would be most concerned if you became someone different just because you had more power or influence."

Gareth's head came up at that. "I would never—"

"I know. I'm merely commenting on the fact that Cadwaladr has acknowledged the inequality between the two of you and doesn't understand it," Hywel said. "It is beyond his comprehension that a man could go from poverty to wealth, from abasement to an exalted station, and remain the same man. That he would not become corrupted or altered. Cadwaladr fears and distrusts—and disparages—what he does not understand."

"I will be careful."

The truth was that Gareth worked very hard never to think about Cadwaladr if he could help it. His dismissal from Cadwaladr's service had been one of the darkest times of his life. His faith in himself had been shaken. Even with the loss of his parents and the later death of his uncle, he'd always landed on his feet. Somehow, until that day, he'd still been one of those people who believed that if he did the right thing everything would turn out all right in the end.

That day, his faith had failed him, but he'd disobeyed Cadwaladr anyway. Sometimes Gareth thought he'd seen too much despair since then, and too many bad things had happened—irretrievable things—for him to have regained that underlying sense of hope. Still, he lived as if he believed it because to do otherwise would betray the very essence of who he was, and what Hywel—and Gwen—and Gareth himself—valued. And as Hywel had pointed out, it had turned out well for Gareth in the end. It had just taken a few years to get there.

With a nod, Hywel went on his way, surrounded by a guard of ten who would protect him with their lives. He left Evan and Rhodri with Gareth. At the sight of their taut shoulders and grave expressions, Gareth made a rueful face. "I see you're taking your duties seriously."

"All our lives may depend upon it," Evan said.

During Gryff's burial, the pair occupied themselves by scouting the periphery of the monastery grounds, and when Gareth left Gwen to begin his duties anew, they fell in beside him.

"What's next?" Evan said.

"With Gryff's body in the ground, the physical evidence of the crime is now out of reach," Gareth said, "but other than the wound that killed him, the prince and I didn't find anything helpful on the body anyway."

"We know how Gryff died," Evan said. "We know where he died. We know roughly when. We just don't have any good idea as to who killed him."

"Nobody seems very worried about us finding out either," Rhodri said. "I watched Iolo and Madlen all day yesterday, and they don't behave like guilty people."

"Nobody looks afraid," Evan agreed.

"Prince Hywel has wrought many changes in Ceredigion over the last three years," Rhodri said. "It looks to me like that's one of them: the people involved—from the monks who found him, to Madlen and Carys, to Iolo and Alun—aren't afraid of his wrath. Another lord—Cadwaladr for one—might have condemned an innocent man simply to close the investigation."

"If he'd investigated the death at all, that is," Evan said.

Gareth was grateful for their staunch support, but their words also made him wary. "In order to lull the murderer into a false sense of security, we've kept to ourselves the knowledge that Gryff was murdered. Perhaps we've done our job too well."

"Our killer threw Gryff into the millpond thinking that Prince Hywel would treat the death like Cadwaladr might have—as that of a common man of no consequence," Evan said. "Unless a lord has someone like you to delve into unexplained deaths, deaths like Gryff's are dismissed as an accident and forgotten."

"So maybe the killer isn't from Aberystwyth after all," Gareth said. "Maybe he doesn't know Prince Hywel or his reputation enough to fear him."

"I don't know how that helps us," Evan said sourly. "Everyone on our list of suspects lives far afield."

"But it might be useful to examine everything we know from that perspective," Gareth said. "If the murderer doesn't live here, he doesn't know how the miller or his pond works, or the daily routine of life in Aberystwyth. He threw Gryff into the pond not knowing that he would be found."

"Which leaves us hundreds of festival-goers to interview," Rhodri said.

"No, it doesn't," Gareth said. "There are hundreds now, but there weren't nearly that many two days ago when Gryff died. That is what we're going to do now."

With renewed enthusiasm for the task, Gareth, Rhodri, and Evan returned to the festival grounds and rounded up twenty more of Hywel's men. Gareth sketched an additional dozen pictures of Gryff and handed them around. "Ask everyone you see if they were here two days ago. We need to question everyone in the festival area, Llanbadarn Fawr, on the road, and around the monastery to find anyone who saw Gryff the day he died. Better yet, we need to find someone besides Iolo and Madlen who saw him that evening."

Gareth then spent a frustrating hour speaking to the vendors around Iolo's booth. Each time he passed it, both Iolo and Madlen were busy with customers. As they already had determined, most of the fair-goers weren't native to Aberystwyth. Most didn't even know where the millpond was unless they'd passed it on the road to the festival grounds. Gareth returned to the monastery for an early afternoon meal, and then spent another three hours interviewing the monks and workers. His only consolation for the complete waste of the day was his proximity to Gwen, who took a moment to relate her conversation with Carys and Alun about the gold cross.

Gareth was pleased to learn she'd discovered something new, but disgruntled that they had yet another mystery to resolve rather than a true piece of the puzzle. This seemed to be one of those investigations that didn't build stone by stone, but in which they discovered dozens of unrelated snippets of information that somehow they had to assemble into a complete story.

Finally, Gareth rode the mile back the festival and called in his men, who, as it turned out, hadn't had any more luck than he'd had. Several merchants had seen Gryff around, but none had noticed him after sunset. Gareth released the men to other duties, leaving him alone with Evan and Rhodri, who'd hung on to him like leeches throughout the day.

"Nobody will admit to anything," Gareth said.

"Could be they have nothing to admit to," Evan said.

Gareth clapped each man on the shoulder. "We have one last destination before I admit defeat to Prince Hywel."

Rhodri visibly straightened. Gareth had learned to appreciate Rhodri's steadiness and occasional insights, and Evan had proved a trusty companion long since. While Gwen wouldn't have enjoyed the last few hours, Gareth missed her companionship. At Aber, she could have been as nosy as he, but she couldn't wander the festival the way he could, and she refused to leave Tangwen for long. It was an attentiveness he didn't understand but had learned to appreciate. Tangwen was happy, healthy, and as bright as Gwen. Gareth wasn't going to do or say anything to interfere with Gwen's mothering.

This was also the first investigation in a long while that Hywel had been too distracted to participate in. Hywel's current need for Gareth to work independently was reminiscent of Hywel's own relationship with his father. In the past, when trouble had come to Gwynedd, King Owain had turned to Hywel, who had turned to Gareth. Now Gareth was playing the same role for Hywel in Ceredigion, doing his job and reporting back, while Hywel attended to more important things.

Hywel had been in near constant motion the last few days, and this hour was no exception. Tossing a coin to a vendor, Gareth snagged a skewer of roasted mutton from a stall and carried it from the festival grounds to the giant pavilion that Hywel had established in an adjacent field. For a crowd this size, it would have been impossible and uncomfortable to hold the musical performances in the castle's hall, and with the sides of the tent rolled up, the onlookers could expand to fill the available space outside the tent's canopy.

Upon reaching Hywel, who was standing by the center pole with his hands on his hips, surveying the grounds, Gareth bowed and presented the skewer. "My lord. It is my guess that you have not eaten recently."

Hywel grunted his thanks, took the skewer, and bit absently into a piece of mutton. He chewed, swallowed, and then wiped his lips on his fist. "What would I do without you?"

Before Gareth could decide what to say—whether to make a jest or to take Hywel seriously—Rhun passed through the tent. He'd been heading in the other direction, towards King Cadell's encampment, but he changed course and came over to them. "Have you news?"

"Not as much as I'd like," Gareth said, but he related what had been discovered since he'd spoken to Hywel that morning.

Rhun looked at his brother. "I don't see either of these women as a murderer, do you?"

"Sioned was strong enough to stab a man," Hywel said. "Neither woman is as tall as she, but passion could have given them strength."

"It's the hour of Gryff's death that makes a scenario with the women more difficult," Gareth said. "Neither should have been out so late at night. Still, it's easier to place Madlen at the scene than Carys."

"From the sound of it, Alun is a more likely killer than Carys, just as Iolo would have been more physically capable of murder than Madlen," Hywel said.

"Though attributing a motive to either is far less easy," Gareth said. "If Iolo was unhappy with Gryff, he could have simply dismissed him."

"Not without harming his niece," Rhun said. "She and Gryff were married."

"The same could be said for Alun and Carys," Gareth said. "Perhaps Alun discovered that Gryff was betraying Carys. The man has a temper. I can see him meeting Gryff in the dark of night and killing him."

Gareth looked at Hywel, who raised his eyebrows at him. "I like it. We need to establish Alun's whereabouts at the time of Gryff's death."

"Haven't Alun and Carys returned to Goginan?" Rhun said.

"I asked them to stay another day," Gareth said. "Alun's wife's uncle lives in Aberystwyth. They said they would stay with him."

"Good," Hywel said. "Are you off to Aberystwyth now?"

"Yes," Gareth said. "Gryff, Iolo, and Madlen lodged at the inn. I would speak to its keeper. I've sent most of the men back to their other duties but the three of us—" Gareth gestured to Evan and Rhodri, "—will run this question to ground."

Rhun stepped closer. "Any sign of ... other trouble?"

The prince was referring to Cadwaladr's threat against Gareth. "Nothing," Gareth said.

"I have sensed nothing amiss either," Evan said.

"Nor have I," Hywel said. "I've kept an eye out for Erik in particular, but either he is wearing a disguise, he is staying well out of my sight, or he has not put in an appearance."

"I could make a sketch of him too," Gareth said. "Pass it among the men?"

Hywel sucked on his lower lip. "No. I would hate for Cadwaladr to get wind that we know he is up to no good or have one of your sketches fall into his hand. We'll keep this between the five of us for now."

Gareth bowed to both princes and took his leave, fording the Ystwyth River with Rhodri and Evan and then heading northwest along the road. They bypassed Llanbadarn Fawr, which lay directly to the east of Aberystwyth, in favor of following a road that led from the castle to the sea and the village of Aberystwyth.

The village was composed mostly of fisher folk but had grown in recent years to include small craftsmen. It was a hub for the whole region, since Ceredigion had a smaller population and fewer villages as a whole compared to Gwynedd. The region around Aberystwyth was suitable for farming, so small crofts and homesteads dotted the landscape to the east of the road. To the southwest lay the escarpment upon which the castle had been built, adjacent to a second plateau upon which could be found the stones of an ancient fortress, which legend said dated back to a time before the Romans conquered Wales.

Once in Aberystwyth, Gareth led Evan and Rhodri to the village inn, which was also its tavern. After three years serving

Prince Hywel on and off in Ceredigion, Gareth knew the proprietor well. The tavern was crowded—mostly with strangers here for the festival—but also with villagers who didn't want to miss the excitement. The tavern was so packed with people that patrons had spilled out into the street.

"We need to keep an eye on this crowd in case someone gets out of hand and becomes more than Pawl can handle," Rhodri said.

"I haven't yet met a man Pawl can't subdue, but he doesn't often have to take on more than one." Gareth eyed the cluster of people with a growing sense of alarm. There were still several hours until dusk. It was early for this kind of rowdiness.

"Pawl could be serving a particularly potent beer today," Evan said. "He might do well to water it down some more."

"We should speak with him," Gareth said.

"Most of these folk should depart for the festival grounds soon," Evan said. "The evening program starts shortly."

Music was sacred in Wales. It would be a lost soul indeed who would miss the opportunity to hear Prince Hywel sing. Unfortunately, keeping everyone else safe meant that Gareth and many of his men might have to miss it. To have so many of the villagers absent from their homes made the village ripe for thievery.

"I hope you're right," Gareth said, "though I'm not sure how many still will be able to stand."

Gareth, Evan, and Rhodri shouldered their way through the crowd. The instant he put a foot through the tavern door, the atmosphere of raucous revelry muted. Gareth didn't have to actually hear the whispers that passed from man to man to know that they were warning each other that Prince Hywel's men were now among them.

"I don't know any of these people. How do they know who we are?" Rhodri said.

"It's the way we carry ourselves, what we wear, and that sword at your waist," Gareth said. "This happens to me all the time."

Rhodri gave a grunt of surprise. When he was with his fellow soldiers, he could let his guard down in a place like this. Since becoming captain of Hywel's guard, Gareth was never treated like one of the men anymore. And he supposed he didn't often want to be.

With Rhodri and Evan in tow, Gareth approached the bar, edging between two customers, who melted away. Gareth didn't necessarily believe that half the inhabitants of the tavern were criminals, but whenever he arrived at a place like this, his effect was to cause people to examine their consciences, and many didn't like what they found. Or thought he wouldn't like what they found. Lies, infidelity, and disputes between neighbors were part of a normal existence, whether in a castle or a village. For the most part, those crimes were of no concern to Gareth until they rose to a level that threatened the social order.

Theft and murder were another matter entirely, and there would be thefts before the festival had finished. He dearly hoped there wouldn't be any more murders.

"I'm looking for Pawl," Gareth said to the barkeep.

The man jerked his head. "In the back, my lord."

Gareth gestured to Evan and Rhodri that they should follow him and went to the far doorway as directed. He knew from past visits that it led to storage areas, the stairs to the guest rooms on the floor above them, and out the back to the kitchen.

"If I've told you once, I've told you a hundred times—" Pawl came out of a passage to the left, full of ire, but he pulled up at the sight of Gareth. "Oh." He bowed. "I apologize, my lord. I thought you were someone else."

"It is no matter," Gareth said. "Is there something I can help you with?"

"No, no," Pawl said. "It's nothing that should concern you. Simply patrons tromping where they don't belong."

Gareth thought the 'you' to whom Pawl had been referring in 'I've told you a hundred times' was more specific than that, but since Gareth didn't at the moment think it had anything to do with his investigation, he let it go. Regardless of what the customers in the tavern believed Gareth thought, people were entitled to their secrets. Most of the time.

"What did you want to see me about? Is the crowd getting out of hand?" Pawl's hands went to the cloth at his waist, working at it to dry his hands.

"Patrons have spilled into the street," Rhodri said from beside Gareth. "Do you need assistance from the castle?"

"Not so far." Pawl looked from Rhodri to Gareth, and then over their shoulders to Evan, who stood behind them. "Is that all?"

"No," Gareth said. "I need to talk to you about Iolo, the cloth merchant. I understand he rents rooms from you when he comes through Aberystwyth."

"That's right," Pawl said. "His are out back. I heard about Gryff. That's too bad."

When Pawl didn't add the usual platitude about how Gryff was a good man or what a loss his death was, Gareth raised his eyebrows and said, "What have you heard about his death?"

"That he died in the millpond, though—" for a moment Pawl looked sideways at Gareth, "—maybe somebody put him there if you're coming around asking questions about it?"

Gareth tsked his disgust. As an inn keeper, Pawl knew too much about people and their dishonorable motives to be fooled for long. "Maybe."

"I can't understand why anyone would do that," Pawl said.

That was more like the response Gareth might have expected. "Did you like him?"

Pawl shrugged. "He was a pleasant enough fellow. He never gave any trouble, even when he was in his cups." Then he grinned. "Though, let me tell you, that man could drink half my tavern and never show it. I've never seen anything like it."

That was what Alun had said. Iolo had declared the exact opposite. Gareth filed that piece of information away for future examination. "Did Gryff get along with Iolo all right?"

"Well enough."

"Meaning?"

Pawl shrugged. "They didn't argue openly, but they weren't close. Iolo knew he'd hired someone who didn't like to work, but he didn't do anything about it either."

"What about Madlen?" Gareth said.

"What about her?"

"Did they get along?"

"Ach. They hardly spoke most days," Pawl said. "They had little use for one another as far I could tell."

Gareth went very still. "How's that?"

Pawl blinked. "How's what?"

Gareth looked carefully at Pawl. "They were a couple. Married."

Pawl's brows drew together. "No, they weren't. That's impossible."

"Why?"

"He had a wife. Carys was her name. Who told you he was married to Madlen?"

Gareth didn't answer. Madlen had lied about being married to Gryff, and Gareth's brain had been working so slowly that he'd missed it. The brazenness of the lie left him both awed and angry.

"Gryff slept with the cart, had no possessions to speak of, just a rucksack. He never ate inside," Pawl said when Gareth didn't answer his question. "Iolo and Madlen treated him little better than a slave."

"Do you have Gryff's rucksack?" Evan said, speaking into the silence that Gareth, still trying to orient his thoughts, didn't fill.

Pawl's brow furrowed. "It's odd you should ask that. Gryff left it with me on the afternoon he died. I put it in the back." Pawl turned on his heel, and the three others followed him.

"Was it unusual for him to leave his pack with you?" Gareth said.

"He never had before." Pawl took a candle from a ledge and lit it. They'd arrived at a narrow doorway with a curtain drawn across it. "In here—"

But as Pawl drew aside the curtain, he stopped dead, his mouth agape.

"What's wrong?" Gareth looked over the inn keeper's shoulder.

He was looking into a narrow storage room, with shelves built along both sides. There was barely enough room between the two walls for a man to turn around. Nothing looked amiss to Gareth, but Pawl was clearly flustered.

"This room has been searched," Pawl said.

"How can you tell?" Gareth said.

"I can tell." Pawl gestured to a blank spot on the bottom of one shelf. "And the pack is gone."

"Are you sure?" Rhodri said from behind them, but Gareth made a swift downward motion with his hand to silence him.

Gareth had no difficulty taking Pawl at his word. The man ran an inn and tavern and rarely needed assistance in keeping his house in order. He obviously liked things well-ordered. "When did you last look in here?" Gareth said.

Pawl took in a breath through his nose, pressing his lips together as he thought. "It was sometime last night. I didn't have a reason to enter here today before now. The night before, I always lay out everything I think I'll need in the room adjacent to the common room."

"So anyone could have taken it?" Rhodri said.

"Anyone who wouldn't have looked out of place back here," Pawl said.

"That means who, exactly?" Gareth said. "Paying guests and your employees? How many is that in all?"

"I employ five: two in the kitchen, one maid, and two in the bar, though the maid helps out in the common room when she's done with her work back here."

"And how many guests do you have this week?" Gareth said.

"We're full up. Counting Iolo's party of three—" Pawl made a rueful face, "—two now, I have four rooms upstairs, all full. So, twenty-two guests."

Gareth nodded. That *was* as he expected. "Have either Madlen or Iolo asked about Gryff's things?"

A wary look came into Pawl's eyes. "Funny you should ask me that. Iolo wondered openly about the location of Gryff's rucksack last night."

"What did you tell him?" Gareth said.

"I told him I had it and was keeping it safe for his wife," Pawl said.

"His wife, Carys?" Gareth said.

"Yes," Pawl said. "I was glad to finally have met her when Gryff brought her by the other day."

Gareth almost laughed. Yet another lie revealed, though this one told by Carys, not Madlen.

"What day was that?" Evan said.

"Come to think on it, it was the day Gryff died," Pawl said.

"Do you remember the hour?" Gareth said, trying to keep the urgency from his voice and undoubtedly failing because Pawl swallowed hard before answering.

"Just after noon it was. I overhead him telling her that she needed to get back to Goginan. He practically pushed her out the door," Pawl said.

"Did they meet with anyone else?" Gareth said.

"Not that I saw," Pawl said. "It seemed to me that he hadn't expected to see her here and was none too happy about it."

"I would ask that you keep this information among the four of us for now." Gareth hated to use up any favors, but now seemed as good a time as any. "We are trying to establish what Gryff did, where he went, and who he talked to on his last day alive."

"So he *was* murdered," Pawl said.

"Yes," Gareth said, deciding he wouldn't withhold that piece of information from the inn keeper, since he'd guessed it anyway.

"I will not speak of it, my lord." Pawl wasn't one to gossip, and like everyone else in Ceredigion, his wellbeing depended upon Hywel. "If you like, I'll keep an ear out."

"Thank you. I'd appreciate it." Gareth had clearly been remiss in not enlisting Pawl earlier. There couldn't be many other men in all of Aberystwyth who knew more about its people than he did. "If you don't mind, I'll check back with you later tonight or tomorrow."

"And we'll send a man or two to keep an eye on your crowd," Evan said. "It wouldn't do for the party to get too out of hand."

Pawl dipped his head. "Thank you. I should look into the potency of the beer. I might have made it a little strong today."

"Maybe a little," Gareth said.

He thanked Pawl and bid him goodbye. Once outside, Gareth was pleased to see that the crowd had, in fact, dispersed somewhat. The sun was heading down into the sea. So far the festival was a rollicking success (even if he hadn't managed to participate in any of it) and people were making their way out of Aberystwyth along the road for the start of the evening program.

Gareth ran his hand through his hair. "This is mad. My head must be as thick as porridge for not seeing this sooner. Madlen made a fool of me."

"Of all of us," Rhodri said.

"You've been distracted by the festival," Evan said.

Gareth rolled his eyes. "You're being charitable."

"It has only been a day since we discovered the body," Rhodri said. "We've come a long way in a short time."

That made Gareth feel a little better. "More lies unveiled anyway. Carys was here when she said she hadn't been, and Madlen and Gryff weren't married."

"Both women had to know their lies would eventually trip them up," Evan said.

"I can't get my head around Madlen's lie in particular," Rhodri said. "Why would she tell you that she was married to Gryff? What could she possibly hope to gain from it?"

"Perhaps she killed him," Gareth said.

"Then I would have thought she would have stayed as far away from the body as possible," Rhodri said. "Why call attention to herself?"

"Maybe she loved him. Maybe she wanted to be married to him so badly that she pretended it was true," Evan said. "She got to play the grieving widow, and if not for that young monk, we never would have known differently."

"On a more devious note," Rhodri said, "playing the widow gave her access."

Gareth raised his eyebrows. "You may have an answer there."

"Access to what?" Evan scratched at his scruffy beard.

"To the body, certainly." Gareth said. "To his purse, since we allowed her to keep it."

Evan nodded. "And to the progress of the investigation."

"Though she may have miscalculated there, since we might never have learned who he was at all if she hadn't come forward," Rhodri said.

"Everybody says Gryff was an affable dreamer," Gareth said, "but it seems more and more clear that there was more to him than we've yet learned."

16

Rhun

"You can't have it! It's mine!" A young woman Rhun didn't recognize shrieked and spat at Madlen as the two women wrestled one another to the ground.

Madlen clawed back at her. "It belonged to my grandmother!"

Rhun didn't understand how he'd managed to go from a pleasant afternoon strolling through the fair with Angharad to breaking up a fight between two women. He and Angharad had listened to a young man with a beautiful voice and no skill with his instrument (but still, one whom Rhun meant to point out to Hywel), purchased several honeyed treats, and up until now had avoided any unpleasantness. He hadn't even seen the Danish spy, Erik, though Rhun was willing to admit that the search for him was a parallel motive to this excursion with Angharad.

Rhun elbowed his way through the onlookers who'd gathered in the aisle between the market stalls and put his arms around the unknown woman's waist. He tugged hard, attempting to wrench her away from Madlen. Each woman clutched the shoulders and arms of the other, scrabbling with their legs for purchase on the hard ground.

"What's going on here?" An enormous man pushed aside three passersby and grabbed the arm of the woman Rhun was trying to pry off Madlen. "Get away from her!" He shoved Rhun so hard with his other hand that Rhun was forced to release the woman and crashed into a nearby stall.

Unfortunately for the big man and the woman he thought he was protecting, Rhun's loss of control gave Madlen the opportunity to pounce once again. While the big man was looking daggers at Rhun, Madlen assaulted the woman whose arm the man was holding, wrestled her away from him, and fell with her to the ground.

Rhun's eyes were watering from the pain in his head where it had struck a tent pole, but he pushed to a sitting position and suppressed the accompanying moan.

The owner of the stall he'd wrecked—a merchant who'd set up his stall next to Iolo's because he sold incidentals for sewing—bobbed up and down beside Rhun, nervously wringing his hands. He was bowing and apologizing profusely at the same time, though what had happened wasn't at all his fault. Rhun allowed the man to help him up, trying to place his feet in such a way as not to further ruin the man's goods, which were on the ground.

While Rhun was getting to his feet, the women continued to roll around on the ground. Now, however, Iolo arrived, and he and the big man waded into the fight together.

"My lord! My lord!" Angharad had been standing with her hand to her mouth, but now she hurried to him. Unlike the merchant who'd helped him up, she wasn't averse to touching him, and she patted him down, feeling for obvious wounds and looking for blood. He'd seen Gwen do the same to Gareth a dozen times.

Out of deference to the warm weather, Rhun had worn only a leather vest as armor today rather than his full mail. With a murderer about and Rhun involved in the investigation, Hywel hadn't wanted him to take the chance of going about without any protection at all. Fortunately, the air was cooler today than it had been yesterday, more like autumn than summer. It might even rain by tomorrow, though everyone in Aberystwyth from Hywel on down hoped that it wouldn't.

Rhun caught Angharad's hands. "I am unhurt, or at least not very hurt."

"You hit the post with your head and you might have broken your ribs! That man should be put in irons!"

Angharad's ire on his behalf warmed Rhun's heart, but he squeezed her hands and smiled, trying to assuage her concern. He looked past her to the fight, which was ongoing. Iolo shouted, "Madlen! Madlen!"

Angharad tried to prevent him from returning to the fray, slipping her hand into his to draw his attention back to her. Rhun brought their joined hands to his lips and kissed her fingers. "I'm well, Angharad. Truly."

Madlen stood up. "Ha!" Her fist was clenched in triumph around something small attached to a jewelry chain.

The other woman screamed. By now Rhun could make a good guess as to her identity. Iolo pulled Madlen back, stepping in front of her and glaring at the big man, who helped the woman on the ground to her feet.

Once upright, however, the unknown woman launched herself at Madlen again. "It's mine! You can't have it. Gryff gave it to *me*!"

Rhun decided it was time to reassert his authority. He put his left hand on the hilt of his sword and strode forward. "Enough!"

The barking tone was one he used to speak to his men. Usually he saved it for the heat of battle, the times he needed to call 'to me!' and had to be heard above the clash of swords and screams of men and horses. Rarely had he used it to call, 'retreat!', though the one time he'd done so had saved the bulk of his men and enabled them to live to fight another day.

Regardless, his order had the desired effect among these less well-armed combatants. Rhun shouldered his way back through the cluster of onlookers to where the two women had frozen in mid-fight, breathing hard and glowering at each other. Three soldiers had also finally appeared, drawn by the ruckus the women were creating. Rhun was happy to see that one of them was his own captain, Gruffydd.

Rhun stepped between the two women and held out his hand, palm flat, to Madlen. "Give it to me."

Madlen was flushed red with temper and heat. "No!"

Rhun didn't ask again, just kept his hand out. It occurred to him that she might be too fired up to recognize him from when he'd questioned her with Gareth.

"Madlen!" Iolo whipped his hat off his head and hustled towards Rhun with bowed head. "Please forgive her, my lord. She is distraught with grief and doesn't know what she is doing."

"Be that as it may," Rhun said, "I want what she has in her hand."

"It belongs to Carys!" the big man said.

Rhun turned his head slowly to look at him, hardly able to believe the man still hadn't realized who he was. But at Rhun's look, the big man's mouth snapped shut, his eyes widened, and suddenly instead of glaring at Rhun he took a step back. "I'm—I'm—" He was prevented from fleeing by the appearance of two of Hywel's men, who buttressed him on either side. The woman he protected, who had to be Carys, clutched her brother's elbow and looked scared.

"I will deal with you two later. Now—" Rhun turned back to Madlen, his hand still out, "—what is in your hand?"

"It's mine." Madlen was still breathing rapidly, her eyes wild with defiance and anger, but under Rhun's calm gaze, she finally blinked and faltered. As Iolo whispered urgently in her ear, the fire left her. Nervous now, as perhaps the realization of the spectacle she'd created occurred to her, she opened her fist and draped what she'd been holding into Rhun's hand. It turned out to be a gold cross on a chain. "Gryff never should have given it to her!"

"No, it's mine—" Carys made a motion as if to dart forward, but the big man—Alun—caught her arm and jerked her back, cutting off her words in mid-breath.

Rhun closed his hand over the cross. With a nod from Gruffydd, the soldiers began to disperse the crowd that had gathered, leaving Iolo and Madlen standing to Rhun's right, and Carys and Alun standing three paces away to Rhun's left.

Rhun studied each person in turn. Alun and Iolo stood rock steady, staring at a point somewhere near Rhun's right shoulder. The two women shifted from foot to foot in uncertainty. "Carys and Alun, I assume," Rhun said, looking at the second pair.

"Yes, my lord," Alun said.

"So you know who I am now?" Rhun said.

"Yes, my lord." Alun swallowed hard. "I'm sorry—"

Rhun held up a hand, cutting the big man off. "We will discuss your transgressions later. For now, I am interested in why you allowed your sister to come within fifty paces of Iolo's stall and Madlen."

"My lord—" Iolo began.

At Rhun's frown, he too subsided. "I have reconsidered. I will bring you before my brother, and you can tell your story to him. Come with me." Rhun held out his elbow to Angharad, who took it. He set off without waiting to see if he would be obeyed.

Cowed, the four culprits followed him towards the market exit, herded forward by the soldiers and Gruffydd. As Rhun had hoped, they found Hywel in the pavilion where he'd left him several hours earlier. Hywel had always demanded perfection from everyone who worked for him, but his current state of frenzy had less to do with his natural proclivities than the fact that their father should be arriving at any moment.

Hywel noted Rhun's approach and came over to the group before Rhun had to hail him. Looking past Rhun to the two angry couples and the guards beyond them, Hywel pressed his lips together for a moment, impatience flashing across his face. "What's happened now?"

"There has been an incident that I believe requires your attention." Rhun opened his hand to show Hywel the cross. "What we have here are two grieving widows, both of whom claim this cross belongs to them."

Hywel picked up the chain upon which the cross was strung and held it up, uncoiling it from Rhun's palm. "Carys was wearing it when she spoke to Gwen this morning," Hywel said.

"Madlen claims the cross belonged to her grandmother, and that she gave it to Gryff as a token of her love for him. She says he had no right to pass it on to Carys."

Rhun had examined the cross on the walk to the pavilion. As Gwen had indicated, an entwined 'C' and 'G' had been etched expertly into the center back where the four arms met.

Hywel looked over at Madlen. "What were your grandparents' names?"

"Catrin and Gwion," Madlen said without hesitation.

"Hmm." Hywel glanced at his brother, half turning his back on Madlen and Iolo. "What do you make of this?"

"I don't know," Rhun said, keeping his voice low so only Hywel could hear him. "I dearly wish that Gryff hadn't managed to get himself killed, because he could have cleared all this up with a few words."

Hywel turned back to the women. "We have many questions about Gryff's death and his relationship with the two of you. When we have a more complete picture, we will make a determination as to whom this cross belongs. Until then, Carys, you must stay far away from Madlen. We have buried your husband. Your children are fatherless. You should be thinking of them. And you—" he looked at Madlen, "—you feel yourself misused in that Gryff played you false. He was not the first man to do so, nor will he be the last. I suggest that before you tie yourself to a dreamer again, you meet his family first."

Madlen and Iolo looked at the ground, indicating that—if not suitably chastened—they were at least willing to pretend they were listening to their lord. Hywel snorted his derision, motioning for everyone to take their leave. Iolo tugged on Madlen's arm, urging her to come with him. She looked as if she was going to call for Hywel's attention again, which would have been a mistake. But after another brief hesitation, she went with her uncle.

"Wait." Rhun pointed at Carys and Alun before they could depart too. "I'm not finished with you two." Gruffydd, Rhun's captain, and the three soldiers still boxed the pair in. Rhun stepped up to the big man. "Did you hope I'd forgotten that you threw me across the fairgrounds?"

Hywel had moved away to return to what he'd been doing before but now hastened back to Rhun's side. "What's this?"

Alun pulled in his chin, looking as if he wanted to flee. "I didn't mean—"

Rhun cut him off. "Don't lie to me. You meant to get me out of the way, and you didn't care who I was. You have a temper, Alun. Was it you who met your brother-in-law beside the millpond two nights ago and murdered him?"

"No!" Alun took a step back in his dismay, bumping into Gruffydd, who shoved him forward again. "I don't know what you're talking about. Nobody ever said anything about murder!"

Carys fell to her knees in the short grass, her arms wrapped around her middle as if she might be sick right there and then.

Rhun eyed the big man, whose eyes had gone wide with shock. "You say you had nothing to do with Gryff's death, and so far that's what everyone's been saying. But I tell you now that someone killed him. I have been wondering all day if that someone was you."

Hywel stepped smoothly between them. "Perhaps a day or two in a cell up at the castle will jog his memory, brother?"

"I think you're right, brother. Everyone has lied to us," Rhun said. "I think it's time this one stopped, don't you?"

Alun choked on his fear and fell to his knees beside his sister. "I haven't lied! My lords, please! I don't know anything about why Gryff died! You have to believe me!" His words appeared heartfelt.

"We really don't." Rhun gazed down at Alun but was spared any more of Alun's denials by a trumpet blast that reverberated all around the festival grounds.

King Owain had arrived.

Hywel spun on his heel, his own eyes widening. Rhun put a hand on his brother's arm. "This is going to go well. You have done brilliantly." Rhun's only goal now was to support his brother, and whatever Alun did or did not know had to be put aside. Rhun jerked his head at Gruffydd. "Put him in the cell."

"Yes, my lord," Gruffydd said.

Rhun looked down at Carys. "Given the circumstances, we still have questions for you too. I expect to be able to find you when I need to ask them."

Carys's eyes were wide. "My children—"

"I understand they are with Alun's wife," Rhun said.

Carys nodded.

"Then they should be fine to stay with her another day." Rhun ignored Carys's gasping protest and headed across the pavilion in Hywel's wake, hastening to catch up.

By the time Rhun reached him, Hywel had come to a halt on the near side of the ford of the Ystwyth River and was smoothing his palms down the sides of his breeches. Though the late afternoon sun had finally fallen below the level of the escarpment to the west, Hywel was sweating at the knowledge that he was about to see his father. Rhun understood the pressure Hywel was under and, for possibly the first time ever, was grateful not to be in his brother's shoes.

As the object of his father's outsized expectations since birth, Rhun had learned to work around and with his father. Hywel, as the second son, had been spared many of those particular burdens, but he had carried other ones. Their father had given Hywel Ceredigion to see what kind of man he had become.

Rhun couldn't blame Hywel for being nervous.

"I was a fool to think any of this was a good idea," Hywel said. "I should have told my father from the start that I wasn't ready to rule Ceredigion."

"You were ready and the festival was a good idea," Rhun said.

"You know very well how difficult this has been," Hywel said.

"I do," Rhun said. "You need to take a breath. Everything is prepared. Even the rain has held off. You will sing tonight, Father will weep, and when you are ready to show him all you have accomplished here, he will be pleased."

Hywel shot him a startled look. "I have made mistakes—"

Rhun scoffed. "Do you think no ruler has ever made mistakes? You are here because our grandfather entrusted Ceredigion to Cadwaladr. Father knows the state the lordship was in when you took it over. Taran has visited here often enough to have given him a clear picture."

"You comfort me." Hywel returned his eyes to the front.

"Father was young once too," Rhun said. "At your age, his father hadn't yet laid the kind of responsibilities on him that he has given to you."

The flag of Gwynedd had just appeared on the other side of the river, so Rhun didn't say the rest of what he was thinking: their father's brother, Cadwallon, had been killed nearly fifteen years before, when their father was in his thirties. It was Cadwallon who had been the eldest and the one upon whom all hopes for Gwynedd had rested. Owain had been trusted, but as a second son, not as much had been expected of him. While Rhun had hope that he would not share Cadwallon's fate, he appreciated his father's desire not to be unprepared for the unexpected.

If Rhun were to die, the future of Gwynedd would rest on Hywel's shoulders. When and if that happened, Hywel needed to be ready. And if Rhun outlived his father and assumed the throne as he and everyone else planned, then Hywel would be just the right-hand man that Rhun needed to rule Gwynedd. Rhun had every intention of keeping his country as strong and united as his father had made it.

As their father prepared to cross the ford of the Ystwyth River, shallow thanks to the lack of recent rains, the two brothers walked forward. Rhun allowed Hywel to get a little ahead of him: this was his lordship, and Rhun was here for moral support only. He caught sight of Angharad out of the corner of his eye. She waved at him, and he fought a smile, though he'd forgotten about her briefly in his anxiety for Hywel.

Then King Owain's horse picked its way through the water, came up the low bank, and halted five paces from where Hywel stood alone in the middle of the path. King Owain dismounted.

Leaving his horse with a member of his guard, he walked to stand in front of Hywel.

"Sire." Hywel bowed, but when he straightened, King Owain stepped forward and wrapped him up in a bear hug, going so far as to lift Hywel's feet off the ground.

"Good to see you, son!"

Hywel managed to grunt an acknowledgement of the greeting, although from past experience Rhun knew their father had squeezed all the air from Hywel's lungs.

King Owain dropped him to the ground and released him, but only so he could hammer him on the back. "This festival is the talk of Wales." King Owain spread his arms wide. "It is quite an accomplishment, son."

"Thank you, Father." Hywel bowed again. "I hope it lives up to expectations."

"I have no doubt," King Owain said.

Rhun could hear the heartiness in his father's voice, and even if the king was putting on a show of a sort, his pride in his son was genuine. Rhun gazed around at the brightly colored flags and jubilant crowd, trying to see it anew with his father's eyes. Rhun felt a rush of pride rise in his own chest at what Hywel had accomplished.

"I trust the journey was uneventful?" Hywel said.

"In the extreme," King Owain said.

"So—slow, I take it?" Hywel said.

"We're two days late." Then King Owain looked to where Rhun waited. Moving past Hywel, King Owain shook Rhun's forearm and then pulled him closer for a brief hug, taking the opportunity to speak to him in a low voice that didn't carry, "I'm glad to see you well, son."

"And you, sir," Rhun said.

His father released him to turn back to Hywel, who gestured that they should begin walking towards the main pavilion. Rhun took a moment to direct King Owain's captain to the field that had been saved for them, where they should pitch their tents, and then he hurried after his brother and father.

Rhun knew why his father had greeted him less exuberantly than he had Hywel. It wasn't because his father loved him less. It was because Hywel had needed that greeting, not only for himself but so his people could see how much his father favored him. Rhun didn't need that kind of attention.

He didn't know why the relationship between Hywel and his father had always been more fragile than Rhun's own. He and his father might look alike, but they were miles apart in temperament, unlike King Owain and Hywel. Certainly Hywel's dedication to winning women's hearts had come from their father. But as long as Rhun could remember, King Owain had looked upon Rhun himself with favor. He might have been found wanting a time or two, but Rhun couldn't remember a day when he hadn't tried to follow his father's example and been rewarded for the effort.

"How fares Gwynedd?" Rhun fell into step beside his father.

"All is quiet in Gwynedd itself," King Owain said, "but I bring news from the east that will interest you."

Rhun felt the corners of his mouth turn down. News from the east was almost never good.

"Ranulf?" Hywel said.

"Ranulf," King Owain agreed. "Word has reached me that King Stephen has released the Earl of Chester from his prison."

"When?" Hywel said.

"Ten days ago now," King Owain said.

"What was the promised price?" Rhun said. "It must have cost all Ranulf had."

"Most of what he cared about, anyway," King Owain said. "Ranulf is required to relinquish all royal lands and holdings, including Lincoln Castle. He must give hostages and swear never to act against the king again."

Rhun nodded. "To Ranulf and the king, the only real matter of importance is Lincoln Castle. This is the only way he could compel Ranulf to release it."

"Stephen's other choice was more bloodshed," King Owain said.

"Along with failure and humiliation," Rhun said. "The king tried twice to take the castle and failed. He needed to find another way."

Hywel laughed sardonically. "If Stephen believes any oath Ranulf swears, he is a fool. The king might get his castle, but Ranulf will turn on him before the year is out."

"Before the week is out," Rhun said. "But my concern is more that he will turn against us."

King Owain nodded. "Ranulf was imprisoned in part because Stephen's other barons mistrusted his motives, thinking he intended to lure Stephen into a campaign against Gwynedd, with the intent to ambush the king instead."

Hywel's eyes widened. "That I hadn't heard."

"I'm not saying Ranulf might not have done so," King Owain said, "but we all know that he has had his eye on our eastern border for years."

"It worries me too," Rhun said.

"Ranulf will turn against Wales," King Owain said, "thinking to appease Stephen. He will want to make the king think he has taken a step back from the war with Empress Maud."

"A step back is not a retreat," Hywel said. "The Earl of Chester is still one of the most powerful barons in England. There's a reason King Stephen hasn't deprived him of his earldom."

"Because he can't." King Owain clapped his second son on the back. "But this is a conversation for a long evening over warm mead. Today is about Ceredigion. To have the pleasure of hearing the voice of my son, the finest poet Wales has ever produced, is something I've been looking forward to for many months."

Hywel looked modestly down at his feet, but not before Rhun caught a glance from him that their father didn't see. Hywel's eyes had snapped with pleasure. "Don't let Meilyr hear you say that."

"Meilyr will be pleased too," King Owain said. "You were his student once, as much as Gwalchmai is now."

Rhun glanced behind them. The bulk of King Owain's party had crossed the river and was wending its way towards the field where they would pitch their tents. The three of them had been walking slowly and had almost reached the central pavilion. Throughout their conversation, many of the onlookers who'd come to see King Owain arrive had remained to watch, some perhaps in hopes of gaining an audience with the King of Gwynedd, however brief.

"Gwalchmai and Meilyr have come too, have they not?" Rhun said.

"They would not have missed this for all the gold in Winchester." King Owain looked at Hywel. "It was wise of you not to compete with the other bards. You are a prince and the Lord of Ceredigion. You stand apart, and yet your voice rules over all others. As does your sword."

"Thank you, Father," Hywel said.

Then King Owain buffeted the shoulders of both his sons together. "After today, all will know that Gwynedd leads Wales not only in might but in music as well." Then he rubbed his hands together. "I can't wait."

17

Gwen

"**H**as anyone so far considered where Gryff might have found the money to buy Carys that cross?" Mari said.

Gwen's friend had miraculously risen from her bed to attend the evening's entertainments. Although pale, she was holding herself well, and the two women walked together towards the high table. Dressed in a tunic of deep green, Hywel stood to one side. He caught sight of his wife, and his eyes lit to see Mari coming towards him. The two nannies followed, carrying Tangwen and Gruffydd, who was asleep.

"It is something to consider," Gwen said. "Gareth is working on it, I know."

The festival had already heard singing from dozens of bards. They included performers at all levels, from men who wandered the length and breadth of Wales, as she had once done with her father, to official court bards. Her father was among the latter again, as he'd been when Gwen was a child. Her chest swelled with pride to see Gwalchmai and her father tuning their instruments a few feet from where Hywel stood. While this was his night, it was also Gwynedd's. Meilyr would play to accompany Hywel's voice, and Gwalchmai would join him in song near the end.

The splendor and wealth of Ceredigion and Gwynedd was on display tonight, and the two women were dressed in their finest garments, as was every person in the pavilion. Food and drink were being served, though not in quantity. The purpose of tonight was not feasting but music, following the saying that was common among them: 'Food is for the stomach, music for the soul.'

"Hywel is so very pleased with how the festival is turning out, but I hope he isn't too nervous to sing," Mari said.

Gwen hurried a few steps to catch up with her friend. "Hywel hasn't been nervous about singing since he was twelve years old."

"Hmmm," Mari said. "He has just learned to hide it better."

Gwen smiled, accepting her friend's knowledge of Hywel's thoughts without feeling hurt. Gwen and Hywel had never returned to the close relationship they'd had as children—it would have been impossible to have done so unless they themselves had married. As a young man, Hywel would have hidden his fears from her, just as every man worked to keep his fears hidden lest they make him vulnerable to the barbs of an enemy.

Gwen had looked into that dark pit herself. Fear was the demon inside all men. To allow it to rise to the surface turned men into animals. A man might fear battle, or poverty, or humiliation as in the case of Hywel tonight, but what woman hadn't lain awake in the darkness, worrying for her man or child? At times Gwen couldn't do otherwise and remain a woman.

King Owain of Gwynedd and King Cadell of Deheubarth sat side by side at the high table. Rhun sat at his father's right hand. Cadell didn't have a son, so his left was taken up by his two brothers, Maredudd and Rhys, who'd arrived for the festival shortly after King Owain. Madog, the king of Powys, had not come, which surprised no one. With the Earl of Chester free again, his kingdom might soon come under renewed pressure from the Normans, who had already carved out large pieces of it for themselves. Whether a particular castle was Welsh or Norman varied from year to year in a constant back and forth for power and land.

Cadwaladr, King Owain's brother, sat at the end of the table, facing down it. Gwen had noted this new habit of his: to keep himself apart rather than assert his rights as a prince of Gwynedd. And in a way, sitting at the end of the table implied that he'd carved out a dominion of his own.

"I see Gareth," Mari said as Gwen escorted her around the back of the high table to her seat. "Later, you must tell me everything he discovered today."

"Of course I will." Gwen smiled at her friend. "Enjoy the music."

Mari chose a seat at the end of the table. It was not an indication of low rank. As Hywel's wife, she was the hostess of the festival. Rather, it was a practical matter of being able to depart the pavilion quickly in case her stomach rebelled against her. It also put her closer to where Hywel stood.

As Gwen headed towards an open side of the pavilion, she neared her father and brother. She hadn't had a chance to greet them properly yet, and even now she only gave them each a peck on the cheek. "You will do wonderfully."

Gwalchmai's face was flushed, and he was sweating in his fine wool tunic. He closed his eyes and took in a long breath, holding it for a moment before easing it out.

Meilyr shot his son a worried look. "Place your faith in your training."

"Yes, Father." Gwalchmai's gaze became focused on a point somewhere in the distance. "You needn't worry about me."

Gwen gave him half a hug, bent over with one arm around his shoulders. When he stood he was taller than she was by several inches. Another month and he might be taller than his father.

"You should be up here too, girl," Meilyr said, ever gruff, but Gwen knew that he meant it.

"Not tonight," Gwen said. "The three of you will do Gwynedd proud."

Gareth was standing off to one side, keeping Prince Hywel and the whole of the pavilion under his watchful eye. She hadn't seen him since they'd eaten together in the early afternoon. As Gwen moved towards him, he took a step back, fading into the darkness outside the tent at her approach. Her heart sped up, not only at the sight of him but because she guessed that he had something important to tell her.

Everybody who could cram into the pavilion had already arrived, and the rest of the festival-goers were spread out around it, seated on blankets in the grass. As Gwen left the pavilion, Hywel raised a hand to gain everyone's attention. Such was the expectation and excitement among the onlookers that silence immediately descended upon the crowd.

Gwen clasped Gareth's hand and turned to look back, sharing the anticipation and delight that was infecting everyone. Some might have expected Hywel to take this moment to welcome his guests, but he didn't. In fact, he didn't say anything, just opened his mouth and released his gorgeous voice. As Gwen's father had proclaimed more times than Gwen could count, a voice like Hywel's came along once in a generation.

Gareth drew Gwen closer, his arm around her shoulders, listening as Hywel warmed to his song. This particular saga told of battle, triumph, and grief, and was one that she and everyone in the pavilion knew by heart, though none could ever regret hearing it again.

As Hywel began the third verse, Gareth gently turned Gwen away from the music, and they threaded their way among the onlookers until they reached the far edge of the crowd. Hywel's voice soared towards the stars that winked above them. Gwen didn't want to stop listening to the singing, but Gareth clearly thought what he had to say was important enough that she needed to hear it now, rather than wait until the evening's music was over.

"This sounds like bad news," she said.

"We uncovered some disconcerting information today," Gareth said and then told her about his conversation with the inn keeper and the disappearance of Gryff's rucksack.

"So Madlen and Gryff weren't married." Gwen shook her head. "Should we detain her, Gareth?"

"I'm thinking about it," Gareth said. "Rhun tells me that he has Alun locked up at the castle. I haven't had a chance to speak to either him or Carys yet, but they've been telling lies too."

"Iolo and Madlen have no ties here. They could have very easily run—far more easily than Alun or Carys could," Gwen said.

"That was one reason I believed Alun and Carys had nothing to do with Gryff's death. After I returned from Aberystwyth, I went by Iolo's booth but like everyone else they had closed it down in preparation for tonight's music. I sent Rhodri back to the inn to see if they'd cleaned out their things, but he has just returned to tell me that they haven't. Still, nobody has seen them."

"The only reason for them to leave now instead of yesterday after the murder was because someone told them you'd visited the inn."

"That was my thought too," Gareth said. "Their informant could be any one of dozens of people who were at the tavern when we visited it. The news could even have been innocently given."

"The inn keeper could have told them," Gwen said.

"I don't see Pawl's hand in this. At least, he promised not to speak of it," Gareth said. "He was very upset at the disappearance of Gryff's rucksack."

"If Iolo and Madlen left Aberystwyth, they could be miles away by now in any direction," Gwen said. "Have you spoken to Prince Hywel about any of this?"

"Not yet," Gareth said. "Tonight was too important to him to distract him with something I mean to deal with myself. I did, however, tell the men to be on the lookout for them."

"Is Iolo's cart still here?" Gwen said.

Gareth made a disgusted sound at the back of his throat. "Why do I never think of these things? It wasn't at the tavern, of that I can be sure."

"Let's go to the market fair and see if it's gone," Gwen said. "All that Iolo and Madlen own is either in that booth or in that cart. Without Gryff to watch over it anymore, one of them must be doing it."

"Is Tangwen all right?" Gareth peered past Gwen towards the pavilion.

"She's with Elspeth." Gwen could just make out the girl sitting with Tangwen in her lap. Gratifyingly, the baby loved music as much as the rest of her family did.

Gareth smiled when he spied his daughter. "Neither of them will miss us. We can go."

To Gwen's regret, the clarity of the music lessened as they navigated among the tents between the main pavilion and the market fair. Still, holding Gareth's hand in the darkness, Gwen wasn't completely let down. She felt like she was sixteen again. In those days, she'd managed to walk off with Gareth illicitly only once, and they'd been caught almost immediately by a nosy matron who'd shooed them back to the great hall. That had been here at Aberystwyth, though in the old castle that Hywel had burned to the ground three years ago.

Gwen mentioned the memory to Gareth, who laughed before pulling her behind a tent with him. Wrapping her in his arms, he kissed her until she was breathless. "We haven't spent as much time alone together recently as I like."

"We haven't spent *any* time alone together." But then Gwen pushed at his chest, putting some space between them. "We have a task, Gareth."

He grumbled, "It would be more fun to forget about it," but he took her hand again and stepped out from behind the tent. Ahead of them lay the long line of carts, dozens of them, which belonged to the traders and merchants who'd come for the fair. Many carts were empty but others were simply battened down. No merchants sat among them. It appeared that all of them were taking advantage of Hywel's assurance that they would be well guarded.

"Do you know which one is theirs?" Gwen said.

Gareth shook his head. "They all look the same time to me." He waved a hand to two of his men who were passing by on patrol. "All is quiet?"

"Yes, my lord," they said together.

"Have you seen any sign of Iolo, the cloth merchant?" Gwen said.

"No, my lady."

"Do you know which cart is his?" Gwen said.

One of the guards pointed with his spear towards a cart halfway along one of the rows. It stood a little apart from the others, as if someone had pulled it forward out of line to better access what was inside. "That one, I believe."

Gwen would have tried to peer inside, but the cart had wooden sides and a rear door that locked. "At least we know he hasn't left."

Gareth jerked his head towards the market fairgrounds, indicating they should keep looking. Thirty yards on, they met a third guard, who turned out to be Goch, a trusted soldier. He'd been patrolling between the carts and the fair itself. Gareth asked him about Iolo and Madlen and at last received a positive response.

"Iolo was just here." Frowning, Goch turned on his heel to look back towards the market grounds. "I think he was walking in that direction the last time I saw him." Goch pointed towards the silent booths. "He's come by twice already, each time with arms heavily laden."

"Do you mean to say that he was carrying his goods from his booth to the cart, not the other way around?" Gwen said.

"That's what it looked like to me," Goch said. "He appeared to be in a hurry."

"He's taking advantage of our attention to the music to pack up." Gareth said with a growl. "I'm glad we thought to check on him."

"If he hasn't come back this way, we can still stop him," Gwen said. "What about Madlen?"

"I haven't seen the girl at all," Goch said.

Gwen looked at Gareth. "I wonder where she went? If she knows that you talked to the inn keeper, she has to be afraid of what you discovered."

"Iolo seems to be." Gareth pointed a finger at Iolo's cart. "Don't let him leave, Goch!"

"My lord, I won't."

Gwen and Gareth hurried down the row of deserted booths. The music from the festival pavilion came more clearly here. A drumbeat resounded among the tents, the low bass carrying through the darkness more easily than the higher tones of Meilyr's lyre or Hywel's voice.

"If he's leaving in the middle of the festival," Gwen said, "he's sacrificing an opportunity for sales."

"Better to lose a few pennies than his livelihood entirely," Gareth said. "Or his life."

"With this, I can't see any way that he isn't involved in Gryff's death." Gwen glanced at her husband. His eyes glinted from the light of a torch smoking nearby. Fire was an ever present danger, so torches were posted only on the ends of the rows. "Certainly he's complicit in Madlen's lies."

"I think it's time we asked him," Gareth said.

They turned the corner and spied the merchant backing out of his stall with his arms full of fabric. Gareth was upon him in two strides, catching Iolo by the back of his collar. "There you are."

"My lord! My lord! I have done nothing!"

"You're doing something now," Gareth said.

Iolo set the cloth on the table upon which his wares were displayed during the day, and then Gareth turned him around to face him, his fists catching the lapels of Iolo's coat.

"Why did you lie to me?" Gareth said.

"I didn't! I didn't! What did I lie about?"

"See, now this is the problem." Gareth unclenched his fists, straightening Iolo's collar and jacket with a few swipes of his hands across the man's shoulders. "You're lying to me again. You know exactly what I'm talking about."

"I—"

Gareth cut him off with a glare. "I spoke today to Pawl, the inn keeper, which I suspect you already knew, or else you wouldn't be trying to leave in such a hurry."

Gwen couldn't tell in the torchlight if Iolo's face paled, but his mouth turned down at the same time that his hands started working together in front of him. "Why should I care if you spoke to Pawl?"

Gwen couldn't believe that Iolo was still trying to brazen out his deceit.

Gareth tsked through his teeth. "Pawl says that he met Carys on the day Gryff died. Gryff introduced her as his wife and at no time would Pawl have said that Gryff and Madlen were married. You lied to me. Worse, you lied to Prince Rhun and indirectly to Prince Hywel. Tell me why I shouldn't arrest you right now for obstructing my investigation into Gryff's death?"

Iolo stuttered a reply that was hardly more than gibberish, and then managed to say, "I'm sorry, my lord. You have my deepest apologies. It was not I who lied, or at least not at first. And it certainly wasn't my idea."

"Explain," Gareth said.

The merchant looked down at his toes as if he might find an answer to his difficulties there. Either that or he intended to lie again and was afraid to look Gareth in the eyes when he did it. Gwen stepped closer, hoping that by watching him carefully, she would be able to tell the difference.

Gareth sensed her presence and put out a hand to keep her back. He looked ready for anything, balancing evenly on his feet with his hands loose at his sides.

With a sigh, Iolo scrubbed at his short black hair with both hands, rubbed at his slightly protruding belly, and hitched up his breeches. He was stalling, but eventually he lifted his head and looked directly into Gareth's face. "It was all Madlen's idea. I didn't even know she had told you she was Gryff's wife until you came to the booth to question us."

And then he sprang sideways to race away into the darkness.

18

Gareth

Cursing, Gareth ran after Iolo.

The merchant had something of a belly, but he was fueled by fear and the knowledge that whatever Madlen had or had not done, he would be blamed.

And rightfully so.

Madlen had lied about her relationship with Gryff, but Iolo had supported her lie. And the moment he was caught, he betrayed her to save himself. Gareth's respect for Iolo—never high to begin with—had fallen through the floor.

Gareth thought back to when he and Rhun had questioned Iolo the first time at his booth on the day Gryff had died. When Gareth had relayed the news of Gryff's death and asked to speak to Madlen as his wife, Iolo had given him a blank stare. Despite the fact that Gareth was currently leaping over lines and weaving between tents chasing after the man, he believed Iolo may actually have been telling the truth when he pointed to that moment as his first indication of Madlen's lie. The question now—or one of them—was why Madlen had lied. The more pressing issue was why Iolo had chosen this moment to run.

The merchant puffed ahead of Gareth, heading for the exit to the market grounds, but Gareth's long legs carried him at speed down the aisles after him. Twenty paces from where Goch stood guard, Gareth threw himself forward, grasped Iolo around the shoulders, and brought him to the ground.

When they hit the grass, both men *whuffed* as the air left their lungs. Gareth was fitter and stronger, however, and Iolo, who was pinned to the ground beneath him, could do nothing to rise.

"I'm here, my lord." Goch left his post to give aid.

Chasing after Tangwen all day kept Gwen fit enough not to have fallen far behind either.

Gareth raised himself up enough to put his knee into the small of Iolo's back. He grabbed each of Iolo's wrists, pulling them down and behind him. Gareth accepted a length of rope from Goch with which to tie Iolo's hands. "Why did you run?"

Iolo didn't answer, so Gareth hauled him to his feet and handed him to Goch. "Take him the castle. He can cool his heels beside Alun for a while until he decides to talk."

"What about my stall? My goods—"

"You should have thought of that before you ran," Gareth said. "Where's Madlen?"

"She couldn't bear to stay," Iolo said, suddenly talkative where before he'd hemmed and hawed. Having one's hands tied behind one's back could do that to a man. "Today broke her heart, working without Gryff, so I sent her to my cousin's house. She lives nearby."

Gwen stepped closer to look into Iolo's face. "You did what?"

Even with his hands tied behind his back, Iolo shrugged, giving off an air of surprising nonchalance, given his flight of a moment ago. There were too many contradictions here, and Gareth was having a hard time figuring out which Iolo he was talking to at any given moment: the affable merchant, the clever strategist, or the loving uncle.

"Where?" Gareth said.

Iolo's face went utterly blank, much like it had during that first interview, and Gareth prepared himself to hear a lie—or something Iolo didn't want to tell him. "Uh ... she went to Borth."

"And what was your plan? You decided to pack up your stall and leave Aberystwyth?" Gareth said. "You would do that without selling all your goods?"

Iolo shook his head. "Without Gryff or Madlen—"

Gareth gave a tsk of disgust. "You're trying to tell me that Madlen is so distraught at Gryff's death that she had to be sent away, but that doesn't explain why she lied about being married to him."

"She loved him. She wanted to be married to him."

"Not according to Pawl, the inn keeper," Gareth said.

Iolo made a *what do I know?* motion with his head and upper body. "That's what she told me. I can't help what other people think."

"How could Madlen think Gryff's real wife wouldn't find out?" Gwen said.

"As I said earlier, Madlen wasn't thinking straight. She loved Gryff, and his death tore her apart," Iolo said. "She wanted the respect and sympathy that comes with being a grieving widow, even if that role wasn't rightfully hers."

"Still, she allowed his real widow to believe that he had betrayed her," Gwen said. "It seems extreme."

Iolo sighed. "I know."

Gwen, too, was looking at Iolo like she couldn't believe the words coming out of his mouth. He'd run rather than talk, but nothing he was saying now was worth running over.

"Why did you run?" Gareth asked again.

"I panicked." Iolo looked down at his feet. "Gryff is dead. Madlen loved him but he's dead. Why can't you let the man rest in peace?" He kept his head bowed.

Gareth studied him. Maybe it was finally time to say a little more. "You must understand. Gryff's death was not an accident."

"What?" Iolo's head came up, and his mouth dropped open. "Gryff killed himself after all?"

"No." Gwen had her arms folded across her chest, and she was gazing at Iolo with an expression akin to hostility.

"Then what?" Iolo looked from Gwen to Gareth. The merchant had been doing a great deal of gaping during their conversation. "Don't tell me that you suspect foul play?"

When Gareth neither confirmed nor denied it, Iolo's jaw dropped further. "Surely not! Gryff was an innocent! Why would anyone want to harm him?"

Gwen raised one shoulder. "That's what we are trying to find out."

"Why do you think it might be murder?" Iolo said.

"We have our reasons," Gareth said. "Thus I'm sure you can see how it would look if everyone associated with him departed before we discovered who killed him. The people of Aberystwyth don't yet realize they have a murderer in their midst, but our investigation will begin to attract attention soon. You wouldn't want Prince Hywel to arrest the wrong man, would you?"

Iolo swallowed hard, realizing full well that Gareth meant *him*. "How can you be sure Gryff was murdered? He was found in the millpond."

"He was stabbed in the chest." Gwen was giving no quarter.

Iolo rocked back on his heels. "You can tell that even after a day in the water?"

"Yes." While Gareth hadn't told any of his suspects about the stab wound, he agreed with Gwen that right now was as good a time as any to let the news out. "Such a wound is usually an indication of murder."

Iolo looked suitably chastened and bowed his head again. "I had no idea. I understand your fervor now and apologize even more profoundly for obstructing your investigation in any way."

"I appreciate your apology," Gareth said, "but it doesn't excuse your lies."

Iolo fell to his knees before Gareth. "Please, I beg you. I will stay in Aberystwyth. I will help you in any way I can. Just allow me to return to my stall."

Gareth rubbed his chin. He had only one cell at the castle into which he might put criminals, and that cell was already occupied by Alun. While it might be entertaining to put Alun and Iolo in together, it wasn't ideal. "For now, I am confiscating your horse and cart. I suggest you ask at the monastery for a local boy who could help you sell your wares tomorrow. He might not be knowledgeable about cloth, but he could be an extra hand and give you the ability to leave your stall at times if you needed to."

Iolo's almost collapsed in relief. "Thank you, my lord. I will do that."

Gareth gestured to Goch, who began to untie Iolo's hands. Gwen's face was a thundercloud, though she didn't openly question Gareth's decision to let Iolo go.

Iolo rubbed at his wrists, easing the place where the rope had rubbed.

Gareth turned away and put a gentle hand on Gwen's shoulder, leaning in close to whisper into her ear. "Trust me." Gwen subsided, and Gareth turned back to Iolo. "I have one more question. Gryff had very few possessions. We're looking for his rucksack. Have you seen it?"

"N-no," Iolo said. "Not since he died. In fact, I asked Pawl, the inn keeper, about it the other day. He said he'd put it away for Gryff's wife to claim. Has it gone missing?"

"Yes," Gareth said.

"Perhaps Carys claimed it," Iolo said.

"Perhaps," Gareth said.

Iolo hesitated and then made a swinging motion with his arm. "Well, I'll be off then." He hurried away without looking back.

Gareth pointed to Goch with his chin. "Find his horse and have one of the men bring it to the castle stables. I want his cart watched and if he goes to it, someone must inspect everything he puts in it or brings out."

"Yes, my lord." Goch frowned. "You're really letting him go?"

"Of course not," Gareth said. "We're going to watch him closely. Tell the others on duty that I want to know everything he does, where he goes, and who he talks to. I'll return to the castle and arrange for more men. We'll need three on duty at any one time."

Goch put his heels together and bowed. "It will be done."

As Goch hurried after Iolo, Gwen took in a breath and let it out sharply. "You had me fooled too for a moment."

"Really, Gwen, would I have let him go, just like that?" Gareth said.

"No." She pursed her lips. "Do you think Iolo believes he's walking free?"

"Not if he's as smart as I think he is," Gareth said.

"Did you believe anything he told you?" Gwen said.

"I think we need to reexamine everything that either Iolo or Madlen has said to us, from the first moment Madlen appeared at the chapel," Gareth said. "Iolo appeared surprised to hear about the stab wound. If he was the murderer, you'd think he'd have been expecting it."

"He was surprised that *we* knew about the stab wound," Gwen said. "That isn't the same thing."

"I bow to your superior observational skills." Gareth placed his arm around Gwen's shoulders. They began walking back towards the festival pavilion.

"Will you go to Borth, then?" Gwen said.

"I'll send someone to collect Madlen first thing in the morning," Gareth said.

"The miller's apprentice went to Borth, didn't he?" Gwen said. "Is that too much of a coincidence?"

Gareth laughed. "With this investigation, I can't tell what's reasonable and what isn't. For now, I intend to deliver you back to our daughter, and then I will have a chat with Alun."

19

Gareth

Gareth was slightly disappointed that Gwen didn't protest about him leaving her again, but he wasn't surprised either. Before their marriage, music had been her life. Even now, nine times out of ten he would arrive home to find her soprano voice filling the house or wherever they were staying. He hoped Tangwen would someday share her gifts, and when they had a son, God would bless him with even half the voice Gwalchmai had been given.

Gareth was sorry to be missing the music too, but this murder was dogging him—less with the emotion of some of their previous investigations, but with its mundaneness. He couldn't honestly say that he cared all that much about Gryff's death. Gryff was one more dead man Gareth hadn't known. His obligation was to Prince Hywel, who expected Gareth's best no matter the investigation, and to himself. The circumstances around Gryff's death nagged him. There was something more here—not only about Gryff the man but the reason for his murder—than met the eye, and Gareth needed to know what that was.

And while in the past he'd sometimes had too many suspects, today he didn't have enough. Surely Iolo topped that list, but they still didn't have a good motive for why he might kill his apprentice. Alun had been locked in his cell more to teach him a lesson than because Rhun—or anyone else—believed he'd murdered his brother-in-law. Gareth believed Alun could have. He had the strength for the deed. But especially now that it was clear Gryff hadn't married Madlen, Alun didn't have a motive that Gareth could discern. And more than anything else, that was what was troubling Gareth about the circumstances surrounding this death.

Still, at the very least, Gareth would be pleased to be able to tell Carys that her husband hadn't betrayed her with another woman. Or, Gareth amended to himself, if he did, it wasn't with Madlen.

"Where do you think you're going?" Evan planted himself in front of Gareth.

"Did you think you could give us the slip?" Rhodri braced Gareth's back as if Gareth were a criminal aiming to flee.

Gareth laughed and shook his head. "I assure you, that wasn't my intent."

"You questioned Iolo without us, with only Gwen for backup!" Evan said. "What were you thinking?"

Gareth held up both hands. "I apologize. I'm not used to needing a guard. I forgot."

Rhodri tipped his chin to Evan. "He forgot."

"A likely story." Evan fell in beside Gareth as they began walking up the road to the castle.

"I hear Iolo ran," Rhodri said, settling into an easy stride on Gareth's other side.

"Goch talks too much," Gareth said.

"Just don't do it again." Rhodri had turned serious. "Prince Hywel would have our heads if something happened to you on our watch."

"I apologize," Gareth said. "I honestly didn't sneak away on purpose. I just didn't think about it."

"Well, think next time." Evan remained uncompromising.

The castle, when they reached it, was nearly deserted except for a small contingent of guards necessary to maintain a minimum of defenses. "My lord." The guard at the gate saluted Gareth as he passed through it.

Rhodri stopped to speak to him while Evan and Gareth continued towards one of the far towers opposite the gatehouse. Both Cadwaladr and Cadell had brought more soldiers with them than the occasion warranted, but they weren't enough to take Hywel's castle if the gates were closed. For that they needed siege weapons or archers, such as Hywel had used to take it from Cadwaladr in the first place.

Like Hywel, Gareth both dreaded the day that Cadwaladr broke the final bonds that bound him to King Owain and hoped for it. Gareth was a soldier, and his gut told him that action was almost always better than inaction. Fortunately for Gwynedd, King

Owain, for all his temper, had more patience than either Gareth or Hywel.

The fortress was built in wood with a stone foundation. Hywel had plans to build the whole of it in stone, as his father was doing at Aber, but he didn't yet have the resources to do it. Alun's prison consisted of a single cell at the base of the west tower, accessed by a door with iron bars at the bottom of a shallow set of stairs. It wasn't a true basement, more like half of one, such that if the prisoner stood at the bars, he could be easily seen from almost anywhere in the courtyard. Another guard sat on a stool in the dirt outside the door, chewing on a piece of bread.

"All is well?" Gareth said.

"Yes, my lord." The guard was one of Rhun's, and Gareth didn't know him well. Hywel's men and Rhun's men had spent most of the summer mixed among one another. Many of the older men had served King Owain before they served Hywel or Rhun, and those Gareth knew better. With the murder, on top of the additional duties required by the festival, everybody was being put to use this week.

Gareth motioned with his head towards the keep. "Take a walk, if you would. I'd like to speak to the prisoner."

The guard got to his feet. "Thank you, my lord."

Before he could leave, however, Gareth put out a hand. "Do you know where Alun's sister, Carys, is?"

"I saw her in the hall before my duty started." The guard rolled his shoulders and stretched after sitting for too long.

"If you see her again, send her to me."

"Yes, my lord." The guard bowed and departed.

Leaving Evan to watch his back, though that anyone would threaten him while inside Hywel's own castle was unlikely, Gareth walked down the steps.

"Come to gloat?" Alun stuck his face up to the bars. The cell was cramped, with only six feet from floor to ceiling, so Alun couldn't straighten up all the way. Gareth had seen cells only four feet in height, so in a way Hywel had been generous in the construction of this one.

"Is that any way to speak to your captor?" Gareth said. "If you give me the answers I seek, you may find yourself released."

"You want my confession? You won't get it no matter how long you leave me here. I had nothing to do with Gryff's death."

"But your behavior has not been that of an honest man," Gareth said.

Alun sneered and turned his back on the door. "I have done nothing wrong."

Gareth rested his forearm above the door and looked through the bars, hunching somewhat in order to do so, since, like Alun, he was over six feet. For the first time ever, Gareth was glad that the cell at Aber he'd once occupied had been at the back of the stables. "You assaulted a Prince of Gwynedd."

"Ach." Alun looked at Gareth over his shoulder, a sheepish expression on his face. "I didn't mean anything by it. I was concerned for Carys."

"Who herself assaulted Madlen," Gareth said.

"That woman is a witch!" Alun said. "Gryff may have been many things that I didn't respect, but unfaithful had never been one of them until she came along!"

"And still wasn't."

Alun swung all the way around to face the door. "What?"

"I appreciate your concern for your sister's wellbeing," Gareth said, "so you'll be glad to hear that Madlen lied about her relationship with Gryff. They were never married, and Gryff was never even interested in marrying her."

Alun came forward to clutch the bars. "You speak the truth?"

"I do," Gareth said.

"Then why—why did she say what she did? Why did she tell the abbot and Prince Hywel that she was Gryff's wife?"

"I will attempt to speak with her on the matter in the morning," Gareth said. "For now, Iolo claims that Madlen loved Gryff and couldn't bear to have that love unreturned. She wanted the recognition that would have come with being his wife—that Carys received, in fact, from the abbot once he learned of her prior claim. With the need to bury Gryff quickly, Madlen hoped that nobody would ever uncover her lie."

Alun pulled a long face. "That's mad."

"I can't say I disagree," Gareth said, "but a woman in love can do strange things."

"That's for true." Alun absently scratched his upper lip in thought and then pushed away from the door. In backing up, however, he banged his head on the ceiling. Cursing, he rubbed the top of his head.

"Sorry." Gareth resisted the urge to rub the top of his own head in sympathy.

"Surely you can't think that Carys had anything to do with Gryff's death now that we know he was faithful. He gave her that cross! What reason could she possibly have to kill him?"

"She lied about being in Aberystwyth," Gareth said. "As did you."

"She panicked at being questioned," Alun said.

"There's a lot of that going around." Gareth snorted his disbelief. "If we're going to learn anything about Gryff's death, I need you and Carys to tell me everything that happened in the days before he died. You pretended you hadn't seen him, and I know now that Carys even went to his lodgings with him. There's more you haven't said—"

"What are you doing? Get away from him!" Carys dashed across the courtyard towards them from the keep.

Evan put out a hand to block her, and Gareth took a few steps up the stairs. At the sight of them both, Carys pulled up, her mouth forming an 'ach' of surprise. Her feet faltered. "I'm sorry, my lord. I didn't see you there—"

"Who did you think you saw?" Gareth said.

Carys swallowed hard.

Gareth signaled to Evan to let her pass. "You thought I was Iolo. I can't decide if I should be offended that you think we look alike."

"It was dark—" Carys reached the top step.

Gareth stepped to one side so she could descend to the door.

When she reached Alun, her brother said, "Sir Gareth reports that Madlen never married Gryff, Carys. She may have wanted to, but he didn't have anything to do with her."

Gareth would have qualified that sentence with *that we know,* and he had wanted to be the one to tell Carys the news, but now that it was done, he wasn't sorry.

Carys stared at Alun, her face paling where before it had been red with anger at seeing Gareth (or Iolo, as she had thought) talking to Alun. "She what?"

"Madlen lied about their relationship," Gareth said. "We still aren't sure why, though Iolo says that she loved him and couldn't resist telling us they were married for the attention it brought her."

"That attention was rightfully mine," Carys said.

"Nobody is arguing with that," Gareth said, "and you may have noted that once you arrived at the monastery, the abbot treated you well."

Carys bowed her head, somewhat chastened. "What does Madlen herself say?"

"I haven't spoken to her," Gareth said. "Apparently she was so distraught that Iolo sent her to a relation's house in a nearby village."

"Not to Goginan?" Carys put a hand to her heart.

"No."

Then Carys' expression turned fierce again, not yet ready to let go of her anger and righteousness. "She had no right to say those things. She had no right to break my heart."

"I know, Carys," Gareth said, "and I regret the role I played in this. Still, you lied too."

"Excuse me?" Carys froze in the act of reaching for Alun's hand. He had stuck it through the bar of his cell so she could grasp it in solidarity.

"You were in Aberystwyth the day Gryff died. Pawl, the inn keeper, spoke to you," Gareth said. "He told us of it, and your brother has all but admitted it."

"Oh." Carys looked down at her feet.

"Now is the time to speak the truth, Carys," Gareth said. "Gryff saw Alun the day before and gave the cross to him to give to you. But then you came to Aberystwyth to see him rather than waiting until Sunday as usual. Why?"

Carys bit her lip and still refused to look at Gareth.

Alun signed. "Tell him, Carys. You can't hurt Gryff now, and it might help Sir Gareth get to the truth of all of this."

"I wanted Gryff to take the cross back to whomever he'd bought it from and get his money back," she said. "I could do so much with it."

Now they were getting somewhere. "He refused?" Gareth said.

"He said that he didn't buy it. He found it and didn't know whose it was," Carys said.

"Did you believe him?" Gareth said.

Carys shook her head morosely. "I assumed he stole it."

The truth, finally. "What do you think now?" Gareth said.

"I don't know," Carys said. "He'd never been a thief. He never cared about money. I want to believe there was something more to it, but he wouldn't tell me what that was."

"But you're still wondering?" Gareth said. "The C and G do represent your names."

"Half of all babies born carry names that begin with those letters," Carys said.

She wasn't far wrong. Alun knew it too. He sighed and said, "Madlen said the cross had been hers. What if she was telling the truth? What if he stole it from her?"

Carys frowned. "She said she gave it to him."

The truth appeared to be as elusive as ever. Gareth motioned to the guard, who'd returned and was standing out of earshot, to come closer, and then he held out his hand for the key to Alun's cell.

"What are you doing?" Alun said as Gareth unlocked the door.

"Letting you go," Gareth said.

"Why?" Alun said.

"You didn't murder Gryff," Gareth said. "Tonight that's all I care about."

20

Rhun

As the music ended and the evening approached midnight, the crowd began to break into smaller groups. Gratifyingly, the majority of people weren't ready to return to their lodgings or tents. Several bards had broken out their instruments to form an impromptu concert around Meilyr and Gwalchmai.

For his part, Rhun kept a wary eye on his brother, who circulated through the crowd, Mari on his arm, accepting congratulations from all quarters. Rhun felt his own blood pumping through him in a way that was typical of a successful performance—usually in his case he felt this way when a fight had gone well. For Hywel, it was when he'd held a crowd in the palm of his hand, which meant that tonight he had to be on top of the world.

Then Gareth appeared near the high table and bent to whisper in Gwen's ear. She held the sleeping Tangwen in her lap, but she turned to look up in evident surprise at her husband's words. Rhun reached them in half a dozen long strides, which he hoped weren't too conspicuous. "What is it?"

"Maybe everything," Gareth said, and gave a summary of his conversation with Carys and Alun. Rhun had already heard from Gwen about Madlen's lies. Strange as they had been, he could almost understand them. As to the rest of the lies they'd been told, he feared he would never make a good king because the common mind eluded him.

"You need to find your bed," Rhun said.

Gareth opened his mouth to protest, but Rhun looked darkly at him, and Gareth snapped his lips together. When he opened his mouth again, he said, "I bow to your command, my lord. I will escort Gwen and the babies home—Mari too if she will consent to come. I'm asleep on my feet." Gareth pointed with his chin to Prince Hywel. "See if you can get your brother to return to the monastery once he comes down from his mountain top."

Rhun smiled. "I'll do my best."

Gwen shifted Tangwen to her shoulder and rose to her feet. "Your father seems happy, my lord."

"My father had the foresight to put Hywel under Meilyr's tutelage." Rhun directed a quick nod in Gwen's direction. "So much joy has come from that simple act."

"It changed my life," Gwen said. "You could even say that it set the course of my life."

"And mine," Gareth said.

Rhun nodded. "I will say your goodbyes to my brother. You'll be of no use to him if you can't think straight, either of you."

As Rhun looked back to Hywel, thinking to detach Mari from him, he felt a tug on his elbow. Turning, he saw that

Angharad's maid had darted towards him from out of the darkness beyond the pavilion, and was already halfway back to it. Frowning, he followed her past the last tent pole and tether line.

"My lord." The woman's forehead was practically on the ground in her obeisance.

Rhun raised her up. "What is it?"

"My lady Angharad asks to speak with you."

Rhun looked at her cautiously. "Why doesn't she return to the pavilion?"

"She fears her uncle's wrath," the woman said.

Rhun growled in dismay. "Lead on."

He followed the maid towards Cadell's encampment. He'd collected Angharad from her tent here earlier that day, but it seemed as if their stroll among the stalls had taken place weeks ago instead of merely hours. As they closed in on the entrance, the woman darted off, this time towards the trees that lined the river. She stopped in the darkness fifty feet from the nearest tent.

Rhun hurried to catch up with her, and when he did, Angharad detached herself from the trunk of an oak tree. She was wrapped in a dark cloak that hid all but her pale face. "My dear." Rhun took the hand she offered him. "What are you doing here?"

"I need you to take me away."

Rhun swallowed and moved closer, lowering his voice. "Why? Are you in danger?"

"My uncle knows I've been speaking to you."

"I know he does. He gave me permission to court you," Rhun said.

"That's not it." Angharad looked at the ground. "He's been asking questions about you. I fear he is using me to spy on you."

Rhun suppressed a smile at her earnestness. "It's all right, Angharad. It is no less than I expected."

"When he questioned me this evening, I became flustered. He knows I'm lying to him."

"What could you possibly lie to him about?" Rhun said.

"I denied that I told you about his men hidden to the south of Aberystwyth," Angharad said.

Rhun made a disgusted sound at the back of his throat. "Angharad, he expected you to tell me. He wanted Prince Hywel to know."

"What?" she said. "Why would he want that?"

"*Cariad,* this is a game we are playing. I know it doesn't feel like it, and perhaps that isn't the right word for what's going on, but this is a contest. Your uncle wants Ceredigion back. My father took it from his older brother, Anarawd, as spoils of war, and as payment for his troubles after the 1136 war. The fifty men he brought were not meant to violate the peace but to show his defiance and strength. We were meant to learn of them. He may even have used you as a way to let us know about them without having to be more obvious."

Angharad looked aghast. "He used me?" Then her expression hardened. "Here I was concerned about your safety and mine, and my uncle is probably laughing at me right now."

"I don't think he's laughing," Rhun said, "especially not at the sight of my uncle Cadwaladr, who also brought a small army with him."

As soon as he said this, Rhun wished he could take the words back. He didn't want to use Angharad as her uncle had, as a conduit between the two of them. He ought to be grateful that he'd impressed Angharad enough with his noble character that she would come to him. He brought both her hands up to his chest and looked down into her upturned face. "I would take you away from here, but I can't defy my father, and I have not asked him for his permission to marry you yet. But with your permission, I will."

Angharad's eyes shone. "Yes! Yes! Oh my lord, yes!"

Tentatively, Rhun bent forward and kissed Angharad gently on the lips. Her eyes widened at first, but then she closed them as he continued to kiss her. After a moment, he took a step back. "I will watch until you are safely back in your tent."

But Angharad wasn't having that. She launched herself at him, throwing her arms around his neck. Her joy was infectious, and he caught her up and spun her around. He wasn't sure how this had happened so fast, but he wasn't sorry either. His stepmother, Cristina, was going to be very disappointed.

Rhun set Angharad down, and she eased back from him a little, just a step, but it was enough to cause him some disappointment of his own. Still, they couldn't remain much longer together here under the trees. They weren't officially betrothed, and until they were, he had to be careful with her.

"Oh, I just remembered," Angharad said. "There was something else I thought you should know: my uncle has placed a spy among you."

Rhun raised his eyebrows. "I would be surprised if he hadn't."

"No, no. He's not an ordinary person," she said. "He travels far and wide for Cadell, and I know for a fact that he has met in secret with one of Prince Cadwaladr's men, if not Cadwaladr himself, as a way to pass messages between my uncle and yours without anyone knowing."

"Cadell and Cadwaladr are working together?" Rhun said.

Angharad looked nonplussed. "You must have suspected they'd been involved in the past."

"Cadwaladr had Cadell's brother killed," Rhun said.

"And who do you think orchestrated that?" Angharad said. "My uncle, of course. He hated his brother."

"You know this for certain?"

"As certain as I can be. At the very least, they are working together now, despite the faces they show in the pavilion. Cadwaladr's man in Ceredigion is a half-Dane named Erik. He has been passing messages to Cadell through my uncle's man. Much of the purpose of their arrival here in Ceredigion was to finally meet."

Rhun felt an understanding growing within him. "So the two armies aren't for the purpose of attacking Hywel and Aberystwyth, but as a show of force and commitment to one another?"

"Unless they intend to join forces here in Ceredigion, but with King Owain's arrival, that seems unlikely, don't you think?" Angharad said. "I confess to several sleepless nights worrying about it."

Rhun rubbed his forehead. "Does Cadell have a target other than Ceredigion?"

"Yes, of course," Angharad said. "He hates the Normans to the south even more than your father. I think, too, that he believes Ceredigion will always be there for him, easily conquerable. For now, he appreciates his alliance with King Owain because it protects his northern border, and he is loath to open a war on two fronts at the same time."

"What could be Cadwaladr's purpose in all this?" Rhun said. "If Cadell gets Ceredigion, what benefit is it to him?"

"That I do not know," Angharad said. "Perhaps he plans to betray my uncle later."

"That I can believe," Rhun said. "Do you know the name of this man who spies for Cadell and meets in secret with Erik?"

"That's what I've been trying to tell you," Angharad said. "It's the dead man's master, Iolo, the cloth merchant from the fair."

"I am troubled, Gruffydd," Rhun said to his captain a short while later.

Gruffydd had tailed Rhun to Cadell's encampment, waited through Rhun's conversation with Angharad, and fell into step beside him once he headed back towards the lights.

By the time Rhun had seen Angharad safely back to her tent and returned to the pavilion, however, all that remained were servants and men too drunk to find their proper beds. Given the warm weather, it was a simple matter to pillow one's head on one's cloak and go to sleep. A few inquiries revealed that Hywel had escorted Mari back to the monastery, King Owain had also retired for the night to his tent in the adjacent field, and Gareth, of course, had been sent away by Rhun himself.

"Murder should always be troubling, my lord," Gruffydd said.

Rhun shook his head. "I can't say that what I just learned has anything to do with the murder, but it is a cause for concern." Rhun briefly relayed to his captain what Angharad had told him. He didn't hesitate to do so: if Gruffydd was going to betray him, then Rhun had no business as a ruler of men and would never trust anyone again.

"If Iolo spies for Cadell, it is hardly a hanging matter, in truth," Gruffydd said. "Your brother and father have many spies, the Lady Gwen among them."

"While what you say is true," Rhun said, "I do wonder what else Iolo has lied to us about. In the morning, Gareth intends to send riders to Borth to collect Madlen. What if he sent her away so she wouldn't waver under our questions? What if she aids in her uncle's work too."

"In which case we have even less reason to believe anything he has so far told us," Gruffydd said. "May I make a suggestion, my lord?"

"Please," Rhun said.

"Sleep feels elusive to me, but perhaps less so to others. Would this be an opportune moment to search Iolo's cart for evidence against him?"

"Evidence that he spies for Cadell?"

"That would be a start," Gruffydd said. "Up until tonight, we had no motive for murder for him, but now ..."

"Gryff came searching for my brother on the afternoon he died." A chill ran down Rhun's spine that had nothing to do with the cool breeze that swept through the field, rustling the flags and tents all around them. "He could have discovered something about Iolo's activities that got him killed."

"A motive, as you say, my lord," Gruffydd said.

Having proposed marriage to Angharad and been accepted, Rhun had been unlikely to sleep either, but with something solid to do, he picked up the pace, heading towards the market fair. When they reached the place where the merchants' carts were parked, he found guards on duty, Goch still among them. Watches in the middle of the night were usually dull, but Goch seemed alert enough. He stood with his hip propped against the side of the last cart on the end. At Rhun's approach, he straightened. "My prince."

"Which cart is Iolo's?" Rhun said by way of a greeting.

"Third one from the end," Goch said. "Some of the merchants have moved theirs around tonight, looking to bring them closer to their stalls to restock, but they've put them back."

"Iolo has not come himself?" Rhun said.

"Not since Gareth let him go. He went straight to his stall and has not left it," Goch said. "I have two men watching, and more are posted at both entrances to the market grounds. Sir Gareth was very specific in his orders. Iolo went in and has not come out."

"Good," Rhun said. "Let's have a look at his cart."

Goch raised his eyebrows, but then quickly rearranged his expression. Rhun thought he knew what that was about, and said, "I may not have the experience of some, but I am loath to wake my brother or Gareth, and this needs doing."

"Yes, my lord," Goch said with somewhat more enthusiasm.

Rhun didn't often feel he had to justify his actions to his men. His authority in battle had been hard won (and was deserved, though he would never say it), but he had never been so actively involved in a murder investigation before. He could appreciate Goch's skepticism, even as it annoyed him.

The cart had been built up on both sides in wood, almost like a little house. It had openings in the sides like a peddler's wagon, for easier access to the wares, and an actual door at the back with hinges and a pin lock. Such locks were designed to stop sneak thieves, however, not determined princes, and Rhun broke the lock off with his belt knife, sparing Goch the duty. If this was a mistake, it was going to be Rhun's mistake.

The door swung open, and the three men peered inside. Rhun could see almost nothing and snapped his finger for a torch. He wouldn't take it inside the cart, but it could shed light on the interior if held at the door. When Goch returned with it, Rhun put a hand on Gruffydd's shoulder to boost himself inside, hunching in the narrow space between the two heavily laden sets of shelves on either side. It was like being in a pantry, except it was in a cart.

Although most of the stacks were neatly ordered, reflecting what Rhun perceived to be Iolo's character, some of the stacks of cloth had fallen off the shelves or had been tossed haphazardly on the floor, as if Iolo had left in haste. Gareth had implied as much earlier, since they'd caught Iolo trying to empty his stall so as to leave Aberystwyth.

Rhun pawed through the various woolens and bolts of brightly colored woven goods, finding nothing that struck him as out of the ordinary. He moved to the front of the cart, finding an open trunk in which was stacked more cloth. After a moment, Rhun realized that he was looking at actual clothing, which belonged to Iolo and Madlen personally. Feeling slightly sick at his intrusion, he searched through their belongings as quickly as he could. Other than an ornate looking glass, Rhun found nothing of particular value or which would implicate Iolo in spying.

"What is that, my lord?" Gruffydd said.

Rhun turned to show the mirror to Goch and Gruffydd.

"Odd that she didn't take it with her," Goch said.

Rhun hesitated, looking back into the trunk again. Two feet deep, it was full of clothing, and in fact, most of that clothing had to be Madlen's. A tendril of concern curled in Rhun's belly. "What if you're right, Gruffydd? What if she didn't go anywhere after all?"

"Then why did Iolo say she did—?" Goch broke off, and the men stared at each other. Spying was one thing. If Iolo had murdered Gryff that was another, but murdering his niece was something else entirely.

Gruffydd cleared his throat. "Surely not?"

"You're thinking what I'm thinking. Don't deny it." But then Rhun frowned and crouched even lower to look underneath the shelf to the left of the trunk. A strap stuck out from behind a stack of linen. Turning himself sideways so more of the torchlight could shine past him, Rhun reached for it and pulled it out. It was a crude rucksack, tied at the top with rope.

"Could that be Gryff's?" Goch said.

"One can only hope," Rhun said.

Rhun had cut the lock with nerves jangling, not so much regretting the commitment, but what he feared might be embarrassment when he discovered nothing. Now he climbed down from the cart, the rucksack over his shoulder, his anticipation rising. Gruffydd closed the door and rigged the pin lock so it closed, even if it would never lock again.

Rhun walked to an adjacent cart with an empty bed and set the bag in the back. While Goch brought the torch close, Rhun untied the strings and laid out its contents. They consisted of spare breeches and shirt, a spoon, and a small box which when opened proved to contain salt. It was a valuable spice but hardly worth killing over.

"Nothing." Gruffydd picked through the few items himself.

"This has to be Gryff's bag," Goch said. "Iolo took it from the tavern."

Rhun rubbed his chin and then dropped his hand with a sigh. "I have no doubt of that, though why we don't know." He gestured to the few possessions. "This is hardly worth stealing, much like Gryff's purse."

"My lord, should we question Iolo?" Gruffydd said.

"We should," Rhun said, "but he is safe for now. It's late, and that can wait until morning. Madlen's whereabouts are of greater concern. We need to find her."

"Sir Gareth was to send to Borth for her tomorrow. We'll know more then," Gruffydd said.

"I feel strongly that we don't want to wait that long," Rhun said.

21

Gwen

Gwen lay in bed, staring up at the ceiling, having woken before the dawn and been unable to go back to sleep. She'd been so tired after returning from the festival that she had fallen asleep right away, but now her mind spun. Her thoughts were focused less on what they'd learned from Iolo, and more on the danger Cadwaladr posed to Gareth. While not exactly dismissing her concerns, her husband had underplayed the threat as more of the same kind of peril he always faced.

But she'd seen the worry in Hywel's eyes, even as he denied there was anything to worry about. And he'd ordered Rhodri and Evan to watch Gareth's back. The prince's actions belied his words. She was almost afraid to start the day.

Then she gasped and sat up. Maybe because her attention had strayed from the investigation, her mind had been free to work on its own. "The cross!"

Gwen had spoken too loudly, given the silence of the hour. Tangwen rolled over on her pallet, which lay beside Gwen and Gareth's own. Elspeth lay beyond her. The girl slept on, and after a few heartbeats, Tangwen did too.

Gwen put out a hand to the space beside her, but Gareth had gone. Then a door banged below her. It was Gareth's departure rather than her thought that had woken her. Either way, Gwen was awake now, and she scrambled out of bed and threw a dress over her shift. Gareth couldn't be allowed to leave without hearing what she had to say.

Gwen clattered down the stairs and burst through the door that led to the courtyard. Gareth stood talking to Prior Rhys and Prince Hywel, and all three men held their horses' reins. Evan and Rhodri stood nearby as they had all day yesterday. She hoped that some of them had managed to sleep a little.

The sun had risen but wasn't yet peeking over the trees that lined the road outside the monastery. The clouds of yesterday had dissipated without releasing their rain. It was going to be another hot day.

Gareth turned as she appeared, a smile on his face even though she was sure she presented a shocking sight, similarly to yesterday when she'd confronted the two monks by the river: her hair was half undone, still in its night braid, and she had no shoes on her feet. She was glad the abbot hadn't risen yet.

Then Gareth's smile faltered. "What's wrong? Is Tangwen—"

Like any parent, his thoughts had flown to fever and illness, which could come upon a child without notice. Gwen shook her head. "No, no. She's fine. This is about the cross."

"What about the cross?" Gareth said.

"If Madlen was never married to Gryff, and he didn't love her, would she have given the cross to him no matter how much she loved him? And if she did, would he have accepted it only to turn around and give it to Carys?" Gwen gazed up at her husband.

Gareth took both of Gwen's arms in his, holding her. "No, she wouldn't have."

"And if Madlen didn't give the cross to Gryff as she said, and Gryff didn't find it as he told Carys, how did he acquire it?" Gwen said. "Did he steal it like Carys thought? And if so, from whom?"

Hywel picked at his lower lip. "From the one who killed him."

"Madlen came to the chapel feigning that she was Gryff's wife, with the purpose of stealing his purse," Gareth said. "She could have been hoping the cross was in it."

"Except it wasn't, because he'd already given it to Carys," Gwen said. "Which makes the cross Madlen's to begin with."

"What is so important about the cross that Madlen pretended to be Gryff's wife to get it back?" Hywel said.

"I think I can answer that." Rhun's voice carried to them as he, Gruffydd, and Goch appeared from underneath the gatehouse archway, having dismounted before the gate rather than wake the house with the clatter of hooves on the cobbles. Everyone turned to him.

"You look like you've been to hell and back," Hywel said, amusement in his voice, perhaps still half-drunk from last night's performance. "Have you even slept?"

"No," Rhun said, "and it's a good thing we didn't."

"Where have you been?" Hywel said.

"Borth," Rhun said. "Looking for Madlen."

Gareth raised his eyebrows. "You saved me the trip, my lord, but there was no need—"

"There was every need. Angharad told me last night that her uncle had placed a spy among us. I told her we knew it already. But then she named him. It's Iolo."

Rhun paused for his words to sink in.

"Iolo is spying for Cadell," Hywel said, not as a question.

Rhun smirked and then said, "What if Gryff carried messages for him? We know he was good at it. Even Alun said so."

"But what does this have to do with the cross?" Prior Rhys said.

"Gryff could have discovered the truth behind what he was doing for Iolo," Gwen said. "Everything that has happened since has been to protect that secret."

"I still don't understand," Prior Rhys said.

Gwen took in a breath. "The letters 'C' and 'G' were etched on the back of the cross that Prince Rhun took from Madlen and Carys yesterday. Carys said the letters represented 'Carys' and 'Gryff' because that is what Gryff told her. Madlen claimed they were the names of her grandparents, but if Iolo really spies for Cadell, then they more likely stand for Cadell ap Gruffydd."

"Gryff took the cross as proof of Iolo's spying and gave it to Alun to give to Carys for safekeeping," Gareth said.

Prior Rhys ran a hand through his very short hair. "So if Iolo is Cadell's spy, and Gryff discovered what he was up to and objected, that would be grounds for murder."

"Yes, it would," Hywel said.

"Gryff must have been terrified when Carys appeared in Aberystwyth wearing it," Gwen said. "No wonder he sent her away so quickly."

"He came looking for me shortly after that." Hywel said. "Do we think he decided to tell me what he knew?"

"That makes sense to me," Gareth said. "What did you find in Borth, my lord?"

"Not Madlen," Prince Rhun said. "If we think Iolo killed Gryff because he threatened to expose him, what might he have done to Madlen?"

"I need to get to the market grounds now." Gareth pulled Gwen to him in a brief hug and kissed the top of her head. Then he mounted beside Evan and Rhodri. "We'll start with his booth." They turned their horses' heads and were away.

Hywel turned back to the others. "What are we missing? Is it really that simple? When has a merchant's spying been worth killing over? You spied for me, Gwen, and I don't see any of the lords whose castles you frequented clamoring for your head. We all take it as a given that any stranger in our midst isn't to be trusted. That doesn't mean we don't provide hospitality. We just keep our secrets the best we can."

"There's another element to it," Prince Rhun said. "Angharad told me that Iolo passed messages from Cadell to Cadwaladr through that half-Dane, Erik."

The others gaped at Rhun, and Hywel said, "Cadell was working with Cadwaladr?"

"She says they plotted Anarawd's death together," Prince Rhun said.

"If Gryff had proof, that would be something worth killing over," Hywel said. "Both Cadell and Cadwaladr have worked very hard to keep that connection hidden. Cadell's brothers would revolt if they knew."

"That's all very well and good," Gwen said, "but why would Gryff have cared what Iolo was doing? By all accounts, he was a dreamer. He didn't know one day from the next. What was it about Iolo's work that caused him to go to such lengths to disrupt it?"

"He hated Cadwaladr," Hywel said. "That's what Alun told Gareth."

Prince Rhun seemed about to say something, but then he looked down at his feet.

"What is it?" Hywel took a step towards his brother, a 'v' of concern between his brows.

"What if Angharad is in real danger from her uncle?" Rhun said.

"If you're worried, go find her," Hywel said, "but I don't share your concern. Cadell knows of your interest in her, but like most men, he underestimates her intelligence. He doesn't even know to fear what she knows. That's why women make such good spies."

"I hope you're right," Rhun said. "When we're done here, I'm going to speak to Father about her hand. I would bring her back to Gwynedd with me."

Gwen's eyes widened. She hadn't realized his relationship with Angharad had progressed that far. It seemed Rhun knew a thing or two about keeping a secret too.

The thought prompted her to put up a hand to the others. "Wait. Just wait. I've had an idea. Don't go anywhere until I get back." She ran towards the kitchen, knowing even as she did so that the monks who cooked in it would be less than happy to see her appear in the doorway.

When she reached it, however, she found Prince Hywel on her heels. "Tell me what you're thinking, Gwen."

"I wasn't going to say anything because it's probably nothing," Gwen said, "but do you remember how Gryff fetched the gatekeeper's dinner on the day he died?"

"Yes," Hywel said. "So what?"

"Why did he do that?"

"Because he was Gryff," Hywel said. "He was a dreamer, not unkind."

"I think there was more to it. He was so anxious to find you that he trekked from Aberystwyth, to the castle, to here, but then he takes the time to carry the gatekeeper's dinner to him? I don't think so."

Gwen stepped through the kitchen doorway to find the head cook three paces away, glaring at her, though his expression softened the instant he saw Hywel at her right shoulder.

"Please, brother," Gwen said, "were you here when the dead man, Gryff, asked to bring Sion's dinner to him the night before he died?"

"I was."

"Did Gryff seem anxious to you at the time?" Gwen said.

"Did he seem anxious?" The cook scoffed. "His eyes flicked from one corner to the next as if he was trying to see the whole kitchen at once. If we had anything worth stealing in here besides food I would have taken him for a thief."

"Could you tell us what he did while he was here?" Gwen said.

"He collected Sion's dinner," the cook said.

"What did he do while he waited for you to fix it?" Hywel said.

"Oh ... well ... I sent him to the pantry to fetch a tray on which to carry Sion's dinner," the cook said. "By the time he returned, I had it ladled out, and I sent him on his way."

"May we have a look in the pantry?" Hywel said.

"Of course, my lord. It's this way."

The cook pointed them to a narrow doorway covered by a curtain. Hywel swept it aside, revealing a small room lined with shelves. It was full of dishware, not food.

"What are we looking for?" Hywel rubbed at his chin, scruffy this morning as he hadn't taken the time to shave.

"Anything out of the ordinary or out of place." Gwen began moving aside the plates and bowls and upturning pitchers to see if anything had been left inside them. "If Gryff left something here, it would have had to have been small—probably small enough to fit inside his purse."

Hywel looked through the items on the other side of the pantry, and then they met in the middle, frustrated.

"You know, we should ask the cook—" Hywel began.

But then the man himself appeared in the doorway. He held out a signet ring. "Are you looking for this?"

Gwen put a hand to her heart. "Dear God."

The cook dropped the ring into Hywel's palm. Hywel's hand shook slightly as he showed it to Gwen, and she felt the same shakiness inside her. Her heart started beating so hard it felt like it was about to explode out her ears.

"The serving boy found that not half an hour ago," the cook said. "The abbot hasn't risen yet, and I was going to show it to him, but I'm thinking that this might be what you were looking for."

"Do you know to whom it belongs?" Hywel's hand formed a fist around the ring. It had to be burning a hole in his palm.

"Of course, my lord," the cook said.

Hywel nodded and took Gwen's elbow, guiding her out of the pantry, through the kitchen, and back into the courtyard.

She walked with him in a daze. "Do you think Iolo knows Gryff took the ring as well as the cross?"

"I'm certain he does," Hywel said.

"If Gryff found out what Iolo was doing and confronted him—" Gwen said.

"I don't know. I don't know what happened." Hywel kept walking.

They reached Prince Rhun and the others, and Hywel silently handed the ring to his brother.

Rhun took it, stared at the signet for a moment, and then looked at Hywel. "What if the letters don't stand for Cadell ap Gruffydd at all—" Like Gwen, he seemed to have trouble finishing his sentences.

"—but for Cadwaladr ap Gruffydd," Hywel said.

"If Uncle Cadwaladr was conspiring with Cadell to take Ceredigion from you," Rhun said, "he wouldn't want any hint of a connection between the two of them to come to light any more than Cadell would."

Hywel nodded. "Gryff could have died because he was willing to stand up and say there was one."

"And he had proof," Gwen said.

22

Gareth

Gareth raced towards the fairgrounds, feeling as if the hounds of hell were at his heels. To know that Iolo had pulled the wool over their eyes so completely—told them lie after lie, probably laughing to himself all the while—burned in his gut. He could stand being wrong. He could even admit it when he was. But he hated being played the fool. And Iolo had played them.

"Almost there, Gareth," Evan said.

Gareth nodded. His friend knew what he was thinking. He might even have been thinking it himself, except that he'd joined the investigation only yesterday, so he hadn't experienced the particular joy of interviewing Iolo or Madlen. Gareth ground his teeth as they splashed across the ford of the Ystwyth River.

Dawn had come and gone, and people were stirring, though fewer than would have been if this were a regular market fair instead of a music festival. Like most of the festival-goers, Gareth had found his bed after midnight. That was fewer than six hours ago. Even merchants whose livelihood depended on an open stall were reluctant to rise.

Rhodri's stomach growled, causing both Gareth and Evan to look at him. Rhodri shrugged. "I can't help it."

"Rhodri has more need to eat than a fifteen-year-old," Evan said to Gareth. "We've grown used to it."

Gareth barked a laugh, and then he slowed his horse to a trot as they approached the entrance to the market fair. He was pleased to see that the men on duty were upright and alert as they should be. The guard would have changed two hours ago in the gray of first light.

They stopped at the entrance and dismounted.

"All quiet here, my lord," one of the guards said. Gareth didn't know his name, but he wore the livery of King Owain.

"Have you seen Iolo this morning?" Gareth said.

"He slept in his stall last night and has not come out," the man said.

"Good," Gareth said. "We'll go check on h—"

A scream split the air—not of joy but of pain and shock. It went on, long and caterwauling.

Gareth pointed at the guards. "Stay there! It could be a diversion."

They had started moving but immediately subsided at Gareth's command. Gareth, Rhodri, and Evan raced down the aisle towards the sound, which had abruptly cut off. They pulled up, having arrived at the aisle that led to Iolo's tent. Gareth didn't see the two guards who were meant to watch the tent itself. Everyone had been so diligent this week, knowing how important the festival was to Prince Hywel, that their absence stood out starkly.

They could be responding to the scream except Gareth was pretty sure the scream had come from somewhere near here, maybe even from Iolo's tent. The air around them still rang with the force of it, even though it had ceased.

"My lord?" Evan whispered. "Where is everyone?"

"That is a very good question," Gareth said.

The food stalls were closer to the market entrance. Back here, nothing moved but a tent flap in the morning breeze. None of the merchants had even made the attempt to open this early. Yesterday their tables had been out at dawn. But again, it had been a late night.

A tent flap flipped up to Gareth's right, and the face of a frightened man looked out. "What was that—?"

Gareth put a finger to his lips, and the man stopped talking. Evan made a soothing gesture with one hand. "Go back inside. We'll take care of it."

"Yes, sir." The tent flap dropped back.

They reached Iolo's stall, and Gareth made a circling motion in the air with his finger to indicate that the three of them should surround Iolo's tent on all sides. As the others moved away to do his bidding, he approached the entrance. It was closed. The grass under his feet made him completely silent, which for some reason he urgently felt he should remain. A crack had opened between the two pieces of fabric that made up the door, and he peered inside.

Iolo lay on the ground near the entrance, his face turned away from Gareth. It was hard to see what was wrong with him in the dim light that came through the fabric of the tent, but Gareth had a pretty good notion that he was dead, especially given who else occupied the tent: a large, blond man lay on his back on the ground. He was wrestling with Madlen, who was on top of him, wielding a knife, her screams having settled into a low grunting as she fought to stab him. With the name, *Erik,* exploding in the forefront of his mind, Gareth launched himself through the tent opening, caught Madlen around the shoulders, and rolled with her off of Erik.

Unfortunately, the tent was a very confined space. Rather than rolling all the way over, which would have brought Gareth on top of Madlen, their roll was impeded by a stack of crates, and Madlen ended up on top of Gareth, still with the knife in her hand and murder in her eye.

"No!" she said as he grasped her right wrist with both hands to stop her from skewering him. "He killed my uncle!"

Gareth managed to shout Evan's name, even as he took a surprisingly strong left cross to the jaw from Madlen's other fist, which he hadn't been paying attention to. Fortunately, that one punch was all Madlen had in her. Just as Rhodri and Evan invaded the tent from opposite directions, Rhodri having half-ripped his side of the tent open, Gareth managed to twist his leg around both of Madlen's and flip her over.

Rhodri and Evan converged on Gareth's position while Madlen continued to buck and twist beneath him. Evan removed the knife from her hand, and then Gareth and Rhodri flipped her onto her front and pulled her arms behind her back to tie them at the wrists.

"I didn't do anything." Madlen gasped the words into the grass. "You don't understand."

Rubbing at his jaw, knowing that Rhodri and Evan were smirking at him for allowing a woman to get the better of him, Gareth stood up. Erik was sitting up too and holding his left bicep in his right hand as blood seeped between his fingers.

"What are you doing here?" Gareth said.

Erik gave him an exasperated look. "It was a mistake to come, obviously."

"The men meant to watch the stall are down, unconscious but not dead," Rhodri said.

"Held around the neck from behind, I'd guess," Evan said. "We would have come inside whether or not you called."

Gareth looked at Erik. Only a strong man could have subdued those men.

Erik shrugged. "My doing. Sorry, but I had to see Iolo."

"How did you get past the guards at the entrance to the market grounds?" Gareth said.

"I have a stall owner who's a friend. I spent the night in the market."

Erik was being surprisingly talkative, which made Gareth very wary. Breathing more easily now, though his jaw throbbed and would surely bruise and swell shortly, Gareth bent to where Iolo lay sprawled on the grass and put his fingers to the merchant's throat, feeling for a beat. It wasn't there, which Gareth had known would be the case before he touched him. Iolo wasn't breathing, and the residue of vomit around his mouth and on the ground beside him told Gareth the cause of death. He'd been poisoned.

Gareth looked back to Evan, who held out the knife.

Somehow Gareth wasn't surprised to see a notch in the narrow blade, which had been worn thin from repeated sharpening.

Gareth squatted in front of Madlen. "This is the knife that murdered Gryff. Would you care to tell me why you took his life?"

"What did you say?" Madlen gaped at him.

Now it was Gareth's turn to be surprised. "Didn't your uncle tell you?"

"No! No! Gryff drowned!" Still on her belly, Madlen was in near hysterics.

Gareth swiveled on the ball of his foot and held up the knife up to Erik's eyes. "I'm surprised a warrior such as yourself wouldn't have exchanged this for a newer blade long ago."

"It isn't mine either." Erik pointed to the leather sheath at Iolo's waist, which was ancient, weathered, and worn. And empty. Gareth handed the knife back to Evan. "Treat this as the murder weapon."

Rhodri had pulled Madlen to her knees, and she knelt in the grass, shaking her head back and forth, much as Carys had done when she'd learned of Gryff's death. "No, no, no. He couldn't have."

"I assure you Gryff was murdered," Gareth said.

"My uncle couldn't have done it," Madlen said.

Gareth didn't really have anything to say to that, so he turned back to Erik. "What about you? You admit to subduing my guards. Why shouldn't I arrest you for murder too?"

"I needed to speak to Iolo in private. I arrived to find him already dead." Erik pointed at Madlen. "She tried to murder me. I fought back in self-defense."

Erik outweighed Madlen by a hundred pounds, but Gareth himself could testify to her determined strength. He looked from Madlen to Erik, uncertain all of a sudden because it felt like both could be telling the truth of what they knew. After all the lies he'd heard so far, it was disconcerting.

Erik indicated his bleeding arm. "Do you think I could get some help here?"

* * * * *

Gareth ordered Evan and Rhodri to truss Erik and Madlen and take them to the castle. Both continued to protest their innocence. Fortunately, the two guards had regained consciousness before Gareth left the tent, with no obvious ill effects. Unfortunately, both Gryff and Iolo were still dead and the problem of determining who'd murdered them remained.

While Gareth sent a rider to fetch Gwen from the monastery, Evan found a cart to transport the body to a place where Gareth could examine it. Once presented with Iolo's death, both Gwen and the castle's healer concurred that Iolo had been poisoned, probably by monkshood delivered in his wine.

"Any fool knows not to touch it," the healer said.

"A few grains are all that would have been needed in the whole bottle, and he'd have been dead," Gwen said. "Anyone who drank with him would have been dead too."

Even though Gareth hadn't dragged anything more about either Gryff's death or Iolo's out of Erik, he allowed the healer to bind Erik's wound, thinking he might get as much out of him with honey as with fists. And then, in the hope that he would learn something that would give him leverage with Erik, Gareth decided to hear Madlen's side of the story first.

To that end, the interested parties crowded into Hywel's office, having evicted the castellan of Cardigan Castle and his large family, who'd been its residents the previous night.

Hywel placed a stool in the middle of the room and then sat in his chair behind his desk. The sleeping pallets that had been spread across the floor were stacked against one wall, and Gwen found a soft seat there. Gruffydd posted himself by the door. Declaring that he'd been in on this from the beginning and wasn't about to miss the end, Prince Rhun brought a stool in from the hall to sit on, and Gareth leaned against the wall to one side. He wanted to be able to see Hywel's face and Madlen's too. He expected her to lie to them again.

"Why don't you start from the beginning, Madlen?" Prince Hywel said.

"What do you know already?" Her hands worked in her lap, nervous and with the appearance that all the fight had gone from her.

"I think I know a great deal," Hywel said, "none of which I'm going to share with you. You lied to me. Your uncle lied to me, God rest his soul. I know more now than I did then." He leaned forward. "I suggest you choose your words carefully."

Madlen put her hands up to her lips as if in prayer. "I didn't kill Gryff."

Hywel sat back. "Go on."

"Uncle Iolo didn't either," she said.

Hywel's expression was stony. "Tell us what he did do."

"He was a spy!" Madlen threw out the words in a sudden burst of anger that was much more like the Madlen they'd been dealing with up until now. "Is that what you wanted me to say?"

"For whom did he spy?" Hywel said.

Madlen's shoulders hunched, and even after all this, Gareth thought she wasn't going to speak, but then she said, "King Cadell of Deheubarth."

"Let's talk about the cross," Hywel said, "the one you claim is etched with your grandparents' initials. That isn't the case, is it?"

"No." Madlen remained slumped. Gareth almost preferred her defiant because at least then she wasn't looking at the floor.

"And Gryff?" Hywel said. "What was his role?"

"He carried messages for my uncle," Madlen said. "People were used to seeing him and ignoring him."

"Like you did?" Rhun said.

Hywel shot his brother a quelling look. Rhun nodded his understanding. It was better not to antagonize Madlen now that she was talking. But Gwen either didn't see the look or had a different agenda. She leaned forward. "You didn't love Gryff, did you? That too was a lie."

Madlen jerked her head to the left to look at Gwen. "You're right. I didn't."

"Talk us through what happened at the chapel when you claimed to be his wife," Gwen said.

Madlen seemed to prefer hearing the questions from Gwen, because she answered readily enough. "It seemed to be the easiest way to gain access to the body. We'd only just discovered the cross was missing, and my uncle was sure that Gryff had taken it."

"Why would Gryff have done that?" Gareth said in a gentle voice.

"Uncle Iolo thought he might have been thinking of going to you." Madlen looked directly at Hywel and then returned her eyes to the floor. "We thought we still had time, because no soldiers had confronted us. We didn't know where he'd put it, so one of us needed to get his purse before anyone opened it and found the cross on him."

"But you didn't tell your uncle what you'd planned until you'd already done it, did you?" Gwen said. "He was genuinely surprised when Gareth and Prince Rhun mentioned that you were married."

"I went to the monastery hoping to see Gryff and ended up needing to improvise," Madlen said. "It should have been easy."

"But it wasn't easy because Gryff had been murdered, which I gather your uncle didn't tell you before you went," Gwen said. "In truth, Iolo should have checked Gryff's purse before he put him in the millpond. It was stupid of him not to."

"My uncle didn't murder Gryff! He drowned. We had nothing to do with it!"

Gwen pressed her lips together in a quick smile. She'd goaded Madlen on purpose by calling her uncle stupid. Iolo had prided himself on his intelligence and his ability to live a secret life. Still, with her uncle dead, it would have been convenient for Madlen to blame him for Gryff's murder.

Madlen calmed herself. "We didn't realize the cross was missing until after he was dead, and it was too late."

"What is the significance of the cross?" Hywel said, bringing Madlen's attention back to himself. "The 'C' and 'G' stand for—"

Madlen sneered. "Cadell ap Gruffydd. I can't believe you didn't figure that out for yourselves. You should have known it the first moment you laid eyes on it. No peasant like Gryff could have afforded it."

Which was why Carys thought Gryff had stolen it—though Gareth didn't say that.

Hywel rested his elbow on the arm of his chair and tapped a finger to his lips, studying Madlen. "What would have been the plan for dealing with Gryff if not to kill him?"

"I don't know," Madlen said. "Gryff didn't show up at the stall, and then my uncle discovered the cross was missing and feared the worst. And then we learned that a body had been found in the millpond."

"And you assumed it was Gryff?" Gareth said.

"He was missing, wasn't he?" Madlen said.

Gareth pursed his lips. She had a point. The miller had expressed the same concern to Prince Rhun when he'd learned of the body, and he'd been relieved to learn it wasn't his missing apprentice.

"What about Erik?" Gwen spoke again from her seat to Madlen's left. "Where does he come into it?"

And to Gareth's astonishment, Madlen flushed pink.

Gwen saw it too and pounced. "He was your lover, wasn't he? Since you obviously didn't go to Borth as your uncle told us last night, was your uncle covering for you when we questioned him?"

Madlen pouted and didn't answer.

"You do realize that you were seen trying to murder Erik," Gareth said. "You really should be talking."

Gwen made to speak again, but Hywel held up his hand, telling her to wait. Most people were incapable of maintaining silence. It was the natural instinct to fill it.

Madlen was no exception, and eventually she broke. She ducked her head in a nod. "That's why he ran from you."

Understanding came to Gareth. "You were at the market last night, weren't you?"

Madlen's expression turned wretched. "My uncle was trying to distract you from Erik and me. He had grown afraid that you knew about his contact with Erik, since you had seen them together at our stall."

"At the time I couldn't understand why he ran," Gwen said. "We weren't that close to finding out the truth."

Gareth pictured the scene in his mind's eye. "Where were you?"

Madlen sighed. "Hidden between the stalls behind you. He'd just told you that I was distraught over Gryff's death. It would hardly have done for you to have turned around and seen me arm-in-arm with Erik.

"Tell me about my uncle's signet ring," Hywel said.

Up until now, Madlen had been alternately defiant and morose, but for the first time she looked genuinely fearful. "You know about that?"

"Was that why Iolo took Gryff's rucksack?" Rhun said. "Because he hoped he'd find the ring hidden in it?"

Madlen wrapped her arms around her middle and bent over. "Prince Cadwaladr passed it to my uncle to show King Cadell, as proof that his words came from him. When my uncle discovered it missing too, along with the cross, I thought his heart would give out."

Again it was Gwen who seemed to understand her best. "You know the history between Cadwaladr and Cadell, don't you? And Cadwaladr and Prince Hywel?"

Madlen gave a jerky nod.

Gwen continued, "It was one thing to spy for Cadell, but quite another to play a role in unseating the Lord of Ceredigion. That your uncle had both the ring and the cross proves that Cadwaladr and Cadell conspired together."

Madlen burst into tears. "I never meant any of this to happen! I've lost everything! What's going to happen to me now?"

Gareth looked down at his feet so Madlen couldn't see his irritation. He shouldn't have been surprised that despite everything that had happened Madlen's greatest concern was for herself.

Gwen leaned forward and spoke gently. "All this time, you didn't know that your uncle had anything to do with Gryff's death, did you?"

Madlen shook her head.

"Or Erik either?" Gwen said. "He confessed to subduing the guards around your uncle's tent. Do you still think the same of him?"

Madlen's head remained down and silent tears dripped onto her lap. She was beyond sobbing now, beyond subterfuge and equivocation. "I loved him." Madlen's words appeared to be only for Gwen, the only other woman in the room. "He said he loved me too."

Every man held his breath as Gwen said, "And yet you tried to kill him. Do you still believe he murdered your uncle?"

Madlen's heartbreak was almost tangible, a physical thing in the room. Both Erik and Iolo had used her and lied to her, though her uncle had tried to protect her in the end.

Madlen nodded and shook her head at the same time. "I do."

23

Hywel

It was one thing to arrest the underlings who'd perpetrated the crime, but it was quite another matter to corner their master. At this point Hywel had little interest in what King Cadell had or had not done, though he knew he should. It was Cadwaladr he cared about. Cadell might be standing on Hywel's doorstep, but Cadwaladr lived in the heart of Gwynedd and still had their father's ear.

"We need to trap him," Hywel said.

"Does Cadwaladr know that we've captured Erik?" Rhun said.

"I don't know." Hywel looked out the window, unable to hide his impatience. He was torn in two. Today's musical events were well underway. He needed to be out there, not dealing with this investigation, no matter how important.

"Leave it to me," Rhun said. "Whatever happens after this, Gryff's murderer is either dead or in custody. We have more to unravel here, but you have people to see to."

Relief crossed Hywel's face. "Don't kill our uncle without me there."

Rhun laughed, but even as he did so, he had to know that Hywel was only half-jesting. "I won't. We need to question Erik again. We need to make him talk."

Hywel sighed. "We could let him go. See what he does."

"What?" Gareth spoke up from the corner where he'd propped himself against the wall, unfolding his arms from his chest and straightening. "No."

"Without more information, we're as stuck as we were before," Hywel said. "We can't place him at the scene of Gryff's murder, and it's Iolo whose knife is suspect. Although Iolo is dead, all we have to hold Erik on are questions about his fight with Madlen, who herself admits that she attacked him, and two guardsmen who remember nothing. Hardly something we can hang him for."

"I don't like it," Rhun said.

"I don't either," Gareth said.

"I'm not saying I *like* it," Hywel said. "We can let him believe Cadwaladr used his influence to get him free, and that we reluctantly agreed."

"And then we follow him." Rhun nodded.

"It's risky," Gareth said. "We could very easily lose him."

"Do you have a better idea?" Hywel said.

All three men looked at the floor, not speaking. Hywel's frustration was almost unbearable. Then a knock broke the silence. Gareth went to the door and opened it. Morgan, Hywel's steward, stood on the threshold. "Sir Gareth, there's some people here to see you."

Gareth's brow furrowed. "To see me?"

"Yes," Morgan said. "Your lady wife is with them in the hall."

Gareth looked over at Prince Hywel, who waved a hand at him. "We all have matters to see to."

Gareth went.

"Have you spoken to Father about Angharad?" Hywel said.

"No," Rhun said. "With all that has happened, there hasn't been time. I need a moment to decide what to say, and then I planned to seek him out."

"Good," Hywel said.

"The music awaits you," Rhun said.

Hywel left his brother staring out the window and followed after Gareth, though he took the rear exit rather than going through the hall. He found Morgan back in the kitchen, talking to the head cook about the preparations for the next meal. Even if the majority of guests would be eating at the festival grounds, dozens remained in the castle and needed to be fed.

Hywel waited for them to finish and then said, "Everything all right?"

"We may spend the winter at half-rations, but supplies are holding," Morgan said. "We may even survive the day."

Hywel managed a laugh and clapped his steward on the shoulder. "Let's hope so."

"It'll be easier now that King Cadell and Prince Cadwaladr have gone," Morgan said.

Hywel froze, his hand still on the steward's shoulder. "What did you say?"

Morgan looked at him warily. "Didn't you know?"

"I hadn't heard." Hywel spared a thought for Rhun, who even now was preparing to ask Cadell for Angharad's hand. "When was this?"

"King Cadell broke camp within this hour," Morgan said. "Your uncle left while it was still dark."

Hywel didn't know what would become of his brother's betrothal now, though he would hold out hope for the best. This was a matter Rhun would have to take up with their father.

Morgan bowed. "I apologize, my lord. I should have brought the word to you immediately, but you were in conference—"

Hywel motioned with one hand. "It's nothing. They're gone."

Morgan picked at his lower lip with two fingers, obviously still concerned about his failure.

"So they didn't leave together?" Hywel said.

"No, my lord. They didn't," Morgan said. "The scouts were clear on that."

That would be the good news. It was bad enough that his uncle was nearly impossible to pin down. Whatever Hywel had expected to happen today, it wasn't this. He paused for a moment, wondering if he ought to feel snubbed, or if their sudden and joint absence boded ill for the festival or his rule. One hundred cavalry could wreak havoc on any domain, but they weren't a true army.

Leaving Morgan to his work, Hywel entered the courtyard of the castle. Evan spied him immediately and hastened to greet him, accompanied by two other men, one of whom was Cadwaladr's man from years back. Hywel didn't know the man on Evan's left.

"My lord." Evan bowed. "I believe you know Sir Aedden. He brings Lord Cadwaladr's apologies for his sudden departure, but the prince had an urgent matter to attend to elsewhere."

That was surely the vaguest excuse Hywel had ever heard, but he took it politely enough. Then the second man stepped forward.

"I am Ralff, cousin to King Cadell, and I bring his apologies as well. He has received word that his uncle is marshalling his forces near Llanstephen in a possible attempt to retake the fortress. My cousin could not wait to make his excuses in person."

"I understand completely," Hywel said. Cadell, at least, had come up with something marginally credible. Ralff bowed again, turned on his heel, and departed.

The first man, Sir Aedden, gave Hywel something of a sickly smile. "If that is all, my lord?"

Aedden made to turn away, but Hywel put out a hand. "Wait. I believe I have some information that might interest your lord."

"Oh?" Aedden turned back.

"We have arrested one of my uncle's men, a half-Dane named Erik, on suspicion of murder. Perhaps you would like to speak to him before you go?" Hywel said.

Aedden frowned. "I know of no such man. Certainly none by that name or description has ever served Prince Cadwaladr."

Evan looked as if he was about to speak, but at a look from Hywel, he kept silent.

"Perhaps I misunderstood his allegiance," Hywel said.

"Indeed," Aedden said. "My apologies for any inconvenience my lord's departure has caused you." It was all very polite, and after another bow, Aedden departed too.

Watching him go, Evan said, "If I may be so bold as to speak, my lord, it seems that your uncle has sold Erik out."

"Whatever my uncle planned with King Cadell, it was worth it to him to cut all ties with a man who's been valuable to him in the past," Hywel said. "Maybe Erik will talk now."

"I fear what might have prompted your uncle to behave in such a manner, my lord," Evan said. "I see it as an indication of his belief that his past cannot hurt him."

"And that means we need to be very careful about our future."

Dismissing Erik's guards, Hywel stood at the top of the steps to Erik's cell, gazing down at the spy, who'd been lying on his back, spread-eagled on the floor. Evan remained nearby, available at a moment's notice should Hywel have need of him. At Hywel's approach, Erik sat up, leaning on this elbows. "What do you want?"

Hywel trotted down the steps to the door. "I have some bad news for you."

Erik sneered. "Whatever you have to say, I've heard worse."

"Cadwaladr has abandoned you," Hywel said. "He claims no knowledge of who you are or that you've served as his spy for three years."

Whatever Erik had been expecting Hywel to say, that wasn't it. For a moment, his expression reflected his surprise, but then he smoothed it. "You can't hold me. You have no evidence against me for Gryff's murder or Iolo's."

"Maybe so," Hywel said. "Perhaps you'd care to provide some?"

Erik scoffed. "I can't do that because I didn't kill either one."

"Murder carries a monetary penalty, payable to the victim's family and sometimes to the victim's lord," Hywel said. "Treason, however, is a different matter entirely. Treason carries the penalty of death."

That seemed to get through to Erik, at least a little. He licked his lips. "I can't help you."

"Really?" Hywel said. "I have a mind to send word on the next tide to Prince Godfrid in Dublin that we have captured you. I'm sure he might have something to say about your service to him and your departure from it."

Erik pushed to his feet and came forward, ducking his head at the low ceiling. He put his hands on the bars that blocked the window in the door. "No."

Hywel raised his eyebrows. "Then it's time you started talking. I'd like to hear in particular about the work you did for my uncle."

Erik's brow furrowed. "I didn't kill Gryff."

"I'm not asking you about Gryff," Hywel said. "I don't care about Gryff anymore. I want to hear about Cadwaladr."

Erik continued to look puzzled. "To what purpose? You already know he plots against you."

Hywel had to struggle to keep his expression mild. "The details are important."

"Cadwaladr wants Ceredigion back. I have no idea why." Erik snickered. "This is a petty lordship with petty people and nothing of importance ever happens here. I could never understand Cadwaladr's interest in it."

Erik's mockery would have been amusing if Hywel didn't care so very much about this lordship and the people in it.

"My uncle hates me," Hywel said.

Erik actually grinned. "You have that right. If you want the truth, my lord, I was charged with discovering what you were doing and how you were doing it: how many men did you have? What was the disposition of your forces? I told him over and over again that the only way he was going to take Aberystwyth back was if he brought an army of at least five hundred men, camped around the castle to starve you out, or burned it to the ground like you did to him when he ruled here. But if he did any of that, he would lose your father's favor forever."

"He would lose his lands in Merionydd too, and then my father would send me or Rhun down here again and take the castle back," Hywel said.

"Exactly. It was a foolish dream." Erik's eyes narrowed at Hywel. "If I tell you more, if I tell you what you really want to know, what do I get?"

"That depends on what you think I want to know."

"You want to know what he's planning now," Erik said.

"Given that he abandoned you, I don't see how you could know that," Hywel said.

"He has his spies, I have mine."

Hywel rubbed his jaw. "You'd work for me now?"

"I would."

"How do I know I can trust you?" Hywel said.

"You don't," Erik said, "but I can be bought, as you well know, and I have no loyalty to Cadwaladr. He paid well, but now he doesn't."

"Why me? Surely you'd be welcomed by King Cadell?"

"Surely I wouldn't. He wouldn't allow me within a hundred yards of his camp now."

"Why?" Hywel said.

"If you're wondering who did Iolo in," Erik said, "I would look no further than our beloved King of Deheubarth."

"You're going to have to be more specific."

Erik's hands were still on the bars, his back bent to look through the window, but now he looked down at the ground. "Iolo invited me to share a drink with him, given to him by Cadell, as an indication of his continued respect. He gave the poisoned wine to Iolo yesterday evening. I promised to join Iolo after the singing ended, and in fact, that was where Madlen and I were going when you and your wife arrived to question him. After that, what with the guards you placed around Iolo, I couldn't get to him easily."

"Why would Cadell poison Iolo?" Hywel said, hoping for confirmation of what he'd already guessed.

"He was, as you say, snipping off loose ends." Erik rolled his eyes. "Prince Cadwaladr might not care who knew that Cadell and he worked together to murder Anarawd, but Cadell surely does. He has two brothers who would turn against him if they knew."

"And Cadwaladr wouldn't want it known that he was working with Cadell now," Hywel said. "Their mutual silence protected them both."

"But if one stone came loose, the whole castle would come crashing down," Erik said. "When Iolo told Cadell that he murdered Gryff and asked for protection, he exposed everyone involved. He was a fool."

Erik seemed to think that many men were fools—including Hywel himself. But Erik was talking now, and his words had enough ring of truth in them for Hywel to remain interested. "You're saying that Iolo told Cadell that he killed Gryff?"

"And Cadell decided that Iolo was a liability he could no longer afford," Erik said.

"Just like Cadwaladr did with you," Hywel said.

Erik grimaced. "Never mistake Cadell's intentions for your uncle's. Cadell is dangerous because he is smart and careful. Cadwaladr is dangerous because he bounces from plan to plan, leaving havoc in his wake. Just ask Iolo."

"So what changed? What made you go to Iolo this morning?" Hywel said. "Subduing his guards was a rash act."

"Your uncle fled Ceredigion in the night, didn't he?" Erik said. "I learned of it from one of my merchant friends. At first I didn't believe it, but he swore it was true. I suddenly feared that everything I knew to be true might not be. Iolo had a good mind. He would have come up with some answers to get us out of this."

"You feared Cadwaladr had sold you out," Hywel said.

"Turns out I was right, wasn't I?" Erik said.

"All right. Tell me about Gryff."

"I thought you didn't care about him."

"Pretend I do," Hywel said. "Did Iolo include him in what you were up to?"

Erik looked affronted. "Of course not. The man was half-idiot. Iolo used him to carry messages sometimes. That is all."

Madlen had said as much. Iolo's mistake was in misreading Gryff's nature and intent. It was perhaps the most overlooked feature of this investigation, but it seemed everything else hinged on it.

"Then why is he dead?"

Erik sighed. "I wasn't there, but Iolo told me later that Gryff followed him to the millpond where he met me. He threatened to expose Iolo as a go-between for Cadell and Cadwaladr."

"Who was Gryff going to tell?"

"You, of course," Erik said. "Cadwaladr and Cadell colluded to murder Cadell's brother three years ago, and they've worked together since then, most recently looking for a way to take you down."

Hywel assumed Erik was fully aware of the potential danger of saying those words out loud. The man had courage, he'd give him that. And the more Erik talked, the more Hywel believed what he was saying. "What about Cadwaladr's plans for Gareth?"

"Oh, well, that would be telling." Then Erik pursed his lips. "All right. I'll give you that too, as proof of my good intentions. Cadwaladr intends to see Gareth dead at the first opportunity."

Though this news was hardly a surprise, an urgency rose in Hywel's chest that he instantly suppressed so Erik wouldn't realize how important his answers were. "How does he hope to do it?"

"In battle would be best, though in the dark, stabbed in the back, would be fine with him." Over the course of the conversation, Erik had turned affable, which Hywel found distasteful given the subject matter. He understood it, however. They had moved beyond Erik's own crimes to theoretical ones. "But as long as it can't be traced back to him, he doesn't care how it's done or who does it."

"Did he offer the job to you?" Hywel said.

"I turned him down," Erik said.

"Why?"

"I'm not an assassin."

"You've killed men."

"I have, but not in cold blood. Not like that." Erik's eyes traced the limits of his cell. "Come to think on it, my refusal is probably why I'm here."

Hywel thought that likely too. "Now that you've told me, if something happens to Sir Gareth, we'll know who's behind it."

"You would have known already." Erik grinned. "And again, knowing that something is true and being able to prove it are two different things."

Hywel pushed away from the door and started up the stairs. He had duties to attend to that couldn't wait, and he was tired of Erik's lack of honor.

"Wait!" Erik grasped the bars, realizing he'd gone too far. "We had a deal. You have to let me out."

"Do I?" Hywel studied the large Dane. "If I let you go, you must tell me everything my brother is planning, everything you know or suspect is in his mind."

"I will, my lord."

Hywel didn't move.

Erik tsked through his teeth. "I didn't kill Gryff, I swear it. And I didn't hurt Iolo."

Slowly, Hywel nodded. Then he took the key from its hook on the wall and slotted it into the lock.

24

Gareth

The hall wasn't as crowded as it had been earlier that morning when they'd brought Erik in. The morning was passing and the guests had dispersed. It was another beautiful day, the last of the festival, and with music all around them, nobody wanted to spend the day indoors. Gareth wasn't a musician, but he was Welsh. He was as proud as anyone of what Hywel had accomplished this week.

Gareth found Gwen near the entrance to the great hall, talking to a gray-haired couple and their son. The son looked as if he'd achieved manhood but was still short of twenty. At Gareth's approach, Gwen turned to him with a smile and gestured to her guests. "They heard about Gryff's death and have come to help us find his killer."

Gareth's expression cleared. Any information would be helpful, given where they were in the investigation. He would have shaken the man's forearm, but instead the woman surprised him by throwing her arms around him. "Thank you! Thank you!"

He looked over the top of her head at Gwen. She grinned at him, and Gareth patted the woman on the back, trying to get her to let go. Finally, her husband managed to pry her off Gareth's chest.

"I'm sorry, madam," Gareth said. "What do you have to thank me for?"

"We never got a chance before, you see," the woman said.

Gareth had no idea what she was talking about. He glanced at Gwen, whose eyes were bright, no longer with amusement but with unshed tears.

The man gestured to his son. "Show him."

The boy held out his left arm. Gareth stared at it. The boy had no left hand. Then he looked into his face. "Don't tell me you're the boy—"

"It was my fault." The mother dabbed at her eyes with a cloth, weeping now. "He never should have thought he needed to steal that pig, but his father had gone to work in the mine, and I was sick. We had nobody to care for us."

"But—" Gareth didn't know what to say.

"We heard what happened to you afterwards," the father said. "You lost everything because you refused to cut off my boy's hand."

Gareth closed his eyes, trying to control his own emotions, and then opened them. "You shouldn't be thanking me. Cadwaladr took his hand anyway. I couldn't protect him from it."

"You did what nobody else did. We have honored you for it all these years. And that's why we're here." The father took in a breath. "Llew works at the mill; he sleeps above it at night. He was there the night that man died."

Gareth's jaw dropped, and his gaze went to the boy. "Where have you been?"

The father cleared his throat. "He didn't come home until last night. He's been afraid of what he saw."

Gareth let out a breath. "Come with me, please." He led the way back to Hywel's office. Hywel was no longer there, but Rhun stood gazing out the window. Gruffydd had propped himself in the same corner Gareth had occupied earlier. Rhun turned as they entered, and Gareth said, "This is our missing mill apprentice. He has something to tell us."

Committed now, Llew stood before Prince Rhun like a soldier—legs spread, arms behind his back—and stared at a spot somewhere near the top of the wall ahead of him. "I was at the mill the night that man died. I wasn't supposed to be there because my father had sent me to Borth to bring food to my aunt who lives alone."

"She lost her husband last year and refuses to come live with us in Llanbadarn Fawr," Llew's father said as an aside.

Llew cleared his throat. "I hoped to meet a girl."

"Llew—" That was from his mother, but Gareth made a chopping motion with his hand, and she stopped.

"Go on," Gareth said.

"I thought the morning would be soon enough to go to Borth. If I left at first light, I could be there and back before anyone noticed I hadn't gone when I said I would," Llew said.

His father looked like he wanted to say something else, but another hard look from Gareth had him closing his mouth too. Gareth didn't want to stop the flow of information now that it had started.

"I was standing in the doorway to the mill, watching for her. It was after midnight by then, and I'd realized she wasn't coming, but I wasn't ready to give up. Then I saw a man pass by on the road, hardly more than a shadow really. He greeted a second man, who was waiting for him in the woods. I followed them." Llew stopped.

"Why?" Gareth said.

Llew shrugged. "It seemed odd to me that they would be out so late. Why meet in the woods? They had to be up to no good, and—" Llew raised his handless arm.

Gareth studied the young man with both pity and understanding. "You have learned to counter those who look down on you or bully you by knowing more about them than they want known?"

Llew had the grace to look sheepish. "I recognized one of them. I'd seen him around Llanbadarn Fawr on and off, though I never learned his name. He was a big man, and in the moonlight his hair was almost white. I didn't like him."

Gareth knew who that was. "Had he come to the mill before?"

Llew shook his head hard. "No."

"And the other man?" Gareth said.

"He was shorter, darker, older too, with a bit of belly," Llew said. "They were talking. I couldn't hear what they were saying. Then the big man left. The smaller man stood at the water's edge for a while. I was afraid he might hear me. I could hardly breathe. But it wasn't me he heard." Llew stopped again.

"Go on, son," Llew's father said.

"The first man said, 'Is that you?' Another man stepped out of the trees and said, 'I know what you're up to. You won't get away with it.' The first man moved towards him. It all happened so fast, I could hardly believe it."

"What did the first man do?" Gareth said.

"I couldn't exactly see, but the man who'd just arrived ended up on the ground. The first man dragged him into the water. I was so scared."

"So you hid," Gareth said.

"He should have come forward sooner, we know," Llew's father said, "but with what happened before—"

"Prince Hywel is not Prince Cadwaladr," Gareth said.

"We know. We know," Llew's mother said. "That's why we're here."

"I know what happens when a body goes into the water. Usually it doesn't come up for days," Llew said. "I didn't think anyone would believe what I'd seen, and I was afraid if I said anything, that man would find me. I always slept in the mill. He could have found out that I'd been there and killed me too."

"Thank you for coming forward at last," Gareth said. "I'll have you know that the murderer will never be able to hurt you. He is dead. You're safe now."

Such was Llew's sigh that he gave the impression of melting through the floor.

Prince Rhun tipped his head to Gruffydd, who took Llew's arm and led him away, followed by his parents. That left Gareth alone with Prince Rhun and Gwen.

"One murder solved." Gwen said.

"What about Iolo?" Rhun said.

A growl formed at the back of Gareth's throat. "With Llew's testimony and the knife, we have all the evidence we need to convict him for Gryff's murder. Madlen, as his heir, will pay *galanas* to Carys for his death."

"I feel bad that I never knew who the boy was." Gwen looked at her feet. "I knew how you'd disobeyed Cadwaladr, of course, but until today, I'd only ever thought about what your decision had done to you and me."

"You do realize that they only came forward because they trusted you," Rhun said. "Everywhere you have gone, you've made an impression."

Gareth shook his head. "All I did was not cut off that poor boy's hand. He lost it anyway."

"And all you did was protect that convent of women in Powys, and in exchange, Godfrid recovered the Book of Kells and we uncovered another murderer," Gwen said.

"What other lives have you changed without knowing it?" Rhun said.

* * * * *

"You let Erik go?" Gareth stared at Hywel. The prince was in between conferring with some of the judges and appeasing two contestants, one who claimed the other had stolen his song. "He will betray you!"

"Maybe," Hywel said, "but since we now have proof that Iolo, not Erik, murdered Gryff, we would have had no reason to hold him anyway."

"You didn't know that at the time. You had only his word!" Gareth knew he needed to get his emotions under control, but it was a struggle. Whatever satisfaction he'd felt at learning the true cause of Gryff's death was gone, replaced by frustration at his lord's relentless practicality. He was still feeling a tendril of guilt at Iolo's death as well. If Gareth had thrown him in a cell, rather than letting him believe himself free, he might still be alive. The investigation had all but concluded, and he felt no triumph.

Rhun was studying his brother. "Only if treason isn't a reason."

"He's hardly committing treason if he's working for me." Hywel looked sternly at Gareth. "You have to understand, Gareth. I have no need to prove a point or waste a man with skills I can use. I would never include Erik in my garrison or my *teulu*, but he can go where I can't and bring me information I need. He already has. You should be grateful he talked, since he told us about Cadwaladr's plans for you."

Gareth ground his teeth. "What's to prevent Erik from running back to Cadwaladr?"

"Why would he do that?" Hywel said. "Cadwaladr cast him off. And King Cadell would have had him dead. It is I who am paying him now."

Gareth hated to concede the point. Only yesterday, Hywel had told him how he valued Gareth's services because of his fine sense of honor, and now his lord went and did this. Gareth looked into Hywel's eyes, both of them seeing this moment for what it was: Gareth was either going to have to concede to Hywel's authority as his lord or walk away from his service.

"Let it go, Gareth," Prince Hywel said after a moment. "I didn't ask you to make this decision. This isn't your compromise. It's mine."

Rhun spoke as if they'd said nothing to each other. "I can see how it all fell out now. Iolo used Gryff as a surrogate spy, passing messages that Iolo wrongly assumed Gryff didn't understand. Iolo thought Gryff wasn't intelligent enough to realize what he was up to and wouldn't have cared if he did.

"But Gryff hated Cadwaladr for something he did three years ago and probably doesn't even remember." Rhun looked significantly at Gareth. "A single, small act can have consequences that ripple outward in an unending circle."

"You never know the measure of a man until he's tested," Hywel said.

Gareth took in a breath, understanding that Hywel's comment was meant as a peace offering. "Gryff was tested, and he wasn't found wanting."

"It just cost him his life," Rhun said.

25

Gwen

King Owain sat in an ornate chair he'd brought with him from Gwynedd and was eating at a trestle table with Mari when his two sons, flanked by Gareth and Gwen, appeared in front of him. The king had raised the sides of his tent to allow whatever evening breeze existed to blow past him. Everyone was thankful the sun had gone down because today had been the hottest day yet. Mari sat beside her father-in-law, nursing Gruffydd, who nonetheless was flailing an arm behind him to reach what was on the table. She'd already finished eating—or, more likely, had given the meal up as a lost cause as long as she had an active one-year-old in her arms.

"It's a delegation," King Owain said by way of a greeting. "I am suddenly worried."

"You have nothing to fear," Prince Rhun said, "though we do have a story to tell you."

"Oh good," Mari said. "I'm tired of being kept in the dark."

Hywel bent to kiss the top of her head. "That was never my intent."

"At least now I'll be able to sleep." Mari lifted Gruffydd from her breast and put him to her shoulder, patting him on the back until he burped.

The festival was over. The last bard had finished his song, and the judges had conferred. They'd awarded the top prize to the bard who'd replaced Gwen's own father at Carreg Cennan. With Meilyr, Hywel, and Gwalchmai not participating in the contest, Gwen hadn't had much interest in the overall outcome. The young man in question, however, had been very good, and both she and Hywel had approved of the choice. He'd beaten out many older men to win.

King Owain plucked a shred of roasted chicken skin from his teeth and leaned back in his chair. "Pull up a stool." He looked at Hywel. "I have wanted to say many times since I arrived that I cannot be more proud of you, son."

Hywel dropped his gaze to his feet, but he was smiling. Gwen was glad to hear King Owain say that. Hywel did deserve whatever accolades were heaped upon him, not only for the festival itself, but for what he'd accomplished in Ceredigion. If nothing else, the resolution of Gryff's murder showed that: a boy who'd lost his hand because of Cadwaladr had come forward because the man who'd refused to take it from him had come to serve Hywel. Whether or not Hywel had made the right decision in releasing Erik, he'd had sense enough to put his trust in Gareth.

Hywel raised his head. "We've had some trouble, and Rhun and I thought it was time we told you about it." He then launched into a summary of Gryff's murder and the subsequent investigation. The four of them had conferred with each other on and off over the course of the day, clarifying the various points to each other as they'd had time to think about them.

King Owain listened intently throughout Hywel's recital, and looked particularly pleased at the discovery that Llew had witnessed the murder itself. As Hywel fell silent, King Owain rose to his feet and began to pace back and forth behind his chair.

It was Mari who spoke first. "I don't understand something. Gryff gave the cross to his wife one day but didn't hide the ring until the next. Why the delay?"

"We may never know," Hywel said. "Perhaps he didn't know himself, except that I can see how the ring—clearly Uncle Cadwaladr's own—wasn't something he could give to someone else for safekeeping. Regardless, at some point he decided to seek me out, and when he couldn't find me to show me the ring, he hid it in the best place he could think of."

"It does seem that Gryff became bolder as time went on," Gwen said. "His final act was to confront Iolo with his treachery. Who knows where that courage came from?"

"From a sense of righteousness," Rhun said. "The man seemed to drift through his life in every other way, but he hated our uncle."

King Owain had continued to pace during their exchange with Mari, but now he stopped and looked at his sons. "So my brother and Cadell have had a falling out?"

Hywel scratched the back of his head and shot Gwen an amused look. His father had latched onto this piece of information as the most important point when he'd hardly blinked at the news that Cadwaladr and Cadell had colluded to ambush Anarawd three years ago. Cadwaladr's future plans, as great or small as they might be, needed to be their concern now.

"It seems so," Rhun said. "Cadwaladr left before dawn, and Cadell departed afterwards, perhaps once he learned of Iolo's death. Our scouts report they went different ways. Whatever may have been the initial reason for Uncle Cadwaladr's presence here, he does not appear to be assisting Cadell with any incursions on Deheubarth's southern border."

King Owain looked at his older son. "And Angharad?"

"She went with him," Rhun said. "I was not able to speak to her before she left."

"We will find a way, son," King Owain said.

"Thank you, Father."

King Owain studied the darkness beyond the tent and shook his head. "Those two will be the death of me—" He turned back to his sons. "Let me see the ring."

Rhun took two steps forward and carefully placed Cadwaladr's signet ring on the table in front of his father.

King Owain glared at it but didn't speak. Gwen hoped his temper wasn't about to rise because he'd likely wake Gruffydd, who'd fallen asleep on Mari's shoulder.

Rhun spoke into the silence. "It seems that Gryff came upon the ring and the cross, whether while fulfilling his role as messenger or when actively searching for them. The latter had been given to Iolo by Cadell to be used as proof that he spoke for him, the former by Cadwaladr to show to Cadell for the same reason. Father, I believe this is the real reason both Gryff and Iolo were killed."

"They were murdered to hide Cadell's involvement in his own brother's murder, and my brother's recent involvement in Ceredigion." King Owain sat heavily in his chair. "He knows that I would not support his designs on this land, and for him to plot to take it, with or without Cadell's help, moves him past mischief to treason."

It was Rhun, not the stony-faced Hywel, who said, "Yes, Father."

King Owain expression was dark as he contemplated his sons. "My brother is like a high wind that blows away everything and everyone in its path. I cannot predict when it will come, only that it is coming. When my brother betrays me, as it seems he must, I ask only that the three of us remain united, whatever the cost."

Gareth stood taut beside Gwen. In a way, this was the moment they'd all been waiting for and made up for all the failures and lack of concord in the past. King Owain had finally spoken out loud what they'd all known needed to be said for years.

"Of course," Rhun and Hywel said together.

"After Cadwallon died, my father made me swear to look after my younger brother. Only we two were left, you see. I have tried ..." Suddenly King Owain looked ten years older than his actual age.

Mari put a hand on the king's arm. "Nobody doubts your loyalty, my lord. You have done more for your brother than he deserved. But some men cannot be saved."

"Especially not from themselves," King Owain said.

Morgan appeared at the entrance to the tent. At first only Gwen noticed him, but then he cleared his throat, and everyone else turned to look. "I apologize, my lords, for the interruption, but I bring grave news."

Hywel raised a hand to his steward, indicating that he should speak.

"A rider has arrived from the east, from Lord Goronwy," Morgan said.

Lord Goronwy was the father of Cristina, King Owain's wife.

King Owain straightened in his chair. "Spit it out, man. We'll never be in a better mood to hear it."

"Earl Ranulf has left Chester in force. He has fortified Mold Castle on Gwynedd's eastern border. Lord Goronwy fears an assault is imminent."

King Owain stood abruptly, tipping back his chair, which Gareth caught before it could hit the ground. "It may be that my brother heard this news and responded, choosing not to share it with us. He seeks glory for himself."

"Or he allies himself with Chester," Rhun said. "He has done it before."

"The festival is over," Hywel said. "My men can be ready to leave tonight."

"Then we go," King Owain said, "and may God have mercy on our souls."

The End

About the Author

With two historian parents, Sarah couldn't help but develop an interest in the past. She went on to get more than enough education herself (in anthropology) and began writing fiction when the stories in her head overflowed and demanded she let them out. While her ancestry is Welsh, she only visited Wales for the first time while in college. She has been in love with the country, language, and people ever since. She even convinced her husband to give all four of their children Welsh names.

She makes her home in Oregon.

www.sarahwoodbury.com

Made in the USA
Lexington, KY
20 September 2014